FULL HART

THE HARTY BOYS, BOOK 4

WHITLEY COX

For my cousin Paula Labelle!
A friend, a HUGE fan and one of my biggest supporters.
Thank you so much for loving my books so hard
And bragging about them to all your friends.
You're amazing and I should have dedicated a book to you sooner.
Thank you again, from the bottom of my heart.
xoxo

CHAPTER ONE
BROCK & KRISTA

"THE MOST WELL-ENDOWED brother gets the biggest tree, right?" Heath asked with a smirk as he hauled his one-and-a-half-year-old son out of his car seat and propped him on his hip.

Brock rolled his eyes at his youngest, cockiest brother. "We didn't cut down a sapling short enough to resemble your Vienna sausage, little brother." He dropped the tailgate of his truck as his wife, Krista, helped their children out of the back of the cab. Rex wandered up, his wife and daughter behind him, while Chase, Stacey, and their two kids, who had parked the farthest up the road, were making their way down the sidewalk.

"Ah," Heath said, chortling, "we *all* know who the biggest brother is. He might not be the oldest, but he's the biggest." He elbowed his wife, then Rex's wife. "If you know what I mean?"

More eyes rolled as they all stood outside their mother's house on December fifteenth, their breath forming puffs in front of their faces with each exhale.

Heath wasn't discouraged at all. He tossed his blond hair off his face with a flick of his head. "I say we go by size. Biggest brother gets the biggest tree, and we work our way down that way. Mum gets the smallest one because—"

"She doesn't have a dick?" Lydia asked, adjusting ten-month-old Maeve on her hip. "Seems like if she had one, it'd be bigger than all of yours. We all know her *cojones* are the size of grapefruits."

Krista, Pasha, and Stacey all nodded and went "mhmm."

The last to slide out of Heath's truck, with a baby in her arms, was Pasha's sister Rayma, she had Heath and Pasha's one-month-old daughter Eve leaned up against her shoulder. "What's this about *cojones?*"

"Just saying that Joy has the biggest of all them. Of all of *us*," Pasha informed her sister.

Rayma nodded, her golden-brown eyes sparkling. "Not gonna argue there. Nana Joy's ovaries are the size of bowling balls. Not sure how that tiny woman can walk, but—"

Brock cleared his throat. "Enough chit-chat. It's cold out here." He heaved the smallest tree—which still stood nearly six feet tall—out from the back of his truck and over his shoulder. Rex went to help him, but Brock grunted him off. "Can do it myself."

More eyes rolled.

Ever since women started joining their family, eventually to outnumber the men, eyes seemed to always be rolling. And it was usually at Brock or one of his brothers.

But they weren't just brothers by blood, they were partners in an elite security and surveillance company as well. His wife had named it, and although Brock's own eyes had rolled at the time, now he kind of liked it. *Harty Boys Security*. It worked, even if it was a little cheesy.

"How come Nana couldn't come to get a tree with us?" Brock's seven-year-old daughter Zoe asked, skipping next to him, her curly red hair bouncing in twin ponytails that sprung out from the side of her head.

"Because Nana had a hair appointment," Krista said, holding

their three-year-old son Zane by the hand as they all approached their mother's front door. "But her car is in the driveway, so she's home now."

"Someone else is here, too," Chase murmured from behind Brock. "Anyone recognize the SUV?"

Heads shook.

It was a light gray Ford Explorer, a new model and with a hefty set of snow tires on it. A glance in through the driver's side window yielded no further information as to who might be visiting their mother.

"Zane want to ring the bell," Brock's son said, having recently entered the stage of his speech where he referred to himself in the third person.

"I'll help him," Zoe said as they all fell in line on the path that ran below the living-room window up to the front door. She went up to her younger brother, hoisted him up around the waist, with his back to her front.

"No need," Brock said, pushing past his kids. "It's Nana's house. We can just walk right in." He turned the knob, but it was locked.

He grunted in confusion.

"I have a key," Krista said, elbowing through her husband and children and fishing her keys out of her pocket. Her blue eyes glittered in amusement as she slipped the key into the hole and turned it. Her cheeks nearly matched her fiery red hair, which was spilling out of her knit cap. She turned the knob and held the door open for everyone to step inside.

"Nana!" Zoe called out.

"Nana!" Zane echoed.

Eight-year-old Connor, Chase and Stacey's oldest, raced through the legs of the adults to meet up with his cousins, then joined in on the call. "Nana!"

"Nana!" Thea, Chase and Stacey's youngest, cried out, pushing out of her mother's arms to join her brother on the ground.

"Where is she?" Chase murmured, the curiosity and unease in his tone mirroring what Brock felt in his gut.

Something wasn't right.

The house was quiet.

Dark.

Cold.

Those were three things it never was when his mother was home. Even if she didn't turn the furnace on, when she was home, there was warmth. And she was almost always humming some tune or puttering in the kitchen making noise. And she *never* drew the blinds to the picture window in the living room, and yet right now they were closed up tight, making the entire house feel like it was enveloped in a shadow.

"Mum!" Heath called out, shoving past all of them, seventeen-month-old Raze still on his hip. "Mum, where are you?"

A clunk and a *"shit"* from down the hall rumbled through the house like thunder.

They all paused.

Then whispers followed. Two voices.

What the hell?

"Mum?" Brock barked louder than the rest of them.

"Anybody packing?" Rex asked.

One by one, they all shook their heads. All of them except Krista. "I have my Glock in the safety box in the truck," she said. "Want me to run and get it?"

Brock nodded but didn't glance at his cop wife.

She nodded and disappeared.

"Get the women and children outside," he said to no one in particular.

Heath turned to his wife and murmured something to her, passing her Raze.

Against the children's wishes, they all started to file back out just as Krista arrived back inside.

The *click* of a bedroom door had them all pausing, including everyone on the threshold.

Brock watched the knob turn and the door open.

His heart was in his throat.

Making *gimme* fingers to his wife, he asked for the gun.

"I'm a better shot than you are," she muttered, elbowing him out of the way.

Holding his breath and not blinking, he kept his gaze focused on where his mother's bedroom door was and the whispers filtering out of it. It was two people. He knew that now.

"Mum?" he barked, making his wife in front of him jump, glance at him over her shoulder, and glare.

A head poked out from the doorway, and his mother's brows furrowed.

Sighs echoed through all of them.

"What the hell are you doing with that, Krista? Put that away right now," his mother ordered, stepping into the hallway, all four feet eleven inches of her.

"Sorry," Krista murmured, stowing the gun in the holster clipped to her belt.

Their mother approached. "What is going on?"

"I'd like to ask you the same question," Brock said, realizing he was still holding the damn tree on his shoulder. He leaned it up against the wall. "Why didn't you answer us? Why is the house cold, dark, and quiet? Why are the curtains pulled? Whose truck is that?"

Color burned in his mother's cheeks.

"Yes," Krista said in what sounded like a hiss. Her smile grew mischievously wide.

Yes?

Brock took in his mother's appearance for a moment.

She was wearing a pair of dark wash jeans and a long-sleeved button-up blouse of some light shade of pink. But the buttons were askew, not fastened properly. The shirt was also wrinkled. Her hair was disheveled, too.

Which was so unlike Joy Hart.

The woman was always put together.

For as long as Brock could remember, his mother had tucked her hair up into a no-nonsense bun on the back of her head and rarely was a hair ever out of place. But the bun on the top of her head now looked like it'd been tossed up in haste.

Her lips were also puffy.

And there was a red rash or something on her cheeks.

A throat cleared down the hallway, and Brock lifted his head.

He could hear his mother swallow as he watched a man about the same height and build as himself walk down the hall, buttoning his shirt.

"What the fuc—"

"Watch it," his mother said.

"Holy crap," Rayma murmured behind Brock. "Have him stripped, bathed, and brought directly to my tent."

Jesus fucking Christ.

"He's old enough to be your dad," Heath scolded her.

"And I'm sure he could help me work through any daddy issues I may have," Rayma retorted. "And for the record, all y'all burly Harty Boys are old enough to be my father. Hasn't stopped the fantasies during the dry spells."

"Rayma!" Pasha admonished, nearly dropping her son as she gaped at her twenty-something sister. "That's my *husband.*"

Brock noticed Rayma's indifferent shrug. "I know, and I'm respectful. It's not like in my fantasies we're cheating. You've been dead a respectable amount of time, and I'm there for Heath to help him raise the children on his own."

"You kill me?" Pasha practically screamed.

"This just keeps getting better," Lydia, Rex's wife, said with a chuckle.

The man from the hallway with the dark, close-cropped hair, facial scruff, and light gray eyes came up suspiciously close behind Brock's mother and rested his hand on her shoulder.

Brock's body turned molten hot.

He heard his brothers grunt and suck in breaths beside and behind him.

Their mother glanced at the man behind her, smiled, and turned back to the rest of them. "Everyone, I'd like you to meet Grant."

———

As happy as she was to see that her mother-in-law was finally getting a little something-something, Krista's thoughts were on her husband and the frightening vein that popped out on the side of his neck as he stared unblinkingly at the man who rested his hand on Joy's shoulder.

"Nana Joy's getting her groove back," Rayma whispered. "And with a freaking demigod, no less."

"Shhh," Pasha whispered. "If I could ground your ass, I would. Having fantasies about killing me. That's some messed-up shit right there."

"I don't fantasize about *killing* you. I fantasize that you're already dead, then I bone your husband as we bond in our grief."

Dear lord, the drama behind her was almost as tantalizing as the potential drama in front of her. Krista wanted to give both her equal attention.

But alas, making sure her husband didn't pop a blood vessel in his eye was her main priority. She slid her hand into his and curled her fingers around his. "You going to say anything, honey?"

Finally, he blinked and cleared his throat.

The man Joy had introduced as Grant thrust his free hand out. "Heard a lot about you kids. Nice to finally meet you."

Oh shit.

Brock was going all alpha.

If she didn't do something to defuse the situation and fast, her husband might whip his dick out and start peeing all over shit.

She was having a hard enough time keeping pants and training underwear on her son; she didn't need him getting any ideas from his he-man, Neanderthal father.

Brock stared at Grant's hand but didn't take it.

For crap's sake.

Not bothering to elbow her husband, because she already knew it wouldn't do much good, she took Grant's hand and gave it a firm shake. "Nice to meet you, Grant. I'm—"

"Krista," he said with a smile. "Joy has told me a lot about you. It's nice to finally meet the fearless cop and Mama Bear."

Well, that made her blush. Heat wormed its way through her, and she fought off the girlie giggle that threatened to bubble up from the depths of her throat. She released Grant's hand and glanced up at her husband.

Brock was glaring down at her.

Crap.

"I'm Stacey, Chase's wife," Stacey said, elbowing her way through and taking Grant's hand. "It's nice to meet you."

One by one, the rest of Krista's sisters-in-law came forward to shake Grant's hand, followed lastly by the young, horny, and filter-free Rayma.

The girl was a great babysitter and had a good head on her shoulders, but she was also young and not quiet about her appreciation for a nice set of dimples or abs.

Krista could certainly hear the young woman sigh when she finally took Grant's hand and introduced herself.

Down, girl.

"How long have you two been seeing each other?" Krista asked, frustrated with her husband and his brothers and the statue status they had all adopted. They were just standing there like big, sexy idiots staring at the man behind their mother.

Joy's blue eyes glittered as she glanced back up at Grant and smiled. "About six months."

"Six months!" Chase croaked out.

Joy's gaze flared, and she fixed her stare on Chase. "Yes, we met this summer at the pool. We were double-booked in a lane for swimming laps and—"

"Decided to share," Grant finished, squeezing Joy's shoulder. "Then I asked her to grab a coffee after our swim."

"And coffee turned into lunch, which turned into a walk on the beach, which turned into dinner ..." Joy went on, clearly twitterpated while glancing back at Grant.

"And we've been together ever since," Grant said with a smile that was quite panty-melting.

If Krista were to guess, she'd probably put Grant around sixty years old. Though the man could easily be younger, because even through his white button-up shirt, she could see muscle and definition. He took care of himself. But the lines around his eyes and wisdom behind the light gray of his irises spoke of years of experience, and also ... tragedy. This man had seen some shit.

Was he former law enforcement?

Retired military, perhaps?

Krista only saw eyes like that on people who had experienced more trauma and hardship in their lives than the average Joe. She was part of a family of those people and was married to a man like that. But the majority of the world didn't have eyes so filled with grief.

Grant did.

"And you're just *now* introducing us to him?" Brock asked, his voice tight, lips barely moving.

Joy's gaze turned hard as she let it fall on her oldest, most stubborn son. "I hadn't planned on introducing him to you today. You all let yourselves into my house."

"Because you said you had an appointment and couldn't come to the tree farm with us," Rex protested, having been the quietest of the bunch up until now. "We figured we'd drop your tree off, but when we saw your car in the driveway, we figured you were home and would want to see your grandchildren." He glanced at Grant. "We didn't expect that you would be *entertaining*. Did you even have an appointment?"

Their mother's cheeks turned an even brighter red.

Grant's lip twitched.

"Don't you play the guilt trip on me, Rex Barry. I see all of my grandchildren and children, and their wives, multiple times a week. Whether I had an *actual* appointment or not is none of your beeswax."

Oh, Krista was sure Joy *"had an appointment,"* all right. An appointment for orgasms from the sexy hunk behind her. Krista bet Joy put that in her planner *multiple* times a week. Probably just circled the whole little square on the calendar with a big promising O.

Rex cleared his throat, which prompted all the other Hart men to start clearing their throats. She rolled her eyes.

"We'll leave you be, Joy," Krista said, turning to her husband and applying some pressure to the side of his arm to get Brock to start moving toward the door. "We're sorry to have bugged you. There's your tree, and we'll touch base in a day or two about going to the gingerbread house display downtown with the kids."

"But we just got to Nana's," Zoe protested. "Nana, did you bake any cookies today?"

"I didn't, sweetheart," Joy said. "Nana was busy—"

"I bet she was," Brock grumbled.

Krista elbowed him hard in the gut.

Joy's blue eyes filled with fire.

One of the many babies that belonged to their ever-growing family made a warbly noise, which did a great job at breaking the heavy awkwardness and tension in the room.

"She's hungry," Rayma said. "My boobs don't work that way."

Pasha rolled her eyes. "I'll go feed her in the truck where there is less distraction." She handed Raze back to Heath and took Eve from her sister, then rested her hand on Heath's shoulder. "We should go."

Just like the rest of the Hart boys, Heath's expression was stony, but when Raze shoved his finger in Heath's ear, the man was forced to snap out of his trance. His blond hair swished as he shook his head and gently swatted away his son's hand. He blinked, nodded once, and followed his wife and their infant daughter outside.

Stacey tugged Chase and the kids out, Lydia dragged Rex out with Maeve, and Zoe and Zane seemed to understand they were not getting to raid Nana's cookie jar—since that was what Grant was doing today—and took off outside after their cousins.

That left Krista and her brooding husband.

"A heads-up would have been nice," Brock said, the tautness of his body reminding her of a cable pulled so tight you could bounce a coin off it.

Joy shrugged. "I'll give you one now, then. Grant and I are seeing each other. It's serious, and I've invited him to Christmas dinner. How's that for a heads-up?"

If she didn't know him so well, Krista would have thought steam would have started spilling out of her husband's ears. His nostrils flared, and the muscle along his chiseled jaw bounced and pulsed. That vein in his neck and the way it was protruding out was starting to worry her though. He needed to take a serious chill pill before he dropped dead from high blood pressure or an aneurysm or something.

Joy turned to Krista. "I look forward to hearing from you later in the week, honey. I've heard the gingerbread houses this year are something special." She smiled at Krista, avoiding her son's heated stare.

Krista shoved Brock's arm as a way to tell him to get moving. "We'll leave you two be. It was nice to meet you, Grant."

Grant nodded once. "Nice to meet you, too, Krista. Hope to see you again real soon."

Brock was near twice her weight, and if he didn't want to move, no amount of her shoving or nudging would have made him budge. But he knew she meant business and that his mother wasn't going to give an inch—not right now.

So thankfully, Brock mustered up the decency to leave, and Krista closed the front door behind them.

All the Hart boys, Krista's sisters-in-law, and the kids were having a little tailgate party on the street out front.

Krista rubbed her hands together and blew on them, watching her heated breath rise up and disappear into the gray sky above.

"Well, that was a Christmas surprise," Rayma said. "Nana Joy is getting her stocking stuffed a little early this year."

All four brothers growled.

"You guys can't be serious?" Lydia asked, bouncing Maeve on her hip. "Are you all pouting right now?"

"We're not pouting," Rex said to his wife, crossing his arms over his chest. He had a black knit cap on to protect his bald head from the cold. The other bald brother, Chase, had a similar gray knit cap on, and his son Connor wore a matching one.

"Looks like pouting to me," Stacey replied, pulling gloves out of her pockets and helping Thea and Connor put them on their hands.

"You wanna think about your mom getting plowed right now?" Rex asked his wife, a glint of frustration in his eyes. His trademark deep twin dimples could not be farther from his cheeks.

"If it makes her happy, yeah," Lydia said. "My dad's been dead for over twenty years. I hope she's getting some. Do I want to hear about it? No. But I hope she's getting her bell rung by a man that treats her right."

Krista, Pasha, Rayma, and Stacey all nodded in agreement.

"Fucker's in our father's home, in our father's bed. Shouldn't be *ringing anyone's damn bell.* Not here, anyway," Brock grumbled.

Krista drew in a deep, lung-tickling cold breath and patted her husband's hard chest. "Well, that's not up for you to decide. It's not your house, your bed or your body. Your mother has control over all of it, and it seems to me, she's doing just fine."

More grumbles and growls from the behemoth peanut gallery.

More eye rolls from the wives.

"I'm cold, Mama," Zoe said, sliding her hand into Krista's. "Can we go home?"

"Zane cold too. Zane go home and have hot chocolate with seven hundred nineteen fifteen five marshmallows." Krista's son shivered a little before stepping up to his father and shoving his hands under Brock's T-shirt.

"Jesus, little man," Brock said. "Your hands are like ice cubes. Okay, everybody in the truck. Let's go home." He scooped their redheaded son up and carried him to the back door of the truck. Krista exchanged glances with her sisters-in-law.

"Drinks at Mickey's later?" Pasha asked.

"I'm in!" Rayma cheered.

Stacey, Lydia, and Krista nodded.

"I'll drive, of course," Lydia said with a small smile.

"And I'll drink," Stacey added.

"Me too," Pasha agreed.

"Me three, obviously," Rayma chimed in.

They all had *a lot* to discuss, and chances were once their husbands got over the shock of seeing their mother with another man, they'd be pissed and ranty and their wives would have to hear about it.

In Krista's opinion, there wasn't enough wine in the world to numb the brain pounding she developed when Brock got in one of his little snits.

Good thing Mickey kept his tequila reserves stocked, because wine just wasn't going to cut it.

CHAPTER TWO
GRANT & JOY

GRANT BLEW out a breath and raked his fingers through his short salt-and-pepper hair as he watched Joy close the door behind her enormous family.

"Well, that was ..."

Joy spun around, her dark blue eyes suddenly appearing very tired. "Really exhausting."

He grinned and encouraged her to come into his arms. She didn't hesitate, and he kissed the top of her head when she pressed her body to his and wrapped her arms around his waist. "I was going to say, not how you were hoping to introduce me to your family."

"Yeah, that, too." She slumped into him, then glanced up the length of his body into his eyes. "I'm sorry."

"For what?"

Her eyes went wild for a moment, then she narrowed her brows and pointed to the front of the house. "For all of *that*. I love those boys, but they can be such buffoons sometimes. Did they not *think* to knock?"

His lips twisted. "I think they did. We just didn't hear them."

Her cheeks turned a gorgeous shade of pink, and a small smile tugged at the corner of her very kissable mouth. "Oh yeah ..."

"The women and kids seem great, and so do your boys."

She chuckled slightly, which caused her whole small frame to shake. "Oh, they are. And they're saintly—the women and kids, that is—for putting up with my boys and loving them as hard as they do. I mean we *all* are. They're a lot of work and require a lot of patience *and* wine to deal with them."

He snorted. "They're looking out for their mum. It's sweet."

"It's annoying. I'm sixty-six goddamn years old. I can take care of myself."

"Good kids don't see it like that, though, and something tells me you raised good kids, if not a little—"

"Bullheaded? Stubborn?"

"I was going to say overprotective, but you know them better than I do." Tracing his fingers gently down her spine, he cupped her butt. It wasn't the most comfortable position for them to stand in since she was so much shorter than he was and he had to bend his old man back in a way that kind of twinged to grab her. But he'd risk the dislocation for a handful of the ass he knew she worked hard to keep tight.

"They're *beyond* overprotective," she said with frustration in her tone as she broke out of their embrace and headed toward the kitchen. He followed her.

He'd follow this woman anywhere.

She filled the electric kettle with water, then plugged it in. "I just had this perfect plan, you know. I was going to invite the boys over for lunch, just the four of them, then introduce you to them. Do it gently. Tell them how much we care about each other, how long we've been seeing each other, and let them know that I have invited you to Christmas dinner."

"And instead, they barged into your house, drew a gun, and practically caught us in the bedroom." He leaned against the counter and faced her where she leaned against her stove, arms crossed in front of her chest, chin tucked.

"The look on Brock's face ..." She shook her head. "It was like he'd caught me cheating on his father or something. The level of betrayal in his eyes. And eyes that are *exactly* the same as Zane's to boot. It ... was gutting."

"But you're not cheating. Neither of us is. There's no betrayal."

She slowly lifted her gaze from where she'd been staring at the tile floor. "I know that. And you know that. And deep down, my buffoon son knows that. But the look on his face said otherwise. And it really, *really* doesn't help that he's nearly the spitting image of his father. I had to catch myself for a moment there, *remind* myself that I am the parent. That I am HIS mother, not his wife, not his child. Because I was going to let his gaze make me feel something I have no reason to feel."

"Like you're betraying Zane?"

She nodded. "But I'm not betraying anybody. Not Zane, not my kids. Not anybody."

He stepped towards her, boxing her in against the stove. "You're not. And you need to keep reminding yourself of that. It might take your boys a little bit to come around to the idea of us, but even though they seemed a little impulsive, they have you as a mother, and you're very level-headed. We'll just give them some time."

The kettle clicked off, and steam rose from the spout.

He stepped away from her, pulled two mugs down from the cupboard, along with a canister of chamomile tea bags. He tossed a bag into each mug, then poured hot water over them. They'd been together six months, and he'd come to know his way around her kitchen pretty well. And not that she stressed out too often, because his woman had a very calm way about her, but when she was feeling a little overwhelmed, he knew she reached for her chamomile tea.

He handed her a mug, and she thanked him for it with a murmur before cradling it in her small hands and pressing it against her chest.

"I don't *have* to come to Christmas dinner if it's going to be too much, too soon," he said. "Your family comes first, and I've had many a Christmas alone. I do just fine."

Her eyes flashed up to his, pain swirling in the blue. "No. That's not happening. You are coming. End of story."

He struggled to hide his smirk at her insistence. He was also really glad she hadn't agreed with him.

He was one hundred percent serious in his offer but had she said yes, it would have really fucking sucked. This was their first Christmas together, and the last thing he wanted was for Joy to not get what she wanted for Christmas. And he knew she wanted him there.

Her expression turned frustrated. "What about *me?* I'm part of this loud, obnoxious, crazy family, too. Why do *they* all get to have their partners and happiness, but I'm just expected to sit alone by myself and watch them all together just because my husband died too soon? I'm just *supposed* to be alone. How is that fair? How is that right? And how is it right that you have to sit home alone on Christmas, both of us miserable without the other, just to make my idiot sons feel *more comfortable?*"

It wasn't right at all. But he wasn't going to say that to her.

He knew a lot about Joy, so he knew how important her family was to her, which meant he wasn't quite sure if he could voice such thoughts just yet. She seemed to slowly be coming around to the notions herself, though, that sometimes, she needed to put herself first. To do what made *her* happy.

She took a cautious sip of her tea, then let out a weighted sigh. "Maybe we left it too late? Maybe I should have introduced you to them sooner so they had more time to adjust and come around to you coming to Christmas dinner."

He didn't have anything to say.

He didn't have any kids of his own, so he didn't know how to handle them. He was completely taking her lead on this.

"I just thought that *maybe* if I waited until a week or so before Christmas to introduce you to them, then they'd be all caught up in the Christmas spirit with their kids and be more open to another person at the table." She blew on the top of her mug. "That backfired."

He leaned back against the counter and blew on his mug before taking a sip. The tea was still really fucking hot, but he liked it that way. He'd never been big into tea before meeting Joy, he'd always been a black coffee guy, but she drank a lot of tea, and over the last few months, she'd turned him into a tea enthusiast, too.

She seemed to be lost in her own thoughts as she stared into her mug with scrunched brows.

So he just took the opportunity to study her.

Fuck almighty, she was a looker.

He'd gone on a couple of dates over the last few years, but nothing amounted to anything serious, then one day he walked toward the lane he'd reserved at the pool, and there she was. She had her bright yellow swim cap on, her blue goggles, and that black racer-back one-piece suit that showed off her fit figure. She'd already set her water bottle down on the edge of the pool, along with her neatly folded towel, and was getting ready to climb in.

He almost thought about just turning around and going to the weight room rather than bother her and tell her she was about to jump in and swim laps in the lane that *he* had reserved.

But when she turned to him, smiled, and said, "Good morning," he was a fucking goner.

Then he had to say something.

Only what he said was really stupid. "Uh, you're in my lane."

He would forever berate himself for such a stupid first line to this incredible, intelligent, beautiful woman.

She'd flipped the goggles off her eyes and leveled him with a gaze so striking, he nearly fell into the deep end—literally.

"Excuse me?" she'd said. Her tone hadn't been harsh, but she also wasn't some shrinking violet.

"I've booked this lane from seven until eight."

She shook her head. "No, I have."

At a public pool, they'd just have to grin and bear it, both dive in and dodge each other for an hour. But one of the perks of paying extra for a private club pool was that when you reserved a lane, you got the whole dang thing yourself.

She glanced at the sandwich board that had the lane number on it. "Number four."

He nodded. "Yes, I booked number four from seven until eight."

Her swim cap impeded her brow from lifting too high on her forehead.

"Well, then, let's go check with Marjorie at the desk." Then before he could argue, not that he planned to, she was pushing past him toward the desk where Marjorie sat.

As it turned out, poor Marjorie had double-booked the lane and they were both on the schedule.

Grant sent Marjorie flowers two weeks later for her wonderful blunder.

"I guess we can share," Joy said, not bothering to hide her approval of his body with the way she let her gaze slowly travel from his toes to the top of his head. He was in a pair of skin-tight swim trunks that fell to his knees. It wasn't a Speedo, because he just couldn't go there, but it still left very little to the imagination. And he also took care of himself. He worked out every morning, ate right, got lots of sleep.

Over the last few years, his health scares had helped set him right. Not that he didn't live a healthy lifestyle before, but he knew he was no spring chicken anymore and needed to take better care of his body.

"I'm Joy," she said, sticking out her hand after scoping him out.

He grinned and took her dainty hand in his. "Grant."

"I don't swim fast, but I'm not a slug either. Please be courteous in the lane."

He grinned. Fuck, he liked her already. "I absolutely will be courteous."

She nodded and spun on her bare feet to head back to the lane. Without waiting for him, she slid into the pool, pulled her goggles back over her eyes, and pushed off.

He gave himself a moment to just watch her. She had nice form, and the way her hips swiveled as she kicked had made him shove down a groan. The woman was a real fucking looker.

By the time they both finished swimming, they were out of breath and had goggle lines around their eyes and grumbling bellies.

She hoisted herself out of the water first, which allowed him to check out her ass again; removed her cap, and draped the towel around herself.

"Well, thanks for not splashing me in the face," she said with a chuckle. "See you around."

But he couldn't let her go. Not yet.

Like Aquaman (or at least that was how he was going to let that memory stay), he sprang out of the water and awkwardly run-walked after her. He gripped her elbow, and she turned around, curiosity in those bright blue eyes.

"Would you like to grab a coffee and maybe something to eat?" he asked, feeling his palm, which was still against her elbow, getting sweaty. He immediately pulled it away from her.

Her eyes narrowed for a moment, but the smile that spread across those beautiful lips made his heart skip a beat. "I'd love to."

Back in the present, he smiled as he watched her sip her tea. He'd replayed that moment over and over in his head a million times since that day, grateful that she hadn't written him off as some bumbling fool. A woman hadn't made him that unsure of himself in nearly fifty years.

"What's got you smiling?" she asked, lifting a brow.

He set his mug down on the counter and boxed her body back in against the stove. She set her mug down, too. "Just remembering."

"How we met?"

He nodded.

Her gaze softened, and a beautiful little smile lifted the corners of her mouth. "You think about that a lot, don't you?"

He nodded, and his thumbs found her spine. She groaned as he started to massage her back, her eyes fluttering shut.

"Hadn't had a woman fluster me like that in damn near fifty years. Still fluster me sometimes, woman."

She opened her eyes and glanced up at him. "Full disclosure?"

He cocked his head to the side. Where was she going with this? "Okay ..."

She nibbled on her lip for a moment and glanced away.

A frisson of unease slid down his back.

Finally, she looked back at him and sighed before speaking. "I'd seen you around and asked Marjorie to make the mistake and put us both in the same lane. I'd been looking for a reason to meet you. Thought you were pretty damn handsome, and I needed a reason to talk to you." She snagged her bottom lip with her teeth again. Her eyes were now like two cut sapphires, the way they glimmered mischievously at him. "Normally men don't make me nervous. I'm perfectly fine asking them for coffee or striking up a conversation. But you left me tongue-tied the first time I saw you climb out of the pool."

Grant tossed his head back and let out a whoop of a laugh. "Damn, woman! You orchestrated the whole thing?"

She nodded sheepishly, but she kept smiling.

"A scheming little thing *and* an Oscar-worthy actor. I never would have guessed based on how aloof you were in the beginning."

"Couldn't seem too eager."

He snorted through his nose. "And you're *just* telling me this now? After six months."

She lifted a shoulder. "You've met my kids. We're serious now. It's high time you learned the truth."

Shaking his head but grinning ear to ear, he scooped her up into his arms with a growl.

She squealed, smiled, and looped her arms around his neck.

"And it's high time you learned the truth of just how crazy I am about you," he said, stalking back down the hallway toward her bedroom as Joy peppered kisses all over his neck.

CHAPTER THREE
GRANT & JOY

"I'LL CALL YOU LATER," Grant said, kissing her one more time before heading out the door to his SUV.

They'd spent the last hour in bed together after she revealed to him that she'd planned their whole meet-cute.

He didn't seem perturbed in the least. He'd gone as far as to say he was flattered and that he'd never had a woman go to such lengths just to meet him.

That made her smile and snuggle deeper into his arms.

Joy wandered over to the big picture window in her living room and pulled open the drapes. She watched him pull out of the driveway. They each waved, then he was gone.

Normally, she never closed the drapes. But when Grant came over, she usually did. Sometimes she just didn't feel like having sex in her bedroom. Just because she wasn't a spring chicken anymore didn't mean she didn't enjoy sex in *other* places besides a bed and her room.

With a heavy sigh that jostled her shoulders, she stared out at the gray sky.

It'd been a hell of a long time since she'd been this happy.

Or as happy as she was when she was with Grant.

Right now, she was worried about her sons. And also pissed off with them—particularly the most bullheaded of them all: Brock.

The way they'd all looked at her, the way *Brock* had looked at her when they saw Grant come out of the bedroom behind her and put his hand on her shoulder—she couldn't scrape that image from her brain even if she tried. It was branded there, and she could still smell the char.

She wasn't betraying Zane.

She would never.

Zane had been the love of her life.

Their romance had been instant, and everything happened at warp speed.

Slowly, she made her way through the house, turning on the lights as she went. She entered the kitchen, checked to see how much water was in the kettle, then turned it back on.

An old, faded picture of Zane with the four boys, all of them in Thetis Lake smiling, hung by a penis-shaped magnet on the fridge. A hilarious friend and colleague had sent her the magnet as a gift. It was their *thing*. They each sent the other genitalia-themed things for Christmas and birthdays. This year, Joy had sent Ingrid a plant pot with all kinds of different women lying on their backs with their legs spread wide open. It showed roughly fifty different sets of labia, clitorises, and anuses. Every one was unique and wonderful in its own way. Some had hair; some didn't. Some were loose; some were tight. She couldn't wait to see what Ingrid sent her this year.

But as much as the penis magnet made her smile, it was the photo beneath it that had her throat growing tight.

Zane.

They'd only had thirteen years together, but they'd been the best thirteen years of her life.

She'd been in a horrible relationship before, an abusive one.

She'd followed Anders over to Victoria from Vancouver for

school, both of them attending the University of Victoria. But they hadn't been over in Victoria for long, living together in a small apartment, when he started to get violent.

And she had nowhere to go.

No friends or family to run to, since everyone she knew and loved was on the mainland and she couldn't just leave school mid-semester.

But one night, Anders got more aggressive and more physical than normal. What used to just be shoves up against the wall, shouting, and bruising around her wrist when he would hold on too tight quickly escalated into him punching and kicking her.

She truly thought she was going to die that night.

Thoughts of her mother and father, her sisters, and the life she wanted to live but would probably never get the chance to flashed through her mind. Only interrupted by the stars she saw with each one of Anders's blows.

She'd cried and screamed for help, but either nobody in their apartment building heard, or they just didn't care.

This was the early eighties, after all. Women had very few rights and were expected to "do as their man told them to."

Curled up in a ball and huddled in a corner to protect herself as best she could, she braced herself for the next blow—but it never came.

Her eyes were swollen shut, so she couldn't see what was happening, and the ringing in her ears distorted things, but when she was lifted up by big strong arms and cradled against a hard chest, all she could do was flop, boneless, against her savior.

She'd landed on a soft bed, and when she made to open her eyes, they resisted. She was able to make out a man through the thin slit of vision, and he was staring at her with so much concern and care that she flung herself into his arms and wept.

That man, of course, had been Zane.

He'd just moved in next door. A retired naval officer and, at the time, a wet-behind-the-ears rookie cop, he'd heard Anders hurting her and came to investigate.

He'd taken care of Anders, had him arrested, then after she stopped soaking his shoulder with her tears, he took her to the hospital.

She moved in with him the next day, and they found out she was pregnant with Brock a month later.

It was a whirlwind, wild, and wonderful romance, and aside from nearly being beaten to death by Anders, she wouldn't change a thing about how she and Zane came to be.

The kettle clicked off, and she poured hot water into the mug Grant previously used for her. No sense wasting perfectly good steeped tea. She could just add to it.

Holding the warm mug with two hands and allowing the heat to seep through her and chase away the chill, she stared at the picture on the fridge.

Zane's smile was electric. He was in his element.

He was with his boys.

The man had been an incredible father.

He was meant to do amazing things, and one of those things was to be a dad.

And his sons had all inherited that trait, too.

Each one of her boys was an absolutely phenomenal father. Their hard outer shells were nothing when their kids were around. They might as well be made of pure marshmallows.

Zane had been the same way.

And he'd supported her career every step of the way.

Of course, when she found out she was pregnant with Brock, she finished that year of her master's but then took a year off. Then she got pregnant with Chase midway through the next year of school and had to take another year off after he was born.

She was close to popping with Rex in her belly when she

finally walked across the stage to accept her diploma for her master's in psychology.

And as much as she would have liked to jump right into her PhD, she had to be realistic and be a mother for a while. Then Heath happened, and she thought her dreams of becoming Dr. Hart would be gone forever.

But Zane kept telling her, "We'll make it work, baby. If you want to get that doctorate, get it. We'll figure it out. Don't give up on your dream."

She'd just been accepted into the PhD program and was excited to tell him the news when he got home from work, only he died before she ever got the chance.

Taking her tea, she headed back into the living room and took a seat in her favorite chair.

Even though she'd lived alone for decades now—besides those two years Rayma lived with her—she never really *felt* alone. She always felt Zane's presence.

Well, not when she and Grant were doing things. Zane respectfully went and haunted someone else.

But when she was alone, she knew he was with her.

So that must mean, if his presence, his energy respectfully gave her space when Grant was over, he was okay with Grant in her life?

He didn't feel betrayed.

She scoffed and mentally chastised herself. She'd never been an overly spiritual person. She believed more in gods and goddesses of fertility and that kind of stuff than she did in the afterlife. But certain things happened from time to time that couldn't be explained. That had to be Zane.

Pressure on her forehead like a kiss, only it was just her standing in front of the sink washing dishes, completely alone in the house. Or when she fell asleep in her favorite chair only to wake up with a blanket on her, but there wasn't one to begin with.

None of these things happened when anybody else was around. So ... it had to be Zane, right? Always, still looking out for her.

"You're okay with him, right?" she said out loud. "We never got the chance to have the conversation because you died too soon, but you'd want me to find someone I care about again, right? Someone who cares about me?"

She held her breath for a moment and glanced up at the ceiling.

Was she expecting a sign? The lights to flicker or the room to shake?

Nothing happened.

"I mean, if the roles had been reversed, I wouldn't want you to live your life alone. We know what we had, and nothing can replace that. But ..." She swallowed. "You don't feel like I'm betraying you, do you, Zane?"

More silence.

She growled. "A sign either way would be nice."

Nothing.

"Just because I care about Grant doesn't mean I don't care about you. That doesn't mean I'll ever stop loving you. He's a widower. His wife was his soul mate, too. But we don't deserve to be alone, not when we make each other happy."

A heady scent of fir wafted toward her, and that's when she realized there was a Christmas tree leaning up against her wall. She needed to untie the string and set it up. She was just about to do that when a text message made her phone and butt vibrate. She leaned over to one side to pull it out of the back pocket of her jeans.

It was from Krista, and it instantly made Joy smile. *I'll deal with my husband. Sorry about today. Grant is hot. You go, girl!*

Chuckling, she responded to her daughter-in-law. *Thank you. I'm sure he'll come around.*

Then, because her daughters-in-law were all of the same mind, cut from the same gorgeous cloth, another text message rolled in. This time from Stacey. *Where'd you pick up that hunk of handsome meat? Ow ow! Nana Joy is getting her groove back. Also, sorry about the guys. I'll deal with Chase. You just do your thang.*

Damn, she loved these women.

As buffoon-like and stubborn as her sons could be, they'd done a hell of a job in picking women. Strong, smart, kind women who didn't take an ounce of her sons' shit without dishing it back tenfold.

Zane would have loved every one of his daughters-in-law as well.

Grant is FINE! Good job, Joy! came from Lydia. Followed by *So sorry we interrupted boom boom time, Joy. I hope you guys were able to jump back into things after we left. He is so damn hot! Nice!* from Pasha.

Now her face hurt, she was smiling and laughing so much.

She counted down from ten. It was only a manner of time until the last woman in the bunch texted her, and this one was going to be a doozy, there was no doubt about it. The woman *was* a doozy, and Joy loved her dearly.

Her phone buzzed again, and of course, there was a message from Rayma. She braced herself. *NANA! You sexy minx, you! Where have you been hiding that silver fox? I want one! Does he have a younger brother? A son? I want ALLL the details. Spare nothing. You know my own sex life is nonexistent. Let me live vicariously through you. I don't care if it's old-person sex. We all need lovin', even senior citizens. I can't wait to come over for coffee after exams are done and hear more. So happy for you. Also, does he GRANT all your wishes? *wink wink* Xoxox*

Yeah, Rayma didn't disappoint.

Dear Lord, she needed to find that girl a man.

Not that Rayma had any problems finding a man herself. The girl was smart, gorgeous, outgoing and a massive flirt. She usually had an endless stream of suitors and flavors of the month. And Joy certainly didn't begrudge or judge Rayma for playing the field. The girl was safe and embracing her sexuality, more power to her.

But she seemed to keep picking real duds of late. Or at least it was the duds that Rayma kept introducing to the family. Preppy boys whose parents own multiple yachts in Oak Bay, or bad boys whose rap sheets were so long, Krista had to send them to everyone in multiple emails because of the 25MB limit.

There had to be a happy medium somewhere.

Even if he wasn't Mr. Forever, Rayma needed to find herself a decent, kind Mr. Right Now. She deserved better.

She texted back Lydia, Pasha, and Rayma while sipping her tea.

Just about to pick up her knitting, since she was behind on scarves and knit caps for all the kids for Christmas, her phone buzzed again.

She rolled her eyes, expecting another text from Rayma.

But it was from Grant. *The beauty of the weekend and being retired is that I don't really have anything I HAVE to do. Once I've finished with this flight lesson, can I come back over?*

She grinned, and her body warmed. A man had not flustered her like this since Zane, and even then, since their relationship had been so unconventional, Zane hadn't flustered her either.

A gasp caught in her throat at the sudden but gentle pressure on her forehead. Then it was gone.

He was okay with it.

Smiling through the tears that brimmed her eyes and with a giggle bubbling up from her chest, she texted Grant back. *I was hoping you would.*

CHAPTER FOUR
CHASE & STACEY

STACEY HUMMED along to a tune in her head as she stood in front of the stove and stirred the freshly grated Parmesan into the tortellini. She would have something to eat at the pub with her sisters-in-law, but first, she needed to make sure her children were fed. Oh, and her husband, too. Not that he wasn't capable of making his own food or feeding the children, but at the moment, the three people she loved most in the world were setting up their freshly cut Christmas tree in the living room. So it was the least she could do.

She could hear the growing impatience in her husband's voice as he kept asking Thea, their three-year-old going on thirteen-year-old, to stop touching the lights.

Then Connor would chime in and tell Thea to stop as well, causing Stacey's little tyrant to stomp her feet and tell Connor he wasn't her daddy.

Stacey just hummed louder to tune them all out.

Her husband had been ornery—well, more ornery than normal —since they'd returned home with their delicious-smelling tree.

She knew why, and she one hundred percent disagreed with it.

He'd made a few mutterings on the drive home about how, at his mother's age, it didn't seem right. And his father would be spinning in his grave if he had a grave and they hadn't cremated him.

She'd remained silent.

She disagreed with his opinion but voicing that before she knew he would be receptive would just be a complete waste of time. She needed to wait until the children were in bed and Chase had food in his stomach and had started to unwind for the night.

It probably also wouldn't hurt if she was drunk and horny and jumped his bones when she came home from the pub. He was always way more talkative after a good orgasm.

But she needed to talk to him, not only for his own sake but for the sake of her mother-in-law.

Joy Hart had welcomed Stacey into the family fold with open arms and so much love. Even when things between her and Chase were rocky, they were never rocky between Stacey and Joy, or Joy and the kids. She insisted they call her Nana Joy from day one, and the kids started doing it like it was just meant to be. Because it was.

But Stacey knew, even though Joy had never voiced it, that her mother-in-law was lonely. She was sixty-six, a successful sex and relationship therapist, incredibly educated and accomplished, but she lived alone and had been alone—intimately—since the boys were very young.

She needed—nay, she *deserved*—to have more in her life.

She deserved love and not just from her family.

She deserved intimacy and orgasms. Devotion and someone who, when all her sons and their families were busy, would keep her company and bring her a mug of tea in the evening while she knitted and watched television.

She deserved that more than any other woman Stacey could think of.

And yet, the way her sons reacted to Grant said they didn't feel the same way. Stacey knew that it would be up to her and her sisters-in-law to convince the men otherwise. It sounded stupid to think it, so she certainly wouldn't say it out loud, but with the news of Grant being invited for Christmas dinner, she knew that if they didn't change the men's minds about Grant before December twenty-fifth, their attitude could very well ruin Christmas.

So, to be cliché ... it was up to Stacey and her sisters in crime to save Christmas.

A big warm palm grazed her butt as she sliced cucumbers and bell peppers into thin strips. "Those kids would give me gray hair if I had any hair to turn gray," Chase murmured next to her ear, the rough timbre of his voice making a shiver race the length of her spine.

"Oh, you have hair to turn gray," she teased. "Come to think of it, I found a few silver strands down there when I was—"

"Mama, I'm hungry!" Thea tugged on the hem of her shirt. "When's supper?"

Chase's hand slipped away from her butt cheek, and he scooped up Thea. "It'll be when your mother calls you, you little turkey. Did you finish the decorations on your side of the tree?" He held her horizontally across his big, muscular arms and blew a raspberry on her belly when her shirt slipped up, causing their daughter to erupt into a fit of giggles.

"Yes, Daddy. I finished. But now I'm hungry. Decorating trees is hard work."

Chase and Stacey both snorted.

"Go wash your hands. Dinner will be ready by the time you get back," Stacey said, dishing up her family's dinner into three individual plates: tortellini, sliced veggies, and homemade turkey apple meatballs that she pulled out of the freezer as soon as she got home and knew she was heading out for a girls' night.

Chase was back behind her, closer than ever.

His scent and heat swarmed her, making her a little lightheaded. "You getting drunk tonight?" he asked, his mouth next to her ear. His hand moved around to the front of her pants and between her legs. She spread them just enough for him to get better access, and with one finger, he pressed against her clit but over her pants.

Her breath hitched. "Do you want me to get drunk?"

"Up to you. But I do *love* tipsy Stacey and how adventurous and amorous she can be." He double-tapped his finger on her clit again, and her knees wobbled.

Two heavy-footed children, bickering as children were known to do, entered the kitchen, and Chase's hand once again slipped away.

"Connor took my stool away," Thea whined. "Now my hands are all wet, 'cause I couldn't reach the towel to dry them."

Connor rolled his eyes as he sat down at the kitchen table. "I didn't take the stool away; I just moved it over so I could wash my hands. I don't need the stool because I can reach the sink without it. Then she started getting all whiny and refused to move the stool back."

"I can't reach the sink without the stool," Thea continued to whine, taking a seat at the table across from her brother.

"Then move the stool back," Connor said blandly.

Thea stuck her tongue out at her brother.

Stacey plopped two plates down at the same time in front of her offspring. "Eat up and stop bickering. There are ice cream sandwiches in the freezer for dessert, but only if your dad thinks you've both eaten enough dinner and you stop arguing."

Chase came back up behind her, his hand once again finding her butt. "Don't stay out too late," he said, his voice a raspy purr next to her ear before he pecked her on the side of the head and sat down at the table between their children with his plate of food.

"What are you going to do while I'm gone and the kids are in bed?" she asked, beginning to tidy up the kitchen while her family ate.

"Brothers and I all recorded the hockey game and will do video chat and watch it once the kids are all in bed. Plus, I took a picture of *Grant's* license plate, and I'm going to run it and see what kind of dirt I can dig up on the guy."

"Is that guy Nana Joy's boyfriend?" Connor asked, spearing a piece of tortellini and popping it into his mouth.

At the exact same time, Stacey said "yes" and Chase said "no."

Connor's brows furrowed.

"Which is it?" Thea asked.

Stacey glared at her husband. He glared back and shook his head.

Stacey rolled her eyes and fixed her attention on her children as she filled the sink up with hot, soapy water. "He is Nana Joy's boyfriend, yes. And I happen to think that it's wonderful that she has found someone she enjoys spending time with and who makes her happy. She said she's inviting him for Christmas dinner, which should be a lot of fun."

"Do they *kiss?*" Thea asked, scrunching up her face in disgust.

Stacey hedged a glance at her husband. The man's entire face was getting redder by the second. Soon, steam would begin to seep from his ears.

"Probably," Stacey said, turning her attention back to her children and away from her irrationally brooding husband.

"Gross," Thea said with a giggle.

"Yeah, gross," Connor agreed.

"It *is* gross," Chase said, his fork making a horrendous noise on the plate as he plunged it into a piece of pasta.

Stacey shot him a look of irritation. "I don't like the idea of you running a background check on your mother's boyfriend. Don't you think she would have asked you to do that if she wanted you to?"

"No," he said, taking a sip of water. "And we're doing it for her protection. She doesn't know this guy's history. Maybe he's leading a double life—"

"Like Ted was?" she asked, cutting him off.

His anger deflated just a touch at the mention of her dead ex-husband and the biological father of her children. Ted had been leading a double life. When he met and married Stacey, he was already married to someone else in another city. But that didn't stop him from having two children with Stacey and promising her a lifetime of happiness. She'd thought nothing of his two-weeks-on, two-weeks-off job. But now, in hindsight, she should have been more suspicious.

"Sorry," Chase muttered.

She shook her head. "No, I get it. Do your background check. Though I doubt he has a second family at his age, but you never know. Just don't go too deep. No medical or financial records, okay? That's none of your business. Stick to the criminal background and work."

The face he gave her said he wasn't promising anything.

She took a deep breath in through her nose and pushed it out a moment later. "Don't ruin Christmas with your antics. And that goes for all four of you. I know none of you are happy to see your mother in a relationship, but really, it's about time, and she deserves to be happy. Do what you need to do—what you do best—to clear your conscience and be okay with your mother's new boyfriend, but don't dig so deep you're all trapped in a hole you can't climb out of."

"Yeah, Daddy, don't ruin Christmas," Thea added. "Santa will put coal in your stocking and reindeer poop in your shoes."

Stacey's lips twitched. "She's not wrong."

Chase's green gaze slid to his daughter, and his expression softened. "I won't ruin Christmas, baby. I promise."

That seemed to satisfy their daughter well enough, and she went back to eating her dinner.

Stacey's phone vibrated on the counter, and she dried her

hands on a dishtowel before grabbing it. It was Lydia, their designated driver. *Five minutes away.*

"That's my ride," Stacey said, pulling the plug in the sink to let the soapy water drain out. She walked up to each of the three people she loved most on Earth and planted a kiss on the top of each of their heads. "Be good. *All* of you. No monkey business. In bed at a reasonable time. Wash behind your ears and between your toes."

"Yes, Mama," all three of them said at the same time before exchanging snickers and smiles across the table.

With a grin, she headed out of the kitchen, but not before glancing once more over her shoulder and snagging Chase's gaze. "Wait up for me?" She bobbed her brows.

His smile stretched clear across his face. "Planned on it."

CHAPTER FIVE
CHASE & STACEY

CHASE PULLED another beer out of the fridge, popped the cap, and carried it back to the living room. Being the tech genius that he was, he had the hockey game on the television, a secondary monitor with a camera on it perched on the coffee table with his brothers' ugly mugs on it, then he had his laptop, which he was using to get dirt on Grant.

His regular laptop wasn't going to do the trick though. He needed the untraceable computer that he bought through an anonymous third party paying only cash. This was the computer he used when he needed to go onto the dark web or hunt down the scum of the Earth. And when he couldn't go sit in some restaurant and pilfer the free Wi-Fi off the café next door to keep his whereabouts a secret, he had to use a proxy server in order to hide his IP address and set up one of his many burner phones as a hot spot. It still wasn't as secure as he would like, but he was home alone with his kids, so he had no other choice.

One thing was for sure though, no way in fuck was he using his home Wi-Fi on the dark web.

Luckily, for various things over the years, he had installed undetectable back doors into a lot of major government servers, which meant he didn't even need to go onto the dark web or do any major hacking. Now it was just as easy as walking in the front door during business hours and unwrapping a hard candy from the bowl on the reception desk.

"Got anything yet?" Rex said, tipping back his beer. His blue gaze bounced back and forth between the television screen with the Canucks vs. Kings game and the computer where they all were.

Each brother was at home in his own houses with their sleeping children. The women were off at Mickey's, because according to Brock, the four of them had "very important things to discuss" so as they sometimes did, they were on a four-way video chat, with the hockey game on in the background.

Chase nodded absentmindedly as he plunked the laptop back on the top of his thighs and settled his beer bottle down on the end table. "Grant Robert Wild. Born October fifth, 1960, to Sylvia and George Wild in Okotoks, Alberta. Two sisters, significantly older—like in their seventies. One is deceased. One is in a care home in Calgary."

"Okay, but does he have any priors? Kids with priors? What does he do for work?", Brock's impatience could be felt through the computers. The man was tightly wound, and it came out in his clipped speech and body language. Chase could see his older brother's thumb twitching against the label on his beer bottle and the paper shavings peeling off and landing on the black leather arm of Brock's recliner.

"I'm still looking," Chase murmured.

"There we go, little duck," Heath murmured. "That better?"

Chase glanced up and focused on Heath's square. He had his one-month-old daughter Eve in his arms and was feeding her a bottle.

"Thank God Pash pumped before she left and had a fresh bottle sitting in the warmer." He pressed his lips to his daughter's forehead as she blinked up at him and guzzled. "What did I miss?"

"Nothin' yet," Rex said. "Just that Grant's younger than Mum and from Alberta. Nothing worth getting your panties in a bunch over—"

"Yet," Brock grumbled.

"Looks like he was in the Canadian Air Force in Cold Lake, Alberta, for several years. Flew helicopters mostly. Became a helicopter mechanic, too. Moved here in ninety-seven, started his own business as a helicopter mechanic and a side hustle as a flight instructor."

"Any kids? Wife?" Heath asked.

Chase was still clicking away on the computer. Stacey had asked him not to go into the man's medical files, but since he'd already built himself a very pretty back door into the records of public health, it was only a few clicks until he was in. And ever since he was seven and had learned to read, it was an impossible skill to just *turn off.*

"No kids. No wife ... wait a sec."

"Don't tell me she died of questionable causes. Like something that was ruled as suicide but we all know could just have easily been murder," Rex murmured, shoving a handful of pretzels into his mouth.

"There *was* a Daphne Wild, but she passed away fifteen years ago," Chase said.

"How?" Brock asked.

Chase clicked a few more times. "Esophageal cancer."

Fuck.

"Jesus," Heath said, taking the empty bottle from Eve's lips, propping her upon his shoulder, and briskly patting her back to work out a burp.

"That fuckin' sucks," Rex breathed out.

Yeah, that did fucking suck.

"Okay, so he didn't kill her. Moving on," Brock said, not an ounce of empathy entering his veins after hearing about a poor woman's battle with cancer.

Chase cleared his throat. "Looks like Grant had a brush with cancer himself a couple of years ago. Prostate. They removed it, and he's now cancer-free."

His brothers nodded. Brock merely grunted the way Brock was known to do.

"That's why we go and get that lubed-up big man finger up our butts, right?" Heath said with an awkward chuckle.

Rex and Chase groaned at Heath's bleak attempt at a joke.

"Address?" Brock grunted.

Unease wormed through Chase. He didn't like the look in Brock's eyes.

He knew how his big brother felt because he felt it, too.

They were looking out for their mother. For their family.

But the glint of almost desperation in Brock's eyes told Chase he wasn't so sure Brock having access to Grant's address was the smartest idea.

"Address?!" Brock barked again.

Chase exhaled, exited the window that had Grant's medical history and returned to the one with his address: "4325 Ellie Jean Drive." He rubbed his palm over his bald head. "But don't go snooping around. If Mum finds out ..."

"You guys don't give me enough credit," Brock grumbled.

Chase exchanged glances with Rex and Heath through the computers and cameras. All three of them were thinking the same thing. They gave Brock a fuck-ton of credit. He was the leader—the patriarch—of their family and the head of their company. So him saying they didn't give him enough credit wasn't meant to convey that he wasn't going to go to Grant's. It meant that he was going to go; he just wasn't going to get caught.

Chase glanced at Heath and Rex again.

"You know I can see you fuckers looking at each other," Brock said with another grumble.

"So?" Heath said, kissing Eve on the side of the head. "You think Uncle Brock is a grumpy bugger, don't you, Evie?" He held the baby's tight little fist and tried to make her wave at the camera. "Yes, I do, Daddy. I also think that out of all the Hart brothers, you are the best-looking and the smartest and the funniest." He brought his voice up several octaves until it was squeaky.

Chase and Rex both snorted and rolled their eyes.

"See, babies are the best judges of character, and even Evie thinks you're being a grumpy bugger," Heath said, kissing Eve again on the baby's little bobblehead.

Surprise, surprise, Brock grunted again.

A car door slammed outside, and Chase stilled, his ears zeroing in on what was happening outside the house. He focused on the front door.

"What's wrong?" Brock asked, sitting up from where he was in his lounger, already on high alert.

Chase's brow dipped, and his lips twisted. "Stand down. Pretty sure it's just Stacey home."

Rex picked up his phone. "Makes sense. Lydia just texted me to say she was about twenty minutes from home. So she's just dropping them all off."

Brock visibly relaxed.

"You need to smoke some weed or have another beer or something, bro. You're wound tight as a fucking top," Heath said, resting Eve down on his thighs, her head toward his knees, and starting to do bicycle movements with her legs. Chase remembered having to do that with Thea when she would get gassy. It was amazing how easily you could work the farts out of them. It was also amazing how cute baby farts were.

Connor's farts as an eight-year-old—not so much.

He heard the key slide into the lock on the front door, and he quickly shut down everything on his computer. Not that he would keep this from his wife—she understood why he needed to investigate Grant—but either way, he knew it would be easier if he wasn't neck-deep in the man's medical records when she got home.

"Gotta go," he said, giving his brothers each a chin lift before canceling the video chat at the same time the doorknob turned and his glazy-eyed wife walked in.

The smile that spread across her freckled face and the way her brown eyes lasered in on his crotch covered in gray sweatpants was enough to get his pulse racing like an Olympic sprinter.

She closed the door without saying a word and flipped the deadbolt.

He'd set the high-end security system he installed before they went to bed, but for now, he had other things on his mind.

It also helped that they lived a bit out in the boondocks on Prospect Lake, so the chance of any crime or a break-in happening out here in the middle of winter was pretty fucking slim.

Stacey let her purse fall to the floor, and removed her coat.

It wasn't exactly a striptease, given how many layers the woman was wearing, but either way, he could watch her take off her clothes every minute of every fucking day.

His cock was already itching to get out of its confined space, and his balls had started to ache.

She licked her lips before pulling her plain white T-shirt over her head, revealing a nude lace bra.

Her jeans were next.

The entire time, she never peeled her gaze from his. Never let that sly, sexy little lopsided smile drift from her lips. She saw only him, and holy fucking hell, did he see only her.

She was his new lease on life.

His saving grace.

His entire fucking world.

Just when he thought he would be lost inside his head, in the darkness with the monsters and the demons forever, she clawed her way across the thorns, battled the monsters, and brought him back out into the real world. She showed him what unconditional love was and how it was a fucking life raft in the white squall of life.

Only Stacey's love wasn't any blow-up dinghy. It was a goddamn aircraft carrier, and it carried him and their children through every rough patch of weather, every swell, and rather than having the hull torn out by a rock or icebergs, it merely split those motherfuckers into two pieces and just kept them all moving forward.

In nothing but her nude bra and black cotton panties, she sauntered over to him. "Did you wear your lingerie for me?" she asked, tracing the tip of her finger along his thigh. "Get all gussied up for mama?"

He snorted and smiled.

That made her grin widen even more.

"You're drunk." It wasn't a question. The glazed-over look in her eyes, the goofy smile, and the way her body kind of swayed said she'd thoroughly enjoyed her night out with her sisters-in-law and Rayma.

He loved that his wife and brothers' wives were so close. Stacey's own family was a piece of shit, so the fact that she fit seamlessly into Chase's meant that they were meant to be together.

She shrugged her freckled shoulder. "I'm not gonna lie. Mickey makes a mean whiskey sour. And you know how Krista likes her tequila shots. And since Lydia isn't drinking right now, Krista, Pasha, Rayma, and I had to drink her share." Her words were slightly slurred, but her don't-give-two-shits expression made his smile grow tenfold.

"As long as you had a good time," he said, reaching up and caressing her bare hip.

"Had a *really* good time. Did you know Mickey got a karaoke machine?"

Brock, who was part owner of Mickey's bar, had mentioned last week that Mickey installed a karaoke machine, but Chase forgot about it when the women said they were heading to Mickey's.

He wasn't sure any of the women could carry a tune, and if Pasha, Krista, and Rayma were as drunk as Stacey, it was probably a pretty entertaining but audibly painful night for the rest of the bar patrons.

His cock in his sweatpants was now hard as granite, and since he wasn't wearing any boxers, a small damp patch where the precum leaked out was noticeable toward his left hipbone.

Stacey zeroed in on it and licked her lips.

"Did you go digging?" she asked.

He nodded.

"And what did you find?" She climbed onto the couch and straddled him but lifted and waited so that he could shove his pants down far enough to release his cock.

"Guy's clean. No priors. No rap sheet. No second family hiding in the woods anywhere. At least not from what I could find." His thumbs stroked her hips, and she rocked against him.

"You going to leave it be now and let your mother be happy?" She reached behind her back and unclasped her bra, letting it slide down her arms and to the floor below. Her raspberry nipples were hard and taunting him.

"Rather not talk about that anymore," he said through slightly labored breathing. The way she was grinding against his cock had his concentration levels waning.

Leaning forward, he latched onto one nipple and sucked it hard into his mouth until she gasped and bowed her back.

She continued to thrust against him, her panties growing damper against the underside of his cock with each tilt of her hips.

He sucked her nipple harder and moved one hand to the other breast to pull and twist the nipple, while the fingers from his right hand moved down between them and pushed her panties to the side so that he could feel just how fucking wet she was.

Stacey's hands tugged at the sides of his white T-shirt, and eventually, he released her nipple with a wet *pop* and let her remove his shirt. Her gaze turned avid and her eyelids dropped as she let her eyes languidly roam his body. Her nails forged a delicate path over his shoulders and arms, causing goosebumps to follow her fingers.

Gathering more of her wetness from her slick heat, he moved his index finger side-to-side over her clit, making her lashes flutter and her breathing grow shaky.

With her hands now perched on his shoulders, she lifted and waited for him to grab his cock and notch it at her center.

They didn't need to speak.

They'd done this hundreds, possibly thousands of times before. Their connection, their language was beyond words.

Their eyes locked. She tipped her head and rested her forehead against his, a small, demure smile curling her lips as she slowly sank down, taking all of him inside her.

Her eyes closed.

His eyes closed.

She moaned.

He moaned.

"So ... good," she breathed out, pausing when she couldn't drop down any farther. She squeezed around him, and he flexed his cock, causing her eyes to open and a sparkle to wink at him in the golden-brown.

"You gonna move, or should we just stay like this until morning when the kids come down for Cheerios and Bluey?" He still had the fingers of one hand on her breasts, and now seemed like the right time to give the nipple a little twist.

Her sharp inhale followed by a smile made him do it again.

"Is it torture, me just sitting here naked in your lap with your cock in my pussy?" she asked teasingly. "Is it *that* terrible?"

"Not terrible at all. Just even better when you start to move. Don't you agree?"

Her teeth raked across her bottom lip before she nodded, made pouty duck lips and, slowly lifted her hips.

Fuck, that felt good.

She lifted even more until just the head of his dick was left inside her. Then she swirled those goddamn perfect hips of hers, and he nearly passed the fuck out.

"Jesus ..." he breathed, twisting the nipple between his fingers again.

"Yeah?" she asked, lifting her forehead away from his just slightly but keeping her head tipped down, her strawberry-blonde bob creating a short curtain around her face.

Releasing her nipple, he cupped her face, sliding his fingers into her hair, and pulled her forward to take possession of her mouth.

She tasted like a combo of whiskey, Mickey's loaded nachos, and all woman. Even though his cock was deep inside her—right where it belonged—he suddenly had the urge to pull out of her, flip her over so her ass was in the air, and dive face-first into her pussy.

The noises she made when he licked her clit, when he laved at her puckered hole or slid his tongue into her drenched slit always made him whimper on the inside for how hard it got his dick.

Keeping their lips and tongues tangled, he kept one firm grip on her head, tightening his hold in her hair, then slid the other hand down to her hip again. Surging up once, he seated himself fully inside her again until she was forced to break their kiss and gasp.

He tugged harder on her hair, making her cry out, then hoisted her off his lap, and just as he wanted, he flipped her around so she was kneeling on the couch. Her belly pressed into the arm at the other end, and after releasing her hair and hip, he spread her cheeks and dove in face-first.

"Fuuuuuck," was all he got from the woman currently soaking his face.

He slipped two fingers inside his wife and began to pump while at the same time flicking his tongue over her swollen clit and thumbing her anus. He felt her pucker beneath his touch for only a moment before she relaxed and let him press it in an inch or so.

Her hips rocked back and forth, pushing her slippery slit harder against his face. From his nose down, he was soaking wet. Which made him a happy man.

Her little whimpers and mewls encouraged him, had him scissor his fingers inside her, then twist them to press upon that spot that made her moan.

His cock and balls ached, but he didn't care.

This was about her right now.

She'd never leave him hanging, and he sure as fuck wouldn't leave her hanging. He wanted her to come more than once tonight, and if the first time was across his tongue, all the better.

He heard her nails rake against the fabric of the couch, and her hip tilts were growing more erratic. She was close. She was also gushing like Old Faithful, filling his mouth with her sweet honey. Her clit swelled against his tongue. Her pussy pulsed around his fingers.

She stilled.

He didn't.

He just kept going, knowing full well what happened next and fucking impatient about getting it.

Her muscles around his fingers squeezed like a fist, her engorged clit pulsed against his tongue, and her anus tightened around his thumb.

"Yesssssssssss," she said on a hiss. "Fuck ... yesssssssssss."

More of her delicious juices fell into his open mouth, and he drank her down like he'd been wandering the desert for days and had finally found the oasis.

She pressed back against him, her body still tight.

He kept licking.

He kept fucking.

He kept going.

She would tell him when enough was enough.

After a few more heartbeats, Stacey's body went lax and she pulled away from his face. He released her underwear and pulled his fingers free while giving her one more thorough lick through her sopping folds.

She spun around, her eyes sleepy, her smile placid and satisfied.

With a smile that matched hers, he sat back against the couch again, and after she ditched those soaked cotton panties, she straddled him, wasted no time teasing, and sank down over his length.

They both smiled as her hands found their way back to his shoulders and she started to bob up and down in his lap.

"Never get tired of fucking you," he said, gripping her hips and helping her move, his balls tightening up and his cock now as hard as it could ever get.

"Me either." She tucked her head and latched onto his bottom lip with her teeth, pulling up slightly before releasing it and sliding her tongue across the seam of his lips. "Never get tired of this cock and how good it feels when you're inside me."

Releasing one hip, he let his hand slowly trail up the length of her spine until he gripped the back of her neck, tilting her head just so until their eyes locked.

Her expression sobered and turned serious, but she kept moving. Kept driving them both closer to that beautiful edge.

"I love you, Chase," she whispered.

I love you wasn't enough for how Chase felt about his wife.

He didn't just love this woman. He needed her. He was not

whole, not himself, not even a functioning man without her by his side holding him up. She was his pillar.

He pressed his forehead against hers as he felt her walls beginning to pulse around his dick. She was close again.

Good. Because so was he.

She lifted and fell on his lap once more.

Twice more.

A third time. She stiffened, shut her eyes.

"Look at me," he demanded.

Golden-brown flashed back at him.

Her lips parted just slightly, and small puffs of air from her ragged breath hit his chin. "I can't breathe without you," he said softly. "My heart doesn't beat without you."

Her eyes widened, then a little squeak rumbled up from the back of her throat as she gave in to the pleasure and came again.

His grip on the back of her neck intensified. He pressed his forehead harder against hers, stared deep into her eyes and finally let go.

CHAPTER SIX
REX & LYDIA

LYDIA QUIETLY CLOSED the front door of the townhouse she and Rex lived in, determined not to wake the sleeping people upstairs.

The lights in the living room were out and all was quiet.

A *woof* from the dog bed by the gas fireplace was all she got as a greeting from their pit bull, Diesel. Once he noticed it was her and not some intruder with nefarious intent, he put his head back down and closed his eyes. Pia, Lydia's calico cat, was curled up as the little spoon. She hadn't even bothered to move when Lydia came in.

Typical.

"Hello to both of you," she whispered. "Nice to know our alarm dog and security cat are worth the biscuits and catnip we pay them." She rolled her eyes at the snoring creatures, made sure to engage the security alarm for the front and back door, then flipped the extra locks. Rex would have already flipped the locks on the back door. Even though those who wanted to hurt them were now in prison and no longer a threat, her husband remained on high alert and ever vigilant. And he'd only gotten worse since Maeve was born.

Not that she could fault him. Lydia's apartment had been broken into by the wife of a locksmith, and Lydia was tied to a bed and force-fed opioids in an attempt to make it look like a suicide overdose.

And since Rex was the one to find her and save her from her fate, she knew seeing someone like that—particularly someone you loved—would be pretty damn impossible to forget and set you on constant alert for threats.

And now with Maeve in their lives, he was the uber *over*protective father. She knew the man would probably wrap their daughter in duct tape and pillows until she was thirty if he could.

So it would be up to Lydia to add some balance to their children's lives because for Rex, safety was the top priority. After shucking her shoes in the hall closet, she ditched her many layers, cursed the damp west-coast winters, and padded softly down the hall.

First, she paused at Maeve's bedroom door.

It was closed, of course, since it was safer to sleep with bedroom doors closed in the event of a fire. She already knew that Rex would have the baby monitor on with the camera pointed directly at their daughter's crib.

Holding her breath, she gently turned the knob.

Not a peep.

Slowly, she stepped into Maeve's dark room and over to where her wild-haired child slept on her belly, her thumb firmly in her mouth.

Ten months had gone by in a flash. One moment she was holding her minutes-old daughter in her arms, staring at the most beautiful thing on the entire planet. The next she had a ten-month-old who was determined to walk and had the most brilliant belly laugh of any baby ever.

Unlike her bald as a billiard ball father, Maeve had hair that was plentiful and unruly—a direct reflection of her personality—because, for less than a year old, Maeve had a big personality.

And it was a beautiful personality.

She had her father's sense of humor, Lydia's kindness, and the perfect combination of both Lydia and Rex's smarts.

Bending over the dark wooden top rail of the crib, Lydia brushed Maeve's feather-soft milk-chocolate-colored hair off her face.

The baby's cheek was a little rosy, and the way her top lip flared out over her thumb and sucked profusely made Lydia's breasts ache.

In her opinion, Maeve had given up nursing much too quickly. She would have gladly continued to nurse until Maeve was two or so if her daughter wished. But ever since Lydia found out she was pregnant again a little over a month ago, Maeve had refused to nurse.

Joy said it was probably because the taste of Lydia's milk had changed when she became pregnant and Maeve didn't like it.

With her hand on her daughter's head and the other on her belly, she closed her eyes and just breathed in the moment.

They hadn't been trying for baby number two. But much like Heath and Pasha, who had kids close together in age, the Hart men were virile and had a difficult time keeping their hands off their wives.

Not that Lydia was complaining. She was over the moon that she was having another baby with the man she loved more than anything. She just wished they'd waited until Maeve was at least a year before they started trying.

She was going to have two under two, and if Pasha and Heath had anything to say about it, it was pure chaos.

Oh well.

Good thing they had so much family around to help with the chaos.

"Goodnight, my love," she whispered, pressing her fingers to her lips, then back to Maeve's cheek. The mattress was too low in the crib for Lydia to bend over and kiss her daughter's head without hurting her belly. So she had to do the next best thing.

Taking another moment to soak up all her daughter's delicious-ness, she rubbed her stomach, sighed contentedly, then made her way down the hall to where her husband slept.

Only when she carefully opened the door to their bedroom, she wasn't greeted with darkness and a big snoring mound on the right side of the bed.

A smile lifted both corners of her mouth as she took in her sexy husband lying on top of the covers in nothing but gray boxer briefs and a smile. His ankles were crossed, and his arms were behind his head, but it was the big ol' circus tent that kept snagging her atten-tion. "'Bout time you got in here," he said.

"Had to go check on our daughter." She pulled her long-sleeved T-shirt over her head and tossed it into the hamper next to the dresser, then her maternity jeans were next. She hadn't had much time to get her old body back and out of maternity clothes before her body was telling her not to bother because she was going to need them again.

Plus, they were crazy-comfy with the elastic waistband and the big fabric panel that went up past her belly button.

Rex yawned. "I had a good night with the sweet beast. She kicks my ass every time at peek-a-boo."

That made her smile. Maeve certainly lived up to Rex's adoring nickname of *Sweet Beast*. She was a hilarious, growling, ferocious, beautiful beast, and every second of every day, Lydia counted her blessings that Maeve's soul chose Lydia to be her mother.

"That's because she cheats," Lydia said, shucking her bra and draping it over the chair that sat on the opposite side of their shared dresser. "She spreads her fingers and looks between them." Her breasts hung heavy beneath her as she bent over to drop her underwear. They'd finally stopped aching about a week ago. That had been the first indication that she was pregnant again. The throbbing ache in her breasts that accompanied getting knocked up.

"She doesn't cheat," he argued. "I asked her if she was cheating, and she shook her head and said *no*. And my perfect angel would *never* lie to her daddy."

Lydia gave her husband a skeptical brow lift. "You're in for a world of disappointment, Rexwell, if you think that. Just wait until she's a teenager."

"You shut that gorgeous mouth, woman. Even when she's a teenager she will always tell her father the truth. Hush now."

His playfulness had Lydia snorting. But when he ran the heel of his hand over his erection and asked, "You want some of this?" she tossed her head back and laughed.

"I need to have a shower first. Even though I didn't drink and you can't smoke inside at Mickey's, I still smell like *a bar*. And fried food."

"Want company?" he asked, bobbing his thick brows eagerly.

"Only if you promise to scrub my back for me," she said, glancing at him over her shoulder as she headed to their en suite bathroom.

"I'll scrub more than your back, woman." The whinge of the mattress and the creak in the floorboards from his impressive size moving said he was right behind her. But the sharp shift of warm air around her as she leaned over the tub and turned the faucet on sent a wave of goosebumps over her skin.

His hands fell to her ass, but he didn't squeeze.

He kissed a scorching trail across her shoulders and upper back, his body a searing heat against her bare skin. A shiver sprinted down her spine, and her toes curled in the plush bath mat.

She thought they were going to step into the shower, but as steam began to fill the bathroom and Rex's hands explored her body, his lips leaving a heated trail across her skin, she realized she didn't even want to wait to get into the shower to have him.

Spinning around so she faced him, she looped her arms around his shoulders and leaped up onto his hips.

There was no surprise in his dark, hooded, midnight-blue eyes. Only passion.

Cupping her ass, he backed up and turned, plunking her butt on the cold granite countertop of the vanity. The mirror behind her was already fogged up, but that didn't matter.

His cock knocked against her inner thigh, and she squeezed her legs around his waist, crossing her ankles so her heel rested in the crevice of his butt cheeks.

Damn, her man had a nice ass.

When she tilted her head back to expose her neck, he took the cue and dragged his tongue up the delicate line of her throat, scraping his bottom teeth over her jaw and flicking her earlobe with his tongue.

Rex's ragged breathing made her pussy pulse and her body turn molten hot. She squeezed again, hoping he would take the hint and surge forward, impaling her as she needed.

"So bossy," he murmured, swirling his tongue back down the side of her neck. "Should I tie you up and show you who's really the boss?'

A moan she had zero control over rumbled up her throat. She *loooved* to be tied up while Rex did wicked and wonderful things to her. But right now, she didn't want to be tied up—though that didn't mean it was out of the question later. Right now, she wanted her big, beefy hunk of man-meat to thrust forward and take her like they hadn't fucked in months, rather than just two days ago.

His chuckle had her nipples pebbling, and her breasts felt heavier than a moment ago. "Ah, who am I kidding? Even when you're trussed up and I'm railing you, we *both* know who the true boss is."

She smiled and closed her eyes.

"You've got me under your spell."

"Waxing poetic rather than hammering your wife? What's gotten into you, Rexly?"

Another chuckle that sounded more like a motorcycle being revved had her clenching her pussy and her impatience growing thin. "Just trying to be romantic," he said, reaching up and twisting a nipple until her mouth opened on a silent gasp. "Do you not want me to be romantic?"

"I want you to fuck me," she breathed, reveling in that delectable snap of pain that radiated outward from the center of her breast where he was twisting. Only the pain didn't last long. It melted into a dull, pleasant throb that spiraled through her down to her toes.

"Well, why didn't you say so?" With another twist to her nipple and a harsh grip on her neck, he impaled her.

Yes.

Finally.

The next groan came because she wanted it to. She pressed her hips forward, and her eyes nearly rolled into the back of her head when his pubic bone grazed her clit. *Yes.*

"This what you wanted?" he asked, giving her hard, quick, deep thrusts. His fingers switched to the other nipple, and he twisted again.

She gasped and bowed her back.

"Yes," she said on a hiss.

His teeth raked up her throat, and he nipped her jaw again.

The pressure of his hand on the back of her neck had her tilting her head back down and opening her eyes. He captured her mouth with his, not wasting a second before he pushed his tongue inside and began to spar with hers.

She inched her butt closer to the edge of the counter, which allowed him to push into her even deeper. They both groaned, swallowing the sounds of the other as he hit the end of her and she tightened her muscles around him.

This was what she missed since Maeve was born. The hot, spontaneous, not-in-their-bed sex that they used to have all the damn time.

Sure, a bed was the most comfortable and logical place to have sex. But there was also something very alluring about getting jiggy with it somewhere *not* comfortable or logical. Like the beach or on a hike. Or in Rex's childhood bedroom up against the wall during Thanksgiving last year. She'd been pretty pregnant, but that hadn't stopped them from sneaking off right before turkey time and banging one out. As Rex put it, they were working up an appetite.

Just because she was a mother now didn't mean she still wasn't a woman and couldn't enjoy the dirtier and more risqué side of sex. She liked sex. She liked sex a lot. And she freaking loved having sex with Rex.

Her sexy Rexy was the best sex of her life, and the way he made her body hum, made the orgasms just explode out of her, was probably another reason why she was pregnant so soon after having Maeve.

He released her nipple with his fingers and trailed them down her sides, a shiver chasing him as he wedged his hand between them and found her clit.

Yes. Two fingers rubbed back and forth over her swollen nub as he continued to buck into her. He was a pretty impressive multitasker, she would admit—for a *man.*

Squeezing her eyes shut, she allowed the melange of sensations to overtake her. Her pulse filled her ears, the scent of sex, Rex, and the steamy bathroom flooded her lungs, and of course, all she could taste right now was Rex's tongue—and like always, it tasted goddamn delicious.

He pulled away and broke the kiss, pressing his mouth to her shoulder. She could tell he was close but holding on for her.

Like a true gentleman, he always let her go first.

His fingers picked up fervor on her clit, and his thrusts, although now slightly erratic, sped up. She plucked at her nipple with her thumb and forefinger, enjoying the snap and zap of pain that quickly morphed into pleasure. The fingers of her other hand held on to Rex by the shoulder, her nails digging in to hold on for dear life as he rocked her body with all his might.

"Close, baby. Real fuckin' close," he murmured against her damp skin.

"Me, too," she breathed.

"Need me to pinch it?" he asked, rubbing her slippery clit between his thumb and finger and giving it a little tug.

"Yes." Her nod was emphatic as she braced herself for the orgasm.

"Fucking love you, woman," he growled against her skin, his teeth making a sharp indent on her shoulder. "So fucking much." Then he pinched her clit, thrust hard and deep into her, and her whole world, her whole being shattered into a million, beautiful tiny pieces.

Everything from the tips of her toes to the top of her head hummed and pulsed as the orgasm crashed through her. Rex stilled and grunted against her shoulder as she felt him finish inside her.

She tightened her muscles around him, enjoying that little bit of extra bliss that came from feeling his cock pulse against her walls.

She milked him, drew him deeper into her body, held on tight so he felt just as good as she did as they came together.

When the orgasm began to wane and Rex released his death grip on not only her clit but her shoulder as well, she sighed and let go of her very sore nipple. She hadn't even realized she'd been tugging so hard on it when she came, but now that she let go of it and it throbbed, she remembered. It resembled the pain she felt after Rex removed the crocodile-teeth nipple clamps they sometimes used.

Usually, he sucked her nipples right after he removed the clamps to help relieve some of the pain. But since he was caught up in his climax vortex, she didn't expect him to do it.

Lifting his head, he smiled down at her, his midnight gaze drifting down to her still achy nipple.

Without saying a word, he tilted his head and drew it into his mouth, sucking and swiping his tongue over it. Relieving the pain and replacing it instantly with immense pleasure.

He always seemed to know what she needed without even asking. He was just that in tune with her.

He released her breast and slowly stepped away, his cock sliding out of her. "We should probably shower. Hot water bill is going to be insane."

"Yeah," she said with a smile. "But totally worth it."

He held out his hand and helped her jump off the counter, then over the rim of the tub. Thankfully, the water in the shower was still marvellously warm, and the moment she stepped under the spray, her already pliant and boneless body grew even more relaxed and sleepy.

Rex stepped in behind her, and she heard the squirt of body wash onto a bath pouf. "I did promise to scrub your back," he said, running the soapy mesh ball over her shoulders.

"That you did," she said on a sigh, closing her eyes and tipping her chin to her chest. "Will you also promise me one more orgasm before we go to sleep?"

One hand snaked around her front and tugged on a nipple while the other one continued to wash her with the pouf. "Of course."

"Promise?" She smiled but kept her eyes closed.

He tugged on her nipple again, hard enough to make her gasp. "Baby, I *always* keep my promises."

She was already in bed when he joined her. Not bothering with underwear, Rex slid beneath the covers and instantly curled up around his wife. She was on her phone, in her email app, most likely doing something that had to do with work. She was always dealing with work-related stuff.

He didn't think owning and running a preschool would be so time-demanding, particularly since she only worked Monday to Friday, eight until three. But after helping her set up her business a little over two years ago, he quickly realized just how much went into running a business like that, and it worried him she was over-doing it—particularly now that she was pregnant again.

She plugged her phone into the charging cord on her night-stand and set it down, glancing at him over her shoulder with a smile.

"Did you ladies have fun tonight?" he asked, letting his hand fall over the slight swell of her lower stomach. Her hand rested over his.

"We did. Rayma can drink, as we all know, but Krista, Pasha, and Stacey made a solid effort trying to keep up."

He chuckled. When the sisters got together, particularly without children or their husbands, they could get a little crazy. Nothing illegal or dangerous *per se*, since Krista was a police officer, Pasha a respected doctor, Stacey a nurse, and Lydia a preschool teacher, but the women knew how to have fun.

And with Rayma in the mix, they were certainly pushed past their comfort zones. That young woman definitely had a penchant for misbehavior.

His thumb rubbed her stomach, and she squirmed. She always squirmed when he touched anywhere on her body that she didn't think was *perfect*. And even though she had given him a beautiful daughter with her perfect body and was going to give him another beautiful child, she was still self-conscious about her shape.

It didn't make a lick of fucking sense to him.

Lydia was the most drop-dead fucking gorgeous woman he'd ever laid eyes on, and the fact that her body had changed after having Maeve only made her sexier. She had more curves, more softness, and even if she did have a gentle swell to her stomach, he didn't care. She was pregnant. Gaining weight was par for the course. And even if she wasn't pregnant and had that little swell, he would still find her to be the sexiest woman alive.

"I think it's a boy," he said, kissing her bare shoulder before resting his chin on it.

"Yeah? What makes you say that?"

"Seems like it's what's meant to be. Brock has one of each. Chase has one of each. Heath has one of each. Now it's our turn."

"And if it's another girl?" The worry in her voice made his chest tighten. Just because he *thought* it was a boy didn't mean he *wanted* a boy. Yeah, sure, having a son would be great, but he was also madly in love with Maeve and had been stoked to be having a girl first. As long as the baby was healthy, he really didn't care what they had, and that was the truth.

"Girl, boy, or gender-fluid, I will love our baby with every fiber of my being," he replied, hoping to quell some of her nerves.

She squeezed his hand with hers. "Me too. Do you want to talk about names?"

They'd had a hard time deciding on Maeve's name. Lydia kept coming to him with lists, and all he'd do was a veto but not add any suggestions of his own. It'd pissed her off something fierce and had actually resulted in one of their first big fights.

"Never mind," she said almost immediately. "I'm not willing to go down that inevitable rabbit hole of frustration until we know what it is and can narrow down the choices by fifty percent like last time."

Laughing, he kissed her shoulder again. "It just makes sense, doesn't it? Since we want to find out what it is, we just wait, then it's a less problematic job picking a name."

She growled. "Even narrowed down by fifty percent, it was still problematic picking a name for Maeve. You are impossible and stubborn and so fucking picky."

He laughed even more. "We need the perfect name for our perfect child. Is it so wrong I need to give it some serious thought to what I will name my offspring? Doesn't that mean I care?"

She continued to grumble barely audible arguments, which just made him chuckle more. "I like Cain," she finally said, going against her own better judgment to wait, which only made him smile. "For a boy. Or Brooke if it's a girl."

Truth be told, he liked both of those suggestions.

Just like Heath seemed to be doing, Rex and Lydia were sticking with the one-syllable names for their children. Brock and Krista hadn't, since they had little Zoe. And since Stacey had named both her children before she met Chase, she hadn't been "up" on the family tradition. Not that it was a tradition, more just preference.

Should he tease Lydia though and say he didn't like either of them and it was back to the drawing board?

Her warm, naked body nestled against his was sending any thoughts that didn't revolve around him being inside her one more time clean out the window.

"Those are both really solid contenders," he whispered, gently rolling her over to her back.

She blinked up at him with soulful hazel eyes, and a small smile curled her lips. "Really? You're not just saying that so you can stick it back in me?"

He snorted.

She saw right through him.

Her smile turned skeptical, and one corner lifted higher than the other, along with one eyebrow. "I knew it. You hate both names and are only agreeing with me because you're worried you're not going to get a second chance to drain your nuts."

He snorted again. "Oh ye of little faith, woman. I genuinely like those names. I was just contemplating pretending that I didn't to tease you but thought better of it because yes, in fact, I would like to drain my nuts again, if you don't mind. You *did* ask me for another orgasm, and I made a promise."

He would recognize that teasing glint in her eye from a mile away. Her lips puckered. "If I remember correctly, I asked you for another orgasm—for *myself.* I didn't ask for more sex. Nowhere in that exchange did I promise or make mention of *you* getting your nuts drained again. I think you only heard what you wanted to hear." She tapped her index finger to her chin and glanced sideways. "Yes, I do believe that's how it went down."

Oh, she was a wily one. A teasing little minx.

And he fucking loved her.

They'd always had such undeniable chemistry. Even from the first time they met when she was drunk off her ass and crying because she'd been fired, she'd been sharp-witted and their banter made him smile.

And over the years, that had only intensified. He never got tired of talking to Lydia or of being around her. She challenged him, made him think, but at the same time, she had this zest for fun and knew how to not take life too seriously all the time. Which he sorely needed given the fact that he was always on high alert and ready for the next threat.

She balanced him out.

Was the yin to his yang.

Best of all, she seemed to know exactly when he needed his space or some quiet time to himself and without a word made herself scarce, never making him feel bad for wanting to be alone.

She understood him. She knew that he was a man with a

scarred past, with demons and hang-ups, and instead of trying to force him to "get better" because there were some scars that would stick for life or change him, she just allowed him to be the flawed person he was and loved him anyway.

Rex smiled down at his wife. "Was that how it went?"

She nodded, beaming, taking his breath away. "I believe it was."

"And I made a promise, didn't I?"

She nodded again, her eyes now glittering in amusement. "Yes, you did."

"So my nuts are going to remain full?"

She shrugged. "Not my call, man. I'm just reiterating the conversation verbatim and letting you know where you misheard things. Filled in the blanks with your agenda." She clucked her tongue. "Seems a bit shady to me, Rextholamew."

Reaching up, she cupped his cheek, her thumb sliding softly over his stubbled jaw. Her gaze turned soft, her smile kind. She was looking at him with so much love, it was going to make his heart explode. "Get to work." Then she released his cheek, her smile dropped, and she pushed down on his head to shove him under the covers.

CHAPTER SEVEN
HEATH & PASHA

H<small>EATH</small> <small>DISCONNECTED</small> the call on his cell phone Sunday morning and scooped up a stinky-assed toddler from where he played on the floor. "Come on, you little stinker. Uncle Rex and Maeve will be over in a bit for a playdate, and we can't have you making the place reek."

Raze had been playing on the floor with his toy cars next to Eve, who slept in the bouncy chair beside him. So far Raze was the perfect big brother. He loved his baby sister so much and was patient when she required his parents' attention or screamed her head off. The only thing that he was finding challenging was the fact that Eve had zero interest in Raze's toys. He was constantly trying to share them with her and play with her, but since she was only six weeks old, she was more interested in sleeping or just watching her big brother play.

Heath pressed his nose to his son's butt, which was encased in navy sweat pants. His ass was huge, too, since Pasha preferred to use reusable cloth diapers when at home with the kids, rather than disposable.

Now *that* had been a learning curve. Heath had infiltrated

criminal compounds easier than it had been to learn how to properly secure a cloth diaper so the shit didn't spill out all over the place.

Seventeen months later and now with *two* kids in the washable crap-catchers, he still had his blunders that resulted in a lot more laundry—for everyone.

"Made big poop," Raze said, slapping Heath's back as he entered Raze's room and plunked his son on his back on the floor.

"I can smell it," Heath said with a grimace. "You're old enough that you can come and tell me when you've pooped yourself, you know. You don't need to leave it until it permeates the house and goes to battle with your mother's oil diffuser."

"But then *I* would end up doing all the diaper changing," Pasha said behind him, causing him to turn around in slight surprise. He had a new diaper and wipes in his hand as he rejoined a reclined Raze on the floor.

"Not true," Heath protested. "I change just as many as you do."

Pasha's expression was skeptical at best. "Perhaps, but he *does* know how to come and tell us that he's crapped himself. The problem is, he only comes and tells me. So, by default, I would be the one changing more diapers."

He wasn't sure her logic panned out, but given the mess he was about to uncover in his son's pants, he was in no mood to argue. He did, however, notice how hot his wife looked.

"Where are you headed looking like a million bucks? You had ladies' night last night. Now you're doing a ladies' lunch?" Bracing himself for the worst, he pulled off Raze's sweats, then unbuttoned his cloth diaper. He held his breath.

Well, holy shit! *Literally*.

It wasn't the explosion he'd been anticipating. His kid had managed to keep it all in his shorts.

"High five for no a*poo*-calypse, buddy. Nice job with the solid—"

"You need to get out more. You're becoming obsessed with our children's bowel movements," Pasha said with a laugh.

"It's important we keep track of color, frequency, and consistency. You of all people, Madame Doctor-lady, should know that."

"I do know that. And I *do* keep track. I just don't think about their shit—or talk about it—as much as you seem to."

"Where are you headed?" he asked again, ignoring her quip about his obsession with his kids' crap.

Maybe he was a little overly invested in their digestive system, but they were his kids and he loved them goddammit and he wanted to make sure they were healthy as new spring foals.

"Christmas shopping with Lydia."

"Ah, is that why Rex and Maeve are coming over?"

"Yeah. When they get here, Lydia and I will go. We're both stumped what to get you men, for Christmas."

Heath finished fastening the new diaper on Raze, slid his sweatpants back up his body and helped his son to his feet. Raze took off out of the room, his little feet making a godawful baby-waking racket as he ran down the wood-floor hallway. "I keep telling you, coupons for blowies and butt sex is all I need. I'm an easy man to please."

She lazily followed him as he went about his routine of disposing of the diaper contents, pulling the inserts out of the pocket, and putting everything into the wet bag that lined the diaper pail in the kids' bathroom. He washed his hands, dried them, then turned to her. "Aren't you always saying that gifts from the heart, *homemade* gifts, are better than store-bought? What's more homemade than coupons for blowies and butt sex? Those gifts will *definitely* come from your heart. And *not* go to waste." He rested both hands on her hips, and she instinctively stepped into his space, her arms magically making their way up to his shoulders.

Golden-brown eyes he loved to get lost in glittered back at him. She looked super fucking hot in her flowy cream-colored blouse and dark green skinny jeans. He knew they were still maternity jeans because she'd worn those exact ones two months ago when she was ready to pop with Eve. But she still rocked them six weeks postpartum. Pregnant, not pregnant, one day postpartum or six weeks postpartum, his wife was the sexiest woman on the fucking planet, and he could not keep his hands off her or his eyes from ogling her.

He'd one hundred percent lucked out when it came to having a smoking-hot partner.

"Speaking of *sex*, how are you *feeling?*" he asked. Since Eve was only six weeks old, they hadn't had sex since before she was born. When she had the energy, Pasha went down on him, but that was it—and rare. She wasn't ready for his fingers, his mouth, and definitely not his cock anywhere near her "baby tunnel," as she expertly called it, seeing as she was a doctor and all and preferred to use the medical terms for things. *Snort.*

Her lips twisted, and she glanced away from him. "Still not feeling it."

He nodded and lifted one hand from her hips to tuck it beneath her chin so she would turn to face him again. "Hey, it's okay. If you need a year—please don't need a year—until you're ready, I can handle it. You gave me a gorgeous daughter and a beautiful son before that. I'm not *so* much of a horndog that I can't wait until your body feels ready. I'm not pressuring you. I want you to want it, too. I want it to feel good for you, too."

Her smile was small and stayed on the lower half of her face, which meant it wasn't genuine. But the love that glittered back at him in her eyes said the hormones were racing through her, and unless he changed the subject, she was going to start crying.

"Besides," he said with a shrug, "my fist has been sending me love letters. It thinks we're getting back together and this isn't just a casual thing. Maybe I've been booty-calling it too much, but it's getting kinda clingy."

That got her really smiling. And snorting.

"I'm serious, though," he went on, "no pressure. Though I am missing hitting you with the dirty one-liners. It feels wrong to say them when you're not ready. Feels like I'm pressuring you."

She blinked, and her eyes grew watery.

Shit.

"Thank you."

Eve squawked from the next room, and their moment of intimacy was broken.

"Ouch," Pasha said, clutching her hands to her breasts and stepping away. "Seriously, the moment that kid makes even a peep, my boobs leap into action. They were never this bad with Raze." She hustled down the hallway toward a squirming and barely awake Eve.

Their daughter always took forever to truly wake up, so she squirmed and bleated with her eyes closed for several minutes—it was fun to watch.

But Pasha didn't stand there and watch Eve. She unbuckled the baby from her bouncy chair, held her to her chest, and wandered over to the recliner, putting her to her breast in under a minute.

Heath's wife was a nursing ninja.

"So what are you and Rex going to do?" she asked, repositioning Eve's head so it was better supported by Pasha's arm. She tucked a strand of her caramel-colored hair behind her ear and welcomed Raze into the chair beside her when he came asking for snuggles. "Oh wait, let me guess ..." She tapped her finger to her chin. "Plot how to break up your mom and Grant?" Her lips twisted, and she gave him a challenging look.

Heath reared back. "What? No."

Pasha's brow lifted. "B.S. Stacey told us last night that you guys were doing a video chat while watching the game and that Chase was going to use Grant's license plate to get information on him. How deep did the computer nerd get? What was the name of

Grant's fifth-grade teacher? What was his final grade in sophomore calculus?"

"First of all, in Canada, we don't use the terms freshman, sophomore, and all that. And no, Ms. Smartass, Chase didn't dig that deep."

"Ah, but he did dig," she replied.

"We're only looking out for our mother. For our *family*. After everything our family has gone through in the last several years, we'd be fools not to do a bit of digging." He made his way into the kitchen and poured her a big glass of water. One thing he'd learned after Pasha had Raze was that when a woman nursed, she grew thirsty very quickly, so as soon as he saw Pasha nursing, he made sure to get her some water.

She thanked him and took a sip before setting the glass down on the side table. Raze was quiet and simply resting his head against Pasha's other breast. Reluctantly, Pasha had weaned Raze a month before Eve was born. She knew she didn't have it in her to tandem nurse and was just grateful that he continued to nurse while she was pregnant. Maeve had already weaned since Lydia announced she was pregnant a few weeks ago.

"Your mother seems happy," Pasha went on. "Don't ruin this for her. All she's ever done since even before your father died has been taking care of you boys, and now she also helps take care of all of your children. She deserves to have companionship, love, and intimacy just like anybody else." She leaned down and pressed a kiss to the top of Raze's shaggy blond head.

"You're curious what we found out, aren't you?" he asked, bending down and doing a small tidy-up of where Raze had spread all his toys out in the living room. He simply put the blocks back in the block bin, the cars in the car box, and the random baby toys in the basket by the bouncy chair.

She shook her head. "I trust your mother's judgment ... and so should you. So should all of you."

He inhaled deeply through his nose and did a very dad-like groan when he stood up straight. "Once we make sure he's not some closet pervert or a serial killer, then we'll let her be."

She didn't believe him for a second, and the way her eyebrow ascended her forehead said as much.

Shit. She knew him too damn well. "That's B.S., and you know it. You're worse than children. You're going to try to break them up, aren't you?"

Not him. But Brock seemed hell-bent on ending their mother's relationship. Heath was always up for some shenanigans, so if Brock needed his help, he'd probably jump on board. Something just didn't feel right about their mother dating. It was weird.

A knock at the door broke their tense moment, and Heath flashed his wife a big, goofy smile. "Saved by the *knock?*"

"Not on your life, bub," she called after him. "This conversation isn't over. All four of us—Krista, Stacey, Lydia and myself, and Rayma too—are on Team Grant. So, if you or any of the Harty Boys do anything to mess up your mother's relationship *or* Christmas, there will be hell to pay times five."

"Times six if you count your mother's wrath," Lydia added, stepping over the threshold. Pasha was in the middle of her monologue when he opened the door for his brother and sister-in-law, so they heard the majority of her lecture.

Rex's lips twitched. Lydia's hazel eyes turned fierce.

Rex had Maeve in his arms along with her diaper bag.

"You getting a lecture, too?" Rex asked with a bland expression on his face as he toed off his loafers and wandered into the living room, plopping Maeve down on the play mat.

"Yep," Heath replied, his tone equally flat. He shot his wife a sideways glance, and she just stuck her tongue out at him.

Rex pulled off his black knit hat, revealing his bald head, and placed it on the side table next to where Pasha was still nursing. She'd switched sides and Raze had abandoned his station as a cuddler and was on the floor showing Maeve some of his toy cars.

Lydia entered the living room, too, and her gaze turned warm as she focused in on Pasha with Eve. "Ah, I miss nursing."

"You'll be back at it again soon enough," Pasha said, tucking her breast away when Eve popped off. Without a second thought, she passed Eve to Heath, stood up and started getting ready. "There are several bottles of pumped milk in the fridge, but you know that if she finishes that and is still screaming to just top up with formula."

Heath knew the drill. He grabbed a receiving blanket off the folded laundry in the basket on the couch and draped it over his shoulder to start burping Eve. "Yes, dear. I have done this before."

Pasha stuck her tongue out at him again.

"Careful, or I'll bite that off," he warned.

"Play nice, boys," Lydia teased. "And no plotting."

"They're actually the two I'm least worried about," Pasha said, pulling on her winter coat. "Krista said Brock has had this giant storm cloud over his head since yesterday and it just seems to be getting perpetually darker."

"Yeah, and we all know how quickly Chase can get sucked down a rabbit hole," Lydia added.

"You saying you're not worried about us because we're not the leader or the tech geek?" Rex asked, pretending to be offended. Meanwhile, Heath was actually a little offended. He'd heard it mentioned within his earshot more than once that out of all of the brothers, many considered him the most deadly and dangerous. He was also the biggest and had done the most amount of risky fieldwork.

But whatever.

He guessed since he was now a father of two, everyone just saw him as a mushy teddy bear who changed twenty diapers a day, burped gassy babies, and released spiders back outside instead of squishing them.

He turned his back to the women at the door and gave Rex an eye roll, but a hand on his butt and a gentle squeeze made him turn around again. Pasha was behind him smiling and all bundled up in her thick black peacoat, a baby-blue scarf that made the gold in her eyes pop, and her knee-high black boots. "You're still the biggest, baddest, *sexiest* man I've ever met." Her lips twitched into a twisted smile before she lifted up onto her tiptoes and pressed a kiss to his cheek. "Behave. Because if you do, tonight *I* won't." Then she stuck her tongue into her cheek a couple of times and bobbed her brows.

Heath's dick instantly jerked in his sweats. "Damn, woman," he breathed.

She grinned, pinched his butt, and kissed Eve before calling their son, Raze, over to hug her goodbye.

Rex was saying goodbye to Lydia, Maeve back in his arms.

Moments later, the women left, and Heath and his brother were alone with the children. He wandered deeper into the living room and put Eve back in her bouncy chair so she could watch her cousins.

He'd only had breakfast an hour ago, but he was already hungry.

He was always hungry.

"Too early for a beer?" Rex asked with a smirk and eyeing the clock on the mantle. It said ten o'clock.

Heath shook his head and headed to the kitchen. "Not if I make nachos to go with it."

Rex was all smiles. "Have I told you lately that you're my favorite brother?"

CHAPTER EIGHT
HEATH & PASHA

"HEATH JUST WANTS coupons for blow jobs and butt sex," Pasha whispered to Lydia as they perused probably the tenth store that morning for "something" to get their husbands for Christmas. "The man is impossible."

Lydia nodded. "Rex did the whole *I have everything I could possibly need—don't buy me anything* schtick when we all know damn well that if he didn't have anything to open Christmas morning, he'd be a pouty little baby."

Pasha made an "mhmm" noise and picked up a pair of gray sweatpants off the table in the clothing store they were in. "More lingerie?"

Lydia snorted and sidled up next to Pasha. "Not a bad idea actually. Rex's favorite pair has a hole right by his crotch. Though isn't that more of a gift for *us*?"

"I suppose ... What about booking a couple of nights away for you and Rex before the new baby arrives? I'm sure either Rayma or Joy would be willing to watch Maeve. I mean we could, too, but I'm only saying the others first because—"

"Their hands are significantly less full," Lydia finished with a grin. "Yeah, that's not a bad idea. He's mentioned storm-watching in Tofino a few times, but I think the peak time for that is November. So maybe somewhere else?"

Even though their quest was not over by a long shot, each of them grabbed two pairs of light gray sweatpants and hooked them over their arms, giggling as they continued through the store.

"So, I texted Joy this morning to apologize for the men's behavior yesterday," Lydia said, running her fingers over a rack of men's chambray shirts.

"Me, too," Pasha added. "Krista seemed frustrated last night with how Brock was handling all of this. Stacey, too, but not so much. She said she supported Chase doing a bit of digging, but after her history—and his—I understand why. I still don't think any of them give their mother enough credit though. It's her life."

"And the woman *definitely* deserves to be getting a little *somethin' somethin','*" Lydia said.

A snort and a cleared throat behind them had Pasha and Lydia freezing. Stock-still beside each other, they glanced sideways and made eye contact.

"You look," Lydia said through her teeth.

"No, you look," Pasha whispered.

"We'll both look. On the count of three."

Pasha nodded. "Okay."

"One ..."

"Two ..."

"Three."

They turned around, and who of all people was struggling not to smile and giving them an opportunity to run away by staring at the label on a T-shirt like it was a *Playboy* centerfold, but Grant.

The Grant.

Shit.

"Hi, Grant!" Pasha said enthusiastically, even though her gut was a nauseous blend of her breakfast oatmeal, coffee, and diced bananas.

Grant's full lips curled into a lopsided grin. "Good morning." He glanced at Pasha first. "Pasha, right?"

She nodded.

"And ... *Lydia?*"

"Good memory," Lydia said with a squeak. "Out shopping?"

The poor woman already had mommy brain again, and she immediately smacked the heel of her palm into her forehead. "Dear God, of course, you're out shopping. Why else would you be here?" Her face turned serious. "Unless you *work* here? I'm sorry. Do you work here?"

Pasha elbowed her sister-in-law. "Shhh. You're embarrassing us *both.*"

Grant was all very sexy smiles and mesmerizing gray eyes. For a man in his sixties—not that that was ancient or anything—he was one fine-looking piece. He certainly took care of himself.

Joy was a lucky woman.

"I don't work here," he said with a small chuckle. "I'm just here looking for some dress clothes. After Joy invited me to Christmas dinner, I went through my closet and realized I needed a bit of an upgrade. And well, everything is on sale this time of year, so I figured *why not?*"

"We're Christmas shopping for our husbands," Lydia said. "They're impossible to buy for. Any suggestions?"

For the briefest of moments, sadness clouded Grant's silver-speckled eyes. But he banished whatever thought had snuffed out the sparkle and smiled through the pain. "My wife used to complain about the same thing. She said I was the hardest person to buy for."

He was married.

Emphasis on the *was.*

What happened?

Divorced?

Widowed?

Was he stepping out on her to hook up with Joy?

"And what did she usually end up getting you?" Lydia asked. "Any suggestions are welcome. Like *anything.*"

Pasha's head bobbed in agreement.

His smile this time was smaller but also wistful and nostalgic. "After our fourth Christmas together and her complaining that I was the most challenging person to buy for, we made a deal. Only consumable products could be purchased for Christmas and birthdays. We are—or I should say *were*—very practical people. And if there was something we wanted, we usually just went out and bought it. Which made it difficult come the time for receiving gifts. So instead, we decided to buy each other things we knew the other liked but that would also eventually get used up. So, she usually bought me different kinds of beer and whiskey, bacon, various salamis, and then one time she bought us a foraging course where we went out into the wilderness with a guide and he helped us gather things from the forest floor and trees to make a meal."

"Like mushrooms and fiddleheads?" Lydia asked.

Grant nodded. "And other things, but yes. And Daphne loved her wine and cheese, so I always made sure to get some exotic cheeses and pick up some nice wine that I knew she would like. So we still put thought into our gifts, but making them consumable ensured things were a lot easier when it came time to give gifts. After that, we were never disappointed, and she was never frustrated. We also found unique little specialty shops around the city and new foods that we both enjoyed. It was a win-win all around."

The man was a genius.

Heath loved food.

Pasha sometimes wondered if her husband loved food more than he loved her and their children. Just kidding. But she knew food came in a close second.

"That's a great idea," she said. "There's a specialty meat shop a couple of doors down. I'm sure I could find something for my bottomless pit of a husband."

Lydia nodded. "Rex will eat pretty much anything." She smiled at Grant. "Thanks for the tip. That saved us a lot of time and grumbling. Now we can go grab lunch."

Grant grinned. "My pleasure and ..." He leaned in toward them just slightly. "I appreciate how supportive you are of Joy. She's told me a lot about the boys, and I knew that it would be a challenge winning them over, so the fact that you ladies support our relationship mean's a lot."

Pasha and Lydia exchanged looks and smirked before turning back to Grant. "They're stubborn and pigheaded and giant buffoons, but they also love their mother more than anything, so we'll try to help calm their shock and apprehension, but know that it all comes from a place of love." Pasha lifted a shoulder.

"And also, the fact that the idea of their mother getting jiggy with someone is probably enough to give them all nightmares. Just saying," Lydia added.

Grant huffed a laugh through his nose, smiled and turned his gaze away from them for a moment. "Yes, well ..."

"Any kids of your own?" Lydia asked.

Grant faced them again, and he shook his head. "Sadly, no. Daphne and I tried for years, and she had many losses, so eventually, we just decided to stop trying. She was more than enough for me."

"I'm sorry," Lydia said, her hand instinctively falling to her belly. Grant's eyes shifted to where Lydia's hand was.

He let out a big, shoulder-slumping exhale through his nose. "Yeah, me too." He lifted the pair of dark gray dress slacks up, and made a motion toward the checkouts. "I'm going to go pay for my pants. But you ladies enjoy your afternoon and lunch. It was nice seeing you."

Pasha and Lydia waved and said similar pleasantries before continuing to wander through the store.

When she was sure Grant had paid for his pants and was out of the store and down the sidewalk, Pasha turned to Lydia. "He kept saying *was*. So does that mean he's a widower?"

Lydia nodded. "That's the vibe I was getting. Did Heath say anything to you about what they uncovered about Grant last night during their video chat and Chase's snooping?"

Pasha shook her head. "No. And I was a little too drunk to remember to ask."

Lydia snorted. "A *little?*"

All Pasha could do was smile. Her sister-in-law wasn't wrong. Pasha indulged perhaps a tad *too* much last night. But it was her first night out since having Eve, and she needed that break. She needed that camaraderie of other women who also understood the demands, highs, and lows of new motherhood. She also wanted a safe space like Mickey's to just let her hair down a little bit and have fun.

Last night had given her all of those things.

And truth be told, when she arrived home and saw Heath asleep on the couch in those gray sweatpants with Eve asleep on his chest, she almost let the alcohol sweep her away to Hornyville, almost took her baby to her bassinet so she could mount her husband.

But she just wasn't ready.

Although Eve's delivery hadn't been terrible, Pasha was feeling rather insecure about her post-baby body this time around. Her labor and delivery with Raze had been long and difficult, but she felt like she got into a routine and was able to schedule time into her day for mini workouts quite soon after giving birth. She didn't get her pre-baby body back before getting pregnant with Eve, but she'd been well on her way.

But now, after having Eve, she felt large, awkward, and frumpy.

And don't even get her started on how she was pretty sure her vagina was one big wind tunnel that would never tighten again.

Maybe coupons for blowies and butt sex were the way to go since she was pretty sure Heath would notice the lack of "tightness" in her pussy right away, and the thought of seeing his reaction the first time they finally had sex again was giving her major anxiety.

"Ready to go?" Lydia asked, having slung a few soft cotton T-shirts over her arm along with the sweatpants.

Pasha grabbed a few shirts for Heath too and nodded. "Yep. Should we hit the butcher shop next?"

Lydia agreed, and they made their way over to the checkout line.

"How are you feeling?" she asked, standing behind an equally bundled Lydia. It wasn't snowing outside, but it was wet and cold. She was still adjusting to west coast winters even though she'd been living in the Pacific Northwest for a few years now. There was something very stick-to-your-bones-and-never-let-go about the kind of cold they got here. It wasn't minus forty, but it didn't have to be to make your teeth chatter.

Lydia rubbed her stomach affectionately. "Okay. Morning sickness hasn't been as bad as it was with Maeve. Mostly just nauseous but no puking."

"That's good." They moved along with the line. "Should we meet at the hotel tomorrow to do the gingerbread house tour, or do you want to convoy?"

Lydia was about to speak when both her and Pasha's phones vibrated and warbled in their pockets.

They grabbed them at the same time. Lydia was probably wondering the same thing as Pasha: Did something happen back at the house? Were the kid's okay?

But the texts weren't from Heath or Rex. They were from Krista.

Brock has taken it upon his stupid self to go and scope out Grant's house. The cop in me wants to track him down and give him a citation for trespassing. The wife in me knows he's just being an overprotective idiot looking out for his mother. Thoughts?

Lydia and Pasha exchanged irritated looks.

Their men could be incorrigible at times.

It really did make her worry about when all the daughters and nieces were of dating age and what kind of overprotective beasts they would be.

Pasha texted Krista back. *Cuff his ass and haul him to the station.*

Lydia replied to their group text as well. *Throw the book at him.*

CHAPTER NINE
BROCK & KRISTA

BROCK KNEW Grant wasn't home. Chase had managed to access the man's phone and hone in on his GPS to track his whereabouts. He was currently out shopping.

Good.

That meant Brock probably had at least an hour to get in, look around and get out.

Plenty of time to uncover all his dirty deeds and hidden proclivities.

The man lived in a modest bungalow in the heart of Saanich, in a neighborhood known as Gordon Head. It wasn't too far from the university or the beach. His yard was well maintained, and it looked like he'd just put a new roof on in the last year or so. Even his white gutters were polished.

So, what was he trying to hide behind the veneer of a manicured yard and house?

He had to have secrets.

Brock just knew it.

A single guy didn't take this much care in his yard without

having an ulterior motive or something to hide. It just didn't add up. How deep were the skeletons buried in his backyard?

Brock sure as shit didn't have shrubs and plants in his front yard before Krista moved in. And even in the wintertime, when the majority of plants were reduced to nothing but sticks, he could tell that come spring, Grant's yard would look very nice.

He made sure to park his truck several doors down to not raise too much suspicion, then he casually walked down the road, shielding his face from the wicked wind and icy rain that hit his cheeks like BB pellets.

Stacey had offered to take all the kids ice skating, and Krista—even though she was hungover as hell and it was her day off—had headed to the police station for a few hours to catch up on paperwork.

Chase was still digging, as per Brock's request.

Making sure nobody in the surrounding houses was watching him, he headed up the small driveway to the lattice-topped fence that separated the front yard from the backyard. There was a big garage-style shop to the side and back of the house with a main door on the left. But he wasn't interested in the shop at the moment. Maybe if he finished in the house in time, he could check out the shop, but right now that would have to wait.

He unlatched the gate and pulled it open just as the *whoop whoop* of a police siren made the hairs on the back of his neck stand straight up.

Shit.

Since he and Krista had gotten together, he'd gotten to know most of the cops she worked with. Unfortunately, since Victoria was divided into thirteen municipalities and each municipality had its own police department, he wouldn't have a clue who was pulling up, since this was not Krista's jurisdiction. She was West Shore RCMP, and this area was served by the Saanich PD.

Had a neighbor called about a suspicious man wandering the street?

The cop had to have been in the area to respond that fast.

He didn't look suspicious. He'd even gone so far as to trade his token black leather jacket for a big navy raincoat in the hopes that it made him look *less* suspicious and intimidating. He also didn't want to wreck the leather in the monsoon rain.

"Hands in the air, sir," came a male voice in the megaphone. "Turn around slowly."

Rolling his eyes, Brock complied.

He was only half turned around when he realized that there were two cops in the car. And he recognized both.

One was a rookie by the name of Jordan Lassiter. He was training with Krista. And the other cop *was* Krista, and she looked pissed.

He dropped his hands and tilted his head.

"You heard Officer Lassiter," Krista said through the megaphone. "Hands behind your head."

He lasered his gaze on his wife and lifted a brow.

"We *will* Taser you, Mr. Hart," she said. "You're trespassing on private property."

With a grunt, headshake, and another eye roll, he lifted his hands back up and tucked them behind his head.

Lassiter got out of the patrol car and pulled the collar of his jacket up as he lightly jogged toward Brock, a grimace on his face. "You know we have no jurisdiction here, right? Sergeant Hart made me come with her."

"I know," Brock grumbled, not taking his eyes off his wife. "Are you supposed to cuff me now?"

"She wants me to," Lassiter said. "But I really don't want to. I respect you too much, sir, and I'm really uncomfortable being in the middle of what is obviously a marital spat. I hated it when my parents were divorcing, and I hate it now." He blinked bright green eyes the long lashes having formed spikes from the rain.

Brock's gaze flicked back to his wife. She was glaring at him so hard; he could almost *feel* the heat radiating off her. With another grunt, he pulled his hands down and held them out in front of himself. "Cuff me then, Lassie. Give the woman what she wants."

Lassiter's lips turned down. The kid was probably no more than twenty-five. A wet-behind-the-ears greenhorn. But he had loyalty and genuineness about him that Brock respected. Once Lassie got some real-world experience under his belt, he'd make a damn fine cop.

"Pitter-patter," Brock said, his face now soaked and dripping. Every so often, a droplet would fall from his chin and into the small gap left open by the top of his coat. It would land on his chest, and he would be forced to fight a shiver.

Shivering showed weakness, and he was not weak.

Lassie cuffed him and, with a hand on Brock's back, ushered him toward the cop car. Lassie hadn't even opened the back door of the cruiser when a gray SUV pulled up, Grant behind the steering wheel, looking crazy confused.

Just peachy.

Grant parked on the side of the road since the cruiser was blocking the driveway. He shut off the engine and was out and around the back of his vehicle approaching Brock and Lassie in seconds.

Krista also got out of the car, her normally wild, curly red hair subdued by a black precinct-issued knit cap that said "POLICE" across the front. She was also wearing her navy, RCMP-issued winter jacket with the Royal Canadian Mounted Police emblem on the shoulder. She didn't have her utility belt on, which made sense since she was off duty. He would have much preferred for her to be in full uniform since it turned him the fuck on, but she was supposed to be off today, and it was the middle of winter, so he'd have to do with his imagination and that fierce take-no-shit-from-anybody look in her electric-blue eyes. She went toe to toe with Brock. It didn't matter that he had a good ten inches of height on his wife. The way she was looking at him right now said she would have no problem and every confidence in the world taking him down right there in the driveway.

And fuck him if he wasn't sporting a half chub just watching her fume.

"Care to explain, Sergeant?" Grant asked, addressing Krista.

Huh. Interesting. He knew her rank, knew to address her by it, and hadn't even bothered to glance at Lassie, even though he was in uniform, and Krista wasn't. That earned him point five percent of respect from Brock.

"Caught this trespasser," Krista said. "Got an anonymous tip a suspicious man was lurking around your property, and we came to check it out." She was all business. Not a lip twitch or an eye crinkle.

Goddammit. His half chub wasn't so *half* anymore. And since his hands were cuffed, he couldn't reach down and adjust himself without drawing a fuck-ton of attention.

They weren't even role-playing right now, but when she went all Mistress Badass Cop, it made him want to scoop her up and carry her back to his cave and his bed of furs and pelts. The woman seriously knew how to turn him full-on horny caveman in under a minute. They'd fought a lot for control in the beginning of their relationship, and even still, he preferred to be the one in charge in the bedroom. But when his woman *did* take charge, it got him diamond-hard in record time.

"I thought you were part of the West Shore detachment?" Grant asked, the corner of his mouth threatening a smile with just the faintest jiggle upward.

"That's correct," Krista said, still all business and not bothering to look at Brock. "But since this is of a bit of a personal nature, I thought it better if myself and Constable Lassiter scoped out the situation rather than bother one of the Saanich cops."

"How considerate of you." Now Grant was smiling. "Well, I certainly appreciate you making the trek all the way here to check out the situation. Did Mister ..."

Fuck, now he was playing.

"Mr. Hart," Krista confirmed.

"Right, right. Thank you. Did Mr. Hart enter my home?"

Krista glanced up at Brock and gave him a look that would melt a Popsicle in Antarctica. "Did you enter Mr. Wild's home?"

Brock shook his head. "No."

Grant shrugged. "Well, then, I have no plans to press charges, Sergeant. No harm, no foul. Not that he would have found anything of worth or interest in my house anyway. I'm a simple man." He pinned his gray gaze on Brock. "An open book."

Brock glared back at Grant and didn't so much as offer him a grunt. That was until his wife swatted him on the arm. Then he was forced to grunt out a half-assed *"Thanks."*

Brock flicked his gaze around the neighborhood. A few neighbors were peering out from behind drapes and through blinds at what was going down in Grant's driveway.

Not even Brock's frustration or embarrassment at the situation was able to warm him now, though. His toes were ice cubes, his head and face drenched, and forget about that half chub. His dick had recoiled back up into his body like a scared turtle.

"What are you waiting for?" Krista's voice brought him back from his freezing thoughts, and he glanced down at her.

"Huh?"

"Get going. Constable Lassiter and I are not leaving until you leave. In fact, we plan to follow you. Make sure you don't double back and come try to rattle Mr. Wild's cage."

Brock fought back a growl. Oh, he'd like to rattle the man's cage all right.

Lassie uncuffed him.

Grunting, he pulled his collar back up around his neck, not that it truly did anything to protect him. He was soaked through, and as hard as he tried, fighting the shivers was downright impossible. Without a second glance at Grant, he headed down the driveway to the road.

"All you have to do is ask, Brock," Grant called after him. "Anything you want to know about me, I'll tell you the honest truth. I care about your mother and would never hurt her. You don't need to break into my house to get the answers you want. Just knock next time, and I'll invite you in for a beer and tell you whatever you want to know."

His hands were frozen, and pain shot through his arms as he clenched his icicle fingers into fists. But he didn't look backward. He didn't even look at his wife as he stalked down the road to where he'd parked his truck.

He heard the doors to the cruiser open and slam behind him, then Lassie started the engine. By the time he got to his truck, they had pulled the patrol car up behind him, the wipers on the cruiser's windshield going faster than a hamster's heart rate.

With a sideways glance and glare at his wife and Lassie, he opened the door to his truck and climbed in.

They waited until he turned over the engine and pulled away from the curb. Then they followed him through suburbia, around Mount Doug, with bluff on one side the ocean on the other, and through Broadmead. He thought for sure they would veer off and head back to the precinct, but they didn't.

They followed him down West Saanich Road until he hit the turnoff for Prospect Lake.

He had to hand it to Lassie. The man was a good driver. Defensive but alert. He never managed to let even one vehicle get between them, but he didn't tailgate and took zero risks, even though he easily could have, given that he was driving a marked car.

They followed him around the lake, and into the area known as Fern Valley.

Brock liked this part of town. It wasn't too far off in the boonies that he felt removed from civilization, but it also wasn't so deeply embedded in suburbia that he felt he could hear his neighbors sneeze even when their doors and windows were closed.

He'd bought his house years ago when the market hadn't gone insane and people could still afford detached homes without offering the bank a severed limb and their firstborn child. And at the time, he'd been one of only three houses on his quiet cul-de-sac.

Now there were ten houses on the cul-de-sac. All of them families. All of them good people. It also helped that the bar he co-owned with a former cop partner of his father's was just a half a kilometer walk, so back in the day, he could stagger home after having a few beers.

Lassie pulled the cruiser up to the curb, and Krista hopped out. She waved goodbye to the rookie, and he pulled away. Brock turned off the engine and opened his door just as his wife walked up, her hands on her hips.

One look at her, her hair still wet, eyes gleaming with fury, and he knew exactly what he wanted to do.

"You have some explaining to do, Brock Hart," she said, venom dripping from her tone. "Stacey snuck a peek at Chase's phone and saw what you two were planning. How could you do that?"

He'd message his brother later and tell him to get better security on his phone, but for now, with their house empty, kids still skating and his wife as angry as a rabid honey badger, Brock only had one thing on his mind.

With a grunt and a growl, he leaped down from the driver's seat and in the same movement tucked low so she was hoisted over his shoulder.

He was up to their front stoop in six strides and used the keypad on the door to open it. He locked his truck with the fob and toed off his wet shoes just inside the foyer.

"I knew you were having issues dealing with the fact that your mother is seeing someone, but this is just ridiculous," Krista went on, obviously resigned to the predicament and deciding to continue lecturing him as he carted her upstairs. "I have half a mind to call your mother and tattle on you."

He grunted again.

"You'd probably be banned from Christmas dinner if she found out. Which we can't guarantee she won't do. Grant could very well tell her. Then what are you going to do? Hmm? Did you think about that? Did you think about how devastated your children would be if they aren't able to celebrate Christmas with their father?"

His mother might get as pissed as a whole truckload of rabid honey badgers, but never in a million years would she ban him from a family dinner. She might spit in his food or banish him to the kiddie table, but she'd never outright ban him.

Brock reached their bedroom door, his cock now a stiff column in his soaking-wet jeans. He nudged the door open and plopped her down on her feet on the floor.

Her hands went back on her hips as he started stripping off all his wet clothes.

"Angry sex?" she asked, her blue eyes wild as he unzipped his jacket and tossed it into the hamper.

He grunted again and peeled off his damp, black, long-sleeved T-shirt.

"It's probably for the best," she said, beginning to strip as well. "Only two things I want or am even capable of doing right now, and that is punching you or fucking you."

CHAPTER TEN
BROCK & KRISTA

DAMN HIM AND HIS GORGEOUS, alpha broodiness. It was like catnip to her, and he bloody well knew it. Just because Krista was revved up and preparing to jump his bones didn't mean that when the orgasms were had and their bodies once again warm, she wouldn't begin her tirade all over again.

Because she certainly freaking would.

Her blood had bubbled like magma in a volcano when Stacey sent her a screenshot of the exchange between Brock and Chase on Chase's phone. Chase was instructed to continue digging into Grant's past—particularly his time in the air force—while Brock took the opportunity of Grant being away from home to go and snoop around his sock drawer.

As uncomfortable as it made Lassie feel, Krista was one hundred percent committed to hauling her husband's fine, toned ass to the police station and putting that fine, toned ass behind bars for a few hours. Teach him a lesson about sticking his nose where it didn't belong and going all vigilante.

All her co-workers would have looked at her like she was certifiably nuts, but they also knew Brock and the secret-service level of protection he tended to devote to things, so they wouldn't have looked at her like she was nuts for long.

Even though it was her day off, without having kids to feed and keep alive—thanks to her awesome sister-in-law—she went into work for a few hours to bang out some backlogged paperwork. So, she hadn't bothered to wear her uniform, since she *technically* wasn't there. But she hadn't been at her desk twenty minutes when Stacey's message about Brock going all cat burglar rolled in.

And after seeing that, like hell would she be able to focus on work.

Nope.

Her SUV was still at the precinct, so she'd have Brock drive her there later to pick it up, but for now, they had the house to themselves and angry sex was on the menu.

Because she was freaking angry with him.

This would not be slow, heartfelt lovemaking between her and her soul mate.

Fuck, no.

This was going to be her trying her damnedest to snap his dick in half with her Kegel muscles and leave bite marks and scratches deep enough to make him bleed.

He was naked now, standing in front of her.

His cock was at full attention, saluting her properly with a translucent bead of precum on the tip. The rest of his skin was mottled red and white from the cold. She knew he thought shivering was for wimps, but she could also tell that the longer he stood there, the harder it was for him not to shiver.

A smile slowly spread across her mouth.

She was enjoying his torture.

She'd only removed her jacket so far, the shirt beneath not overly damp but not dry enough to put back on after she clawed up his back like a tigress.

"Get naked, woman," he grumbled, though the slight quaver to his voice was unmistakable. He was cold.

Ha!

Good.

Served him right.

However, she was also cold, and it didn't serve her right.

She was just looking out for a mother-in-law she adored and a man who she was pretty sure was *not* the serial killer, puppy-drowner that Brock was convinced Grant to be.

She quickly unbuttoned and shimmied out of her jeans, the tops of her thighs wet and cold, which made pulling those damn skinny bastards to her knees a bit of a struggle. But with a few Brock-like grunts, she managed, then shucked them to the side along with her socks.

That left just her open red, black and white flannel and the black tank top under it.

Though, to be fair, she would rather leave them on, since she was extremely freaking cold and he didn't deserve to see her fully naked after the stunt he pulled.

However, that was also punishing her, since there was very little she loved more than having her nipples nearly bitten clean off.

Oh, the dilemma.

Brock stretched his fingers a few times before taking his cock in his palm and giving it a few sexy-as-hell tugs. With his thumb, he swiped the precum off the crown and swirled it around the tip.

Krista fought back her groan and bit the inside of her cheek rather than her lip, but there was no way she couldn't watch. It was just too hot.

"What's the holdup, woman?"

She rolled her eyes.

Did he honestly think he was in control here?

That this angry sex thing was *his* idea?

Pffsst.

Please.

Why did he think she had Lassie drop her off at home and not back at work, where her SUV *and* a mountain of paperwork waited for her?

Because she planned to fuck some sense into him, that was why.

She couldn't fuck him senseless, because he obviously already was senseless, so she needed to try to fuck some sense *into* him instead.

Grumbling at just how irritating the love of her life could be, she tugged off the flannel and let it fall to the floor behind her, then she pulled the tank top over her head.

She was just reaching behind her to unfasten her bra when he growled in impatience and surged forward, cupping her ass and hoisting her up onto his hips.

She was still in her underwear, but at this point that was just semantics.

He'd shredded plenty of her panties before and would most likely do it again.

"Taking too fucking long." He grunted and spun them around, plastering her back to the bedroom wall, his teeth scraping their way down her neck.

She finished removing her bra and let it flutter to the ground. "Maybe I like seeing the frustration in your eyes. You deserve to be tormented."

"You deserve to be properly fucked," he said, reaching one hand between them and pushing her panties to the side enough so that his cockhead brushed her wet, warm center.

"And you deserve to have your nipples twisted the fuck off." She reached between them and did just that.

Well, not completely.

But she twisted pretty damn hard.

Hard enough to make him grunt out in pain and paint the air

with a few lovely curse words at the same time he thrust his cock
deep and hit the end of her with enough force to make her feel it in
her toes.

Yes.

She sank her teeth into his shoulder and tugged on his nipple
again.

"Fucking Christ," he breathed out, swatting her hand away
from his chest. He hammered into her harder.

"You deserve every ounce of pain, baby. You knew what you
were doing was wrong."

"Protecting ... my ... family," he said, each word coming out as
her head hit the wall from the force of his pounding. "Not ...
wrong."

"From what? The big bad helicopter mechanic?"

"From ... the ... unknown."

With a gruff nudge, he pushed her head out of the way, made
her tilt it to the side so he could drag his bottom teeth up her neck.
She sucked in a sharp breath when he nipped her earlobe.

"Oh, give me a break. You don't think your mother *knows*
Grant?"

"Stop ... fucking ... talking ... about ... my mother ... when ... I'm
... fucking you!"

The hand that still cupped her ass regripped, and his fingers
dug painfully into her flesh.

But she liked the pain.

She'd always liked a little bit of pain with her pleasure.

Sometimes more than just a little.

When he readjusted, that also changed the angle, and now his
pelvic bone was scraping against her clit with every luscious pound,
driving her body closer to that edge of existential bliss. Every
thrust, every plunge was like a little firework going off in her lower
belly.

She squeezed her eyes shut and envisioned his cock, thick and veiny and so damn perfect the sight of it undoubtedly made angels cry, sliding into her channel, splitting her open and grazing her walls.

It didn't matter that they'd been together nearly eight years. Brock was the best sex of her life. And one might think that they were in the seven-year itch where the sex was getting dull and predictable.

It was anything but that.

The sex between Krista and her husband just kept getting better.

Sure, it wasn't as frequent as it had been before Zoe was born—but then, they'd only just gotten together since their daughter was from a whoopsie one-night stand. As soon as Krista found out she was pregnant, she knocked on Brock's door and told him.

They hadn't seen each other since the night Zoe was made.

She'd been a rookie cop and had pulled his speeding ass over. Only her radar gun was glitchy, and he claimed to be driving with the cruise control on.

She'd found him impossibly frustrating and impossibly gorgeous the moment she laid eyes on him, and when he drove away with just a warning, she hoped she never saw him again but secretly prayed she would. And when she found herself next to him at Mickey's later than night, as she drowned her sorrows in tequila, he wasn't nearly as cocky or irritating, but he was certainly just as sexy—if not more.

She propositioned him, then followed him home, where they tumbled into his bed with such one-track minds and enough liquid courage in their systems for them both to forget about a condom.

Five weeks later, those two little lines appeared on a stick, and she knew her life would never be the same.

The funny thing is, she had no idea how amazing her life would get after agreeing to move in with Brock so he could help her through the pregnancy and take care of the baby once it was born.

Of course, with a generous offer like that, his lickable abs, fine toned ass, and tongue of a god, it'd taken very little time for her to fall in love with the hard Hart, even though he drove her crazy, and eight years later continued to do so. And the sex—oh mama, the sex just kept getting better.

Her breasts were mashed against his hard chest, but she wanted them in his mouth. She wanted his teeth tugging on her nipples, sinking into her areolas, his lips creating enough suction to cause a hickey.

She wanted hard and dirty. Rough and greedy.

They hadn't even kissed yet, and they probably wouldn't.

She wanted his mouth elsewhere.

She wanted it everywhere.

If she wasn't so hell-bent on the orgasm that was climbing the cliff inside her, she'd grab his head with two hands and force him to his knees and his tongue between her legs.

But the kids wouldn't be home for roughly another hour. They had time for that.

Stacey had texted when Lassie was driving Krista home that the kids were being good as gold and she offered to take them all out for pizza.

Krista wouldn't say no to her kids being exercised and fed in a million years. If she did ever say *no* to an offer like that, Stacey already knew to have Krista committed.

Brock's pounding was relentless, but his cadence was beginning to wane.

He was close.

His grunts were growing more guttural. More distressed. Like he was holding on by a thin thread, waiting for her thread to snap first so he could let the final fiber unravel.

But she wasn't going to let him get his release.

Not yet.

She was close, but she'd also gotten very good at skirting the edge.

As a cop, her job was risky, but she rarely took risks she didn't have to take. She rarely walked on the wild side of life anymore. Particularly not after having children.

But she had gotten very good at tiptoeing along the edge of an orgasm.

It was a torturous bliss she could get lost in until time seemed to no longer exist. Seconds, minutes, hours, she had no idea how long she treaded along the ledge. How long she danced with danger.

But either way, it felt amazing, and she tried to dance along it whenever she possibly could.

With his hips digging into the insides of her thighs, she squeezed her legs around him, pulling him deeper, harder against her. The heel of her foot wedged between his flexing ass cheeks, and she tilted her head forward and scraped her teeth along his shoulder cap, feeling it bunch and flex as she dug in for a bite.

His hiss of pain made her smile, and she released her chomp and swept her tongue across the bite marks.

"Fucking savage, woman," he grunted out, continuing to hammer into her.

"Serves you right," she growled, biting his neck this time.

He grunted again, and his thrust faltered.

She laughed. "You're close, aren't you?'

It was a rhetorical question. She'd had sex with this man thousands of times. She knew when he was close, and right now, her husband had one toe over the ledge.

He only offered her another grunt.

She laughed again and squeezed her internal muscles around him as hard as she could. His grip on her butt intensified, and she reached between them and tugged on his nipple again.

With a growl, he released her, stepped away from the wall, and she fell to her feet, eyeing him with confusion.

But he gave her nary a second to voice her frustrations before she was gruffly gripped by the hips, flipped around to face the wall, made to bend over, and he was sliding back home behind her.

She scrambled to grip the wall, planting her palms against it to absorb the impact of his pounding.

Her breasts jiggled and swayed beneath her, and her pussy pulsed from the new angle and the way his cock filled her just right. He was able to get so damn deep when they fucked in this position, so damn deep it nearly made her cross-eyed.

His hard chest pressed into her back as he leaned over her, his grunts of passion mixed with frustration, a tune she was very much familiar with, right next to her ear. "You think you're in charge?" he said, sliding one hand around her and between her legs. "Think you're the one calling the shots?"

She smiled and her body jolted when his middle finger found her clit and stroked it.

"I'm protecting my family. Protecting what's *mine*." He hammered into her harder, enough to make her teeth rattle against each other.

But oh, she could take more.

She wanted more.

He knew exactly how far to push her and that he could push her just a little more. Never had Brock gone beyond what she would handle or was comfortable with. He knew just how far she could go, just how much she could take, and then he went half a step over that line, which was the sweet spot. The place where her skin tingled, her soul left her body and her pulse raced like a cheetah's after taking down an impala.

As hard as she tried, the whimper that bubbled deep in her throat broke free, and she squeezed her eyes shut.

He'd taken control of not only her but of her orgasm as well.

She was caught up in a pipe dream to think she could hold on to the reins for long. He always took them.

But nine times out of ten, she was so enthralled in the pleasure that she willingly handed them over to him.

And today was one of those days.

Yes, she was still angry as fuck with him, still determined to make him wait to come as long as she could, but when he raked his teeth up her neck and wiggled her clit between his thumb and index finger, a sob clawed up her throat and little sparks of pure euphoria ignited in her body.

"You'll come when I tell you to come," he murmured, dragging her earlobe between his teeth and tugging. "And *only* when I tell you." Brock pinched her clit, and her hips jerked back into him, which made him groan.

"You're such an asshole," she ground out. "Such a fucking control freak."

"And you love it."

Goddamn him, she truly did.

But she also hated it.

Because she was also a control freak.

They were always butting heads. Always.

But what made their marriage, their partnership work so well was that at the end of the day, they never went to bed angry. And as much as everyone else who knew him would say Brock was a tight-lipped beast who barely spoke when Krista and Brock had a problem, they talked it out. Or fucked it out, like right now.

He wiggled her clit between his fingers again, pausing his thrusting to just exist inside her to the hilt, pulsing against her walls but otherwise not moving.

In frustration, she grunted and wiggled her butt against him before trying to pull forward and ride him herself. But the position he was in, hunched over her and holding her in place, made any major movements impossible.

She was at his whim.

And he knew it.

His chuckle sent a waft of warm air skittering across her bare shoulder. "Do you want to come?"

He damn well knew she did.

Brock cleared his throat, still not moving even an inch. His cock, however, flexed inside her, and her eyes threatened to roll back into her head. "I asked you a question."

Dear sweet baby Jesus. He knew how that authoritative tone and demand would just push her closer to the edge. He fucking knew it. And he was using every tool in his arsenal to prove a point. That *he* was in charge of this family. That *he* was in charge of her. Orgasms and all.

But he also knew he hadn't married a shrinking violet, and with a growl, she felt all the way down in her baby toe, she tore out of his grasp and away from him. The hollow ache inside of her from no longer being filled by his cock was something that actually made her heart hurt.

Rounding on him, she shoved him hard in the chest, knowing full well that he was only going to move if he wanted to. But he obliged and fell back onto the bed, inching up enough so that when she climbed on top and straddled him, she wasn't at risk of falling off the bed.

His hands rested on her hips and impatience shone in his green eyes as she lifted up and hovered over his erection. The head of his cock was notched at her center, but she didn't sink down.

No.

With a wicked grin, she swirled her hips around, relishing the way her sensitive entrance was teased by his thick crown.

If she did this for another minute, she could easily come.

She was that close.

Teetering so precariously on the edge that the rocks beneath her feet were beginning to crumble and fall away.

Brock sucked in air through his teeth and growled, his grip on her hips tightening as he tried to encourage her to take him.

But the anguish in his eyes was intoxicating, and rather than sink down, she slid backward a few inches and lifted higher onto her knees. Gripping his cock in her hand, she slid the bulbous crown back and forth between her pussy lips, using it like she would a vibrator to tease and rub her clit.

Brock's nostrils flared, and his fingers dug into her hips.

Their eyes locked, and when she swirled the head of his cock around her clit once more, the heat that had been building in her belly ignited into an inferno, and fireworks went off inside her.

Quickly, she angled him back at her center, taking him to his base and grinding down hard so she got every single inch of him.

Just as she knew it would be, her orgasm was intense. Mind-altering. Life-affirming. Soul-claiming. Her toes curled behind her, her nipples tightened to painful points, and her pussy pulsed like it had its own heartbeat.

Her eyes were closed, but she opened them when Brock's hands found her breasts and he scraped his thumbnail over her tight buds, the jolt of pain and blossoming pleasure making her moan.

"You gonna let me come?" he asked, giving her nipples a twist as if he were trying to snap his fingers.

She gasped, then whimpered from the second snap of pleasure, the high from her orgasm taking its sweet time coming down from the summit.

She smiled lazily and squeezed around his cock. "A nice wife would, wouldn't she?"

He grunted. "She would."

Krista flexed her hips and rocked against his pelvis once, twice and three times, then, when the orgasm took its final bow before the curtain dropped, she lifted up on her knees again and climbed off him. "Too bad I'm not a nice wife then, eh?" She slid onto her butt on the bed and stood up, but she hadn't even made it two steps to the bathroom before he had her by the wrist, whipped her around to face him, and crushed his mouth to hers.

She smiled as he forcefully thrust his tongue between her lips, then she bit his bottom lips enough to feel the growl rumble his throat.

"You love it when I come inside you," he said, pulling away from her mouth, flipping her around again and bending her over the bed. "Always makes you come again." He slid inside her once more, and when her sensitive clit hit the edge of the bed, she saw stars.

His grip on her hips was tight but not brutal, and in about five pumps, he was coming. And just as he predicted, so was she —again.

When he finally finished and her second climax waned, he pulled out of her, and she stood up and spun around to face him. His face was dark and stormy, but the love that glittered back at her in those intense green eyes would be unmistakable a mile away.

"I know you're doing what you think is right, but you're going about it the wrong way," she said, the anger in her tone having sloughed off with that last toe-curling orgasm. She reached up and cupped his cheek, and Brock instantly leaned into her touch. "Promise me you won't do something like that again. Don't break into Grant's house. Give your mother the benefit of the doubt. I'm not saying you need to start calling the man *Dad*."

He instantly bristled when she said that and pulled away from her hand, bending down to retrieve his clothes.

She huffed out an exasperated sigh. "At least give the man a chance. And your mother deserves some credit for knowing how to pick a decent companion. She picked your father, didn't she?"

Brock stood back up to his full height, all his clothes in his hands now. "And he was the love of her life. Now she's trying to replace him. She's trying to replace my father in her house, her bed, and her heart. I would never replace you. Would you replace me?"

His lips twisted, and his nose twitched. The man was one loose brick away from a full-on crumble.

Her heart broke at the thought of what he must be feeling right now, especially since Brock had been in the car with his father when he died. It was a trauma he'd never fully recovered from. And perhaps for all these years, he'd somehow taken solace in the idea that since his mother had never brought any men home or dated to his knowledge (even though Krista and her sisters-in-law all knew that Joy went on dates), she had also never recovered. That they were both forever caught up in the grief of their loss and that Zane Hart was irreplaceable.

But now, in Brock's eyes, Joy was finally able to replace Zane, leaving Brock all alone in his grief. Perhaps he even thought that because he'd been the leader of the family for so long, the patriarch, that by finally introducing everyone to Grant, Joy was trying to replace Brock as the head of the family as well.

It wasn't a far-fetched thought. Even though she'd only met Grant for a few moments, she'd been around enough alpha-male protectors to know that Joy was dating one. The testosterone that filled the air in Joy's house yesterday was as thick as an autumn fog. Brock was the silverback, and he felt like another male was coming in and trying to take over the family.

Of course, he would get his back up. Of course, he would feel threatened and alone and like his mother was trying to replace him —and his father.

Tears stung Krista's eyes, and her throat grew tight. She stepped toward her stormy husband, took the clothes from his hands, and let them fall back to the floor. Then she wrapped her arms around his big frame, pressed her cheek to his heart, and held him.

Slowly, she felt him relax, and his arms came around her, too. His cheek rested on the top of her head, and when a shudder coursed through him, she knew he was finally letting all that anger he felt burning inside twist itself into what it really was—pain. Confusion. And of course, sadness.

They didn't say anything.

Not a word.

The anger that had buzzed between them since they arrived home had evaporated, and all that remained between them was pure love and understanding. She wouldn't always agree with her husband's tactics or the way he went about things, but she would always support him and knew that everything he did was done to protect those he loved the most.

She wasn't sure how long they stood there, wrapped up in each other's embrace, but when the doorbell chimed and there was impatient knocking and yelling at the door, they pulled apart, smiled up at each other, and went about getting dressed.

She was on his heels when he bounded down the stairs to open the front door for Zoe and Zane, but just before he turned the knob to welcome in chaos, Brock glanced up at her, graced her with one of his rare but heart-melting smiles, and said, "I love you."

CHAPTER ELEVEN
CHASE & STACEY

It was Monday afternoon, and after picking Thea up from preschool and Connor up from school, Stacey joined the convoy of her sisters-in-law downtown to the Empress Hotel to see the gingerbread house display.

Since she joined the Hart family, it had quickly become a tradition. Sometimes the men came, but most of the time, it was just Stacey, her sisters-in-law, mother-in-law and, all the children. They'd all grab a hot chocolate and delicious candy-cane-flavored cookies from a kitschy a delicious bakery on Government Street and nibble and sip as they walked to the Empress.

As she always did, Stacey had invited Chase to join them, but he was on an assignment. Apparently, some celebrity was visiting the island and had fallen ill and was now at Victoria General Hospital. But because of the nature of the ailment and how it could *ruin* their career, they hired a security detail to stand outside their room so no lookie-loo media or overly curious Georges uncovered the secret.

Stacey had probed Chase for clues on who was in the hospital and what ailment they had for a solid five minutes, but her husband was the utmost professional and refused to even say whether it was a man or a woman.

Of course, she had her guesses and waited for his eyes to shift or lips to twist and confirm her suspicions, but the man's poker face was top-notch, and she got nothing out of him.

This was one of the few times she was cursing herself for being a nurse at a dermatology office rather than a nurse at the hospital. If she worked at the hospital, she'd for sure have the skinny on the VIP patient in no time. And since Pasha was still on maternity leave, she would be of no help either. She was also a pediatrician and *definitely* wouldn't reveal anything about a patient even if she knew who the celebrity was.

Stacey would just have to pay attention to her newsfeed and see if anything popped up there, then quiz her husband more when he got home.

Chase's lack of excitement about playing bodyguard to a celebrity could be felt around the house before he left. He'd dragged his feet leaving and said he'd be home late after Heath relieved him at midnight.

Did Pasha know about Heath's graveyard shift?

Banishing her wandering thoughts and relieved that her children were for once *not* bickering in the back seat of her minivan, she breathed out a sigh of relief that she'd found a parking spot in the parking garage and pulled into the stall. Krista was behind her in her SUV, and Pasha was behind Krista. Lydia said she was running late, and Joy was apparently already downtown and would meet them all at the bakery.

She turned off the ignition and spun around in her seat. "Coats, gloves, hats and, scarves, please. We're down on the water, and you know how windy it can get." She glanced at both children's feet. "Did you guys kick off your boots?"

Connor and Thea grinned at her.

Stacey rolled her eyes. "Boots on, too."

The kids went about unbuckling themselves and pulling on all their winter gear. Thea had been covered in mud when Stacey picked her up from school, claiming that if she opened up her Muddy Buddy and dumped mud inside, the mud warmed up, then helped keep her body warm. Although this wasn't necessarily *wrong,* it was, however, really freaking messy and unnecessary since Thea could have just put on her winter coat under her Muddy Buddy instead.

Since Lydia owned the school, she wouldn't have let Thea get away with something like that, but Lydia was still on her one-year maternity leave with Maeve, so she wasn't at the school.

Her daughter made Stacey face-palm more in the last few years than Stacey had in her entire lifetime.

Fortunately, she had a plethora of backup clothing in a bag in her van and had promptly changed Thea in the back of the van before they went to pick up Connor.

Now her van smelled like mud and wet clothes.

Lovely.

Opening the door, she pulled on her own winter coat, grabbed her leather driving gloves from the side panel on the driver's door, and tugged her black knit cap farther down over her strawberry-blonde bob. She still had her baby-blue scarf on but just pulled it tighter around her neck. By the time she slid the van door open, both children were ready.

Fortuitous!

Connor and Thea climbed out, and Thea was just about to run out into the middle of the parking garage, eagerly calling for her cousin, Zoe, when Stacey managed to grab her wildling by the hood and haul her back, causing her to make a small strangled noise in her throat.

She was just helping Thea zip up her coat when a black Jeep came careening around the corner way too freaking fast.

"Hey! Slow the fuck down!" was followed promptly by a loud *bang*, which was most likely a big palm on the hood of a vehicle.

Ah, Heath had come.

He'd made his presence known in typical Heath fashion, too.

Tires screeched in the garage.

"You got a problem with me, buddy?" Heath asked as Stacey took her children's hands and steered them around the van to go and meet up with the rest of their group.

Pasha was fastening Eve into the carrier on the front of her body, while Krista was busy helping Zane get his fingers into the right columns of his gloves. Both women were struggling not to smile as they kept their heads down.

"N-no," the twenty-something man-boy behind the wheel of the Jeep stammered, his eyes taking in Heath's monstrous size, only amplified by his big black peacoat.

"This isn't *Tokyo Drift*. Slow the eff down. You wanna ruin somebody's Christmas and yours by running them over?" The venom in Heath's tone had receded a touch but not enough to add any color back into the man-boy's face.

Man-boy shook his head. "N-no. I'll slow down. I'm sorry." He glanced at Stacey, the other women, and children, murmured another apology before fixing his terrified gaze back on Heath. "C-can I go? I-I'm going to be late for work."

Heath's eyes became laser-focused and his jaw muscle bounced, but he nodded. "Yeah, go. But drive slow."

Man-boy nodded. "I will. I promise." Then he quickly rolled up his window, put the Jeep back into gear, and climbed the spiral parking garage at the speed of a sloth who had just taken a bunch of Valium.

Stacey and her sisters-in-law all snorted as Heath went about fastening another child carrier to his back and helped Raze climb on.

"That guy was driving *so* fast," Connor said, using his free hand to make a *zooming* motion. "Uncle Heath got mad at him."

Stacey nodded and glanced down at her son. "He did. Because he loves his family and wants to protect them."

"I'll never get hit. I would jump out of the way. I am a super-fast and super-high jumper, Mama. Don't worry," Thea said, her posture and tone radiating with confidence and leaving zero room for argument.

Stacey simply rolled her eyes.

"Thanks, for protecting your family, Uncle Heath." Thea beamed.

Heath finished strapping Raze in, then patted Thea's head. "Anything for my little niece."

Thea beamed even brighter.

Krista glanced at her phone. "Just got a text from Lydia. She found parking closer to the bakery so is just going to meet us there. Joy is there, too. So, we can get a move on."

Everyone nodded, grabbed children's hands, hit fobs to lock doors and headed to the stairwell.

Connor, Thea, Zoe, and Zane were all animatedly chatting. Since Connor and Zoe were in the same school and Thea and Zane were in the same school, and the fact that they were cousins and the closest in age, they all got along swimmingly. The boys were jumping and kept saying, "Watch this," while the girls were discussing which gingerbread house they were going to see first.

Krista sidled up next to her since they were the only two without children strapped to their bodies, and now that they were in the stairwell, the kids didn't need to hold their hands. "I didn't say anything, but Joy brought Grant." She winced. "How do you think Heath is going to react?"

Stacey shrugged, then glanced back at her brother-in-law, who was quietly chatting with his wife. "No idea. I don't think Chase would be too happy if he was here and found out Grant was going to be participating in one of our family traditions. But then again, my husband is a perpetual walking grump, so ..."

"As is mine," Krista confirmed. "And I *know* that if Brock were here and saw Grant standing on the sidewalk, he'd throw the mother of all toddler tantrums. Complete with arms and legs flailing as he writhed on the ground on his back and screamed."

Stacey snorted at that conjured image. "I would *pay* to see Brock do that. Like good money."

Krista chuckled. "I think a lot of people would. But how do you think Heath will react? He's a bit of a wild card. He could go either way. Be chill or turn into a baby."

Stacey twisted her lips in thought. "Do we prep him?"

Krista nodded. "I'll take care of it."

They exited the stairwell and emerged onto the sidewalk.

"Hands, please," Stacey said to the kids. "Either a grownup's or in buddies together, and remember to stop and look both ways even when you cross a driveway."

"We know, Mama," Thea said with teenager-level impatience before shooting her mother some serious attitude in her gaze. Stacey shot it right back at her offspring and held it until Thea's expression changed and her sassy recoiled a bit. "Sorry, Mama." She reached for Zoe's hand.

Stacey hastened a glance back at Krista, who was talking with Heath and Pasha, and Stacey knew the exact moment Krista told Heath that Grant was going to be there because the man stopped in his tracks and his mouth dropped open.

Shit.

Pasha and Stacey exchanged looks, and both of them grimaced.

"You can't be serious?" Heath said, his blue eyes growing fierce. "This is a family outing."

They were almost at the bakery, and Stacey could see Lydia, with Maeve in the carrier on her back, standing and talking to Joy. But Grant wasn't there.

Had he left?

Did Lydia say something to him?

No, Lydia would never do that. She had messaged Stacey and Krista to let them know that she and Pasha ran into Grant at the clothing store yesterday and said how lovely he was. Lydia would never ask him to leave. And frankly, if she did, Stacey would give her sister-in-law a stern talking-to.

Heath's grumbles continued, and Stacey glanced back again at the conversation, but the screech of tires, blaring horn honk and a child's scream had her whipping her head back around.

Her heart climbed into her throat as she took in the scene.

From out of nowhere it seemed, Grant had swooped in and shoved Thea backward; otherwise, Stacey's child would have stepped into a crosswalk without looking and been hit by a gray sedan.

Thea was on the ground, crying. Zoe was standing over her with a look of terror on her face, and Connor and Zane were both yelling at the car in much of the same fashion as Heath had at the Jeep earlier.

Like she'd actually been struck by the car herself, Stacey fell forward, collapsing to the ground on her knees next to Thea. "Baby, are you okay?" As a nurse, she knew better than to touch someone who had fallen and was lying down in case of a back injury. But she ran her hands over all of Thea's limbs. "Are you hurt?"

Thea's lips trembled, and tears stained her rosy cheeks. She leaned up on her elbows and launched herself into Stacey's arms, clutching her mother around the neck in a vice grip.

The driver of the car rolled her window down. "I am so sorry. She just stepped out." She glanced worried eyes up at Grant. "Thank God you were there."

Grant grunted.

"Need to watch where you're going, buddy," Connor said. "There are people walkin'. Families and kids."

"Yeah, buddy. You almost hit my cousin," Zane added.

The woman's eyes widened, and she glanced at the boys. "Y-yes, you're right. I'm so sorry. Is she okay?"

Stacey ran her hands over Thea's back and spoke gently into her ear. "Are you okay?"

"I think so," Thea blubbered. "My butt hurts a little."

"Can I touch your butt to see if you've broken anything?"

"Yes, Mama." Thea sniffed.

Stacey softly prodded and squeezed Thea's lower back and butt. Her daughter didn't cry out in agony like she would if her coccyx was broken. She might have a bruise, but she would probably be okay. Lifting her head, she nodded to the woman in the car. "I think she'll be okay."

"Pull over to the side of the road and I'll get your information just in case," Grant ordered, leaving the woman zero room for argument. And she didn't argue. She found the first available cutout on the busy, cramped one-way street and pulled over.

"Forgot my wallet and ran back to get it from the car," Grant said, lifting his chin at Krista, who passed him on her way to go speak with the woman in the sedan. He joined her, his stride confident and long.

"Thank God he was there," Pasha breathed out. "Talk about the right place at the right time."

Joy and Lydia had made their way over to the rest of them by this time, horror streaked across both of their rosy faces.

"Is my darling all right?" Joy asked.

"I'm okay, Nana," Thea blubbered, now sitting on Stacey's lap and burying her face in Stacey's neck. Stacey's knees ached from how she was kneeling on the cold concrete, but the pain barely registered in comparison with the fear and relief that were embedded in her heart like a railway spike.

"You need to stop and look both ways, sweetheart," Stacey said, kissing the side of Thea's head, her silky hair soft beneath her lips and smelling of lilac-scented shampoo.

"I'm sorry, Mama. I forgot," Thea said. "I saw Nana and Aunt Lydia and I was just so ... excited." Each word came out like a forced sob, and her little body shook in Stacey's arms. "Nana's man-friend saved me."

Stacey glanced up at Pasha and Heath, who were standing over them. "Yeah, baby, Nana's man-friend saved you."

———

"AND THEN GRANT *flew* in the air and knocked Thea back like he was Superman and my squirrel-head of a sister was one of those clown things that when you hit it, it just bounces back but doesn't fall over. Only Thea *did* fall over. It was *so* cool." Connor's animated explanations and facial expressions as he recounted the events of the day for Chase that evening were rather entertaining.

Chase found himself chuckling more than once as Stacey prepared dinner in the kitchen while he sat in the living room with the children, keeping them "out of their mother's hair."

Thea was snuggled up in his lap, petting his bald head as she was prone to do when she needed to calm down.

"I'm sorry I didn't look both ways, Daddy," she said, doing little swirls with her index finger on the very top of his head. "I just saw Nana and Aunt Lydia and I got excited and forgot."

Chase pecked his precocious daughter on the side of the head. "You still have to remember to be safe even when you're excited though, kiddo. We still need to wear our life jackets even though we're excited to go out in the kayaks off the dock, right?"

Thea nodded. "Yeah, I just forgot."

"I know you did, baby."

"Thank goodness for Nana Joy's man-friend, eh? Grant saved my life."

Chase grunted.

"And then Grant picked me up when I couldn't see over all the giants."

Chase scrunched his brows in confusion and glanced down at his daughter.

Connor was doing karate kicks in the air but paused to translate. "She means because the crowd at the gingerbread house display was so big, she couldn't see over all the people, so Grant picked her up so she could see."

"Ah." Chase nodded.

"He's tall and strong and very nice," Thea said. "And when nobody was looking, he snuck me the last piece of his cookie. Said he was too full to finish it. But I wasn't too full. Almost getting hit by a car makes you *very* hungry, 'specially for cookies."

Chase's lip twitched, and he locked eyes with his son. Their expressions said the words they didn't have to say out loud, then Connor grinned and rolled his eyes.

He wasn't sure how he felt about everything he'd just been told, except maybe immense relief that his daughter was safe and unharmed. Besides the sore butt, she periodically complained about, of course. But Stacey said there was just a small bruise and no chipping or breakage to the bones, which was good.

He grabbed his phone from the arm of the couch and shot off a text to Heath.

Just got the details of the day. What's your side of the story?

Heath messaged back in less than two minutes. *Grant saved the day. Flung himself in front of Thea to stop her from stepping in front of a car. He was really great with all the kids. Didn't try too hard and wasn't fake. Pisses me off that he's getting harder to hate.*

Chase grunted. Yeah, it was pissing him off, too.

The fact that Grant had thrown himself in front of Thea and pushed her out of the way of getting hit earned him some serious brownie points in Chase's book. Stacey already seemed to be won over by the man, the kids, too. But Chase was still skeptical.

Less skeptical than before but still skeptical.

It also didn't help that his in-depth search on Grant regarding his time in the air force proved to be fruitless. The man was an exemplary soldier. Served two tours, flew helicopters, and repaired them. Didn't have a black mark, not even a smudge on his record, and was honorably discharged with various medals of valor.

That earned him more brownie points and Chase's respect.

Fuck.

He really wanted to hate this guy.

But fucking Grant was making it hard to do so.

"Grant said he has a big bus that we can all fit in to go see the Christmas lights," Thea said, dropping her finger from the top of Chase's head to circle the shell of his ear. "We can make popcorn and have hot chocolate and sing songs together. Zoe and I are so excited."

Chase glanced behind him on the couch into the kitchen. Their house was open concept and very spacious with minimal furniture and a lot of windows. It was what he needed to feel calm. Too many times in his life, he'd been shoved into tight, confined spaces, so much so that he'd developed a debilitating case of claustrophobia. But it was something his family was acutely aware of and did everything they could to help him when the panic started to settle in.

Nearly every night—at least during the summer—he and Stacey slept with the French doors on the master bedroom balcony open so the breeze and openness helped squash the demons that haunted him.

It helped.

Most of the time.

And when it didn't, he went and slept outside. He had an arctic-expedition-worthy sleeping bag and a canopy on the deck for if it was raining. Sometimes he just needed no walls, not even windows, to settle his muscle-clutching nerves.

Neither Stacey nor the kids ever questioned why they would wake up some mornings and find him asleep on the sundeck, even in the winter. It was just an accepted way of life for all of them. They didn't try to fix him. They just accepted him and helped him in whatever ways they could.

His wife had her back to them and was humming in the kitchen, rocking her hips back and forth to the tune. The smell of fried onions and bacon wafted through the house, and his mouth watered at the exact same time his stomach grumbled.

Thea giggled. "Daddy's hungry, Mama. I heard his tummy growl. It was like a bear!"

Stacey turned around, the spatula in her grasp. "He's hungry, is he?"

Thea nodded. Chase nodded, too. He was actually pretty hungry. He hadn't eaten anything since lunch, and even then, his lunch hadn't been very big: a meatball sub from the grocery store that was almost too soggy to eat.

"What's for dinner, Mum?" Connor asked, having abandoned his karate kicks and now practicing doing "the worm" on the floor in front of the fireplace. He looked more like a spastic armless sala-mander to Chase.

"Pan-fried gnocchi with fried onions, turkey bacon and garlic, Caesar salad, and roasted chicken thighs. Like three minutes and it'll be ready. You lot can go wash up, then come finish setting the table."

Connor and Thea glanced at each other, then in a flurry that nearly cost Chase his nuts with the way Thea climbed off him, both children were running down the hall to the bathroom. Neither of them particularly liked washing their hands, but they *did* like to help set the table. They just weren't allowed to touch the utensils until their hands were clean.

Bickering, along with running water from the downstairs powder room, echoed back into the living room and kitchen.

"Knock off the fighting or I'll set the table myself," Chase called to his children before prying himself off the couch and lazily making his way into the kitchen. He was about to cup his wife's butt, but she spun around with something white between her fingers and told him to open his mouth.

He did as he was instructed.

"Is the gnocchi ready?" she asked.

It was hot, but it was delicious. Anything cooked in fried onions and bacon was delicious. He nodded. "Seems ready to me."

"Grab some water glasses and fill them for me, please," she said, turning off the burner for the stove.

He once again did as he was instructed. "So ... Grant ..."

She turned around a bowl of the steaming gnocchi now in her hand. She walked toward their unfinished-edge wood table with the copper light fixtures hanging overhead. Stacey had gone with a bit of a country house, an almost barn-like theme for their décor, with lots of white accents and, of course, windows. "Yes? What about Grant?"

"He's ..."

"Not the evil monster you men think he is. But *I* already knew that. He didn't have to launch himself in front of a car to save our daughter to prove that. At least not to me. Not to Lydia, Krista, or Pasha. Just *you,* apparently. And Heath. Heath seemed to have warmed up to just above freezing toward Grant by the end of the day."

Chase grunted just as a herd of wildebeests in the shape of his two children came running heavy-footed down the hallway.

"I hope you didn't set the table yet, Daddy," Thea said, "'cause I want to."

"I didn't," he said dryly, setting the full water glasses in front of where each of them sat.

Thea grabbed the step stool from the pantry closet and went about getting down plates. Connor was grabbing the utensils from the drawer.

Chase had to hand it to his wife; she'd trained these kids well. Somehow tricked them into *liking* chores.

Of course, he was skeptical how long the novelty would last, but for the moment, he and Stacey planned to foster and encourage their children's willingness to pitch in as much as possible.

As if they didn't even know how to bicker, the two kids set the table together beautifully and peacefully.

"What's this I hear about Grant having access to a bus?" he said to Stacey, grabbing the bowl with freshly dressed Caesar salad and taking it over to the table.

She had the chicken thighs on a plate and followed in his wake. "Yeah, doesn't it sound like a great idea? Grant is licensed to drive thirty-passenger vans. He moonlights as a backup driver for one of the retirement homes. You know, the luxury ones that shuttle their residents around town? He said he could borrow the van for no charge—just gas—and we could all go see the Christmas lights together instead of our usual multi-car convoy and walkie-talkies."

"We can't have walkie-talkies?" Connor asked with disappointment.

Stacey rolled her eyes. "No need when we're all in the same vehicle."

Connor pouted.

"I think it's a great idea," Stacey went on, returning from the kitchen with a big tray of cut-up raw veggies and placing it on the table before taking a seat.

The kids took seats, too, and Chase pulled out his chair at the head of the table.

"So he's just invited himself along to the Christmas lights, then?" Chase asked, spearing a piece of chicken with his fork and letting it drop to his plate.

Stacey rolled her eyes again and helped dish some gnocchi onto Thea's plate for her. "No. Your mother invited him, then he offered up the van." The heated and almost angry glare she gave him next made his asshole pucker just a touch. "Knock it off. He saved your daughter. He's not a bad guy, and your mother really likes him. You don't have to like him, but I don't want to hear any more of this crap." She pointed at the kids. "Particularly in front of these two."

Thea and Connor exchanged confused expressions.

Thea picked up a piece of gnocchi and popped it into her mouth. "You don't like Grant, Daddy? You don't like the man who saved me? Are you mad at him for saving me?"

Stacey fixed him with a "You made this mess" face.

Ah, fuck.

CHAPTER TWELVE
REX & LYDIA

"I'm just pulling into the Root Cellar to grab some brussels sprouts," Lydia said through the Bluetooth hookup on her phone as she pulled into the grocer's parking lot. "Anything else you can think of that we need?"

It was Thursday mid-morning, and Rex was on his way out to Sooke for an all-day plumbing job. Their phone conversation was getting more and more staticky the farther away he drove.

"Get ... yams ... marshmallows ... spaghetti ... limes."

She turned off the ignition. "Get yams so I can make a casserole with marshmallows, then spaghetti and limes? I missed that last bit."

"Spag ... squash ... limes ... Caesars. Celery ... and pick ... ed ... eans."

Ah, now she got it.

"Roger!" she said with a nod. "Good thing we're so in tune with each other, eh? Otherwise, you'd be disappointed when you got home and I didn't have spaghetti squash and all the ingredients to make Caesar cocktails."

"That's ... love ... you."

"Love you, too. Drive safe, and I'll see you when you get home."

He disconnected the call, and she pulled her phone out of the holder fixed to her dash. She glanced in the mirror and saw Maeve in the other mirror, sitting in her rear-facing car seat, aggressively gnawing on her fist. The baby was teething something fierce. She only had one tooth so far, but there were a lot of almost erupted ones in her mouth, and it was driving Maeve—actually, their entire household—crazy. Poor kid had been up most of the night crying in pain and pulling on her ears.

Acetaminophen only seemed to help a little bit, as did chewing on a cold wet washcloth. By the end of it, Lydia had taken Maeve out of her crib and gone and cuddled with her on the couch in the living room. They both dozed, but Lydia wasn't nearly as rested as she hoped to be.

When they got home and Maeve went down for her nap, Lydia was going to make sure she took a nap, too. This pregnancy was kicking her butt. She might not have nausea anymore, but she definitely had the fatigue. Between the baby growing inside her and the mischievous one she looked after all day, her energy was completely zapped.

The rain had let up and it was just a heavy mist now, but even so, with it being cold and flu season, she made sure to pull her knit cap over her auburn locks, zipped her down vest up to her neck, and mentally patted herself on the back for donning wool socks that morning. Otherwise, her toes would probably turn into frozen sausages in her black knee-high leather boots.

She climbed out of the driver's side, opened up the back seat and went about the long but now down-to-a-science routine of getting Maeve out of her car seat and bundled up in all her own gear. If Lydia's daughter lasted ten minutes with her hat on, Lydia would consider that a victory. Maeve hated hats.

Once they were both ready to climb Mount Everest and not just walk across the parking lot to the grocery store, she grabbed her reusable shopping bags and headed to the carts, where Maeve could sit and resume chewing on her fist.

As it was all day, every day, The Root Cellar was packed with people.

A locally owned small produce store, it boasted a large variety of fruits and veggies—many locally grown that weren't necessarily found at chain grocery stores—as well as specialty items from local vendors. Their deli was also somewhere Rex would die a happy man after gorging himself on all their different kinds of meat.

But she was on a mission.

She followed The Root Cellar on social media and saw that they had a flash one-day sale on brussels sprouts for seventy-five cents a pound. She hoped because it was only ten o'clock in the morning and midweek, there would still be some left. She always made her mother's "famous" pan-roasted brussels sprouts for Christmas dinner, and since they were such a good price, she'd buy extras for their own house for dinner.

Rounding the corner past the tomatoes, she located the bounty.

Of course, it was shoulder-to-shoulder people around the bin of sprouts.

Her belly wasn't big enough to play the preggo card yet and politely bump people out of the way, laughing as she apologized and inched her way to her destination. Besides the benefit of getting a baby at the end, knocking people out of the way with your belly was one of the real benefits of getting pregnant.

But alas, she was still in her first trimester, not showing—at least not to the world. She'd have to wait her turn like she taught all the children at her preschool to do and refrain from sighing loudly with impatience.

A person right in front of her stepped away.

Ah-ha! An opening.

Grabbing a reusable mesh produce bag from her bag of bags in the cart, she made her way forward to sidle up to the bin but bumped shoulders with someone else who had the exact same idea.

"Oh, I'm sorry," he said, his voice deep and familiar.

"I'm sorry," she echoed, glancing up at him. "Grant!"

His smile made her insides tingle and grow warm. "Lydia, fancy meeting you here."

Another person stepped away, and now they both had room to begin loading their bags with sprouts.

"Can't beat this deal," she said with a chuckle.

"No, you certainly can't. I'm cooking dinner for Joy tonight. I'm making my mother's famous truffle and Parmesan roasted sprouts. What about you?"

She continued to fill her bag, chuckling. "I'm making *my* mother's famous sprouts recipe for Christmas dinner. But we all love them roasted—even Maeve—so I'll probably roast some up tonight for dinner, too. Truffle and Parmesan sound delicious. You're pulling out all the stops for Nana Joy."

He winked. "She's worth it."

"That she i—" Pain erupted in her belly and between her legs, as if someone had just thrust a machete into her abdomen.

Dropping the bag of sprouts to the ground, Lydia hunched over and held her stomach.

Something wasn't right.

Something wasn't right at all.

Grant's hand landed on her shoulder, panic coating his tone. "Are you all right?"

Glancing up at him, her vision blurry from the pain, she shook her head. "I don't think so. I ... I'm ten weeks pregnant—today."

His eyes widened in horror. "Do you think you're ..." Slowly, nervously, Grant let his gaze drift down her body, and when those stormy gray orbs closed, she knew that what he saw confirmed what she felt.

Blood.

She was wearing light gray yoga leggings, so if the blood was substantial enough, he'd be able to see it.

Apparently, it was.

Another stab of pain shot through her, so much so she thought she might pass out.

No!

This couldn't be happening.

She wanted this baby.

Rex wanted this baby.

They wanted this baby so badly.

"We need to get you to the hospital right now," Grant said softly. "Where are you parked?"

She was barely able to get the words out through the pain and the clawing ache in her throat from trying to keep the tears and fear at bay.

Stupidly, she brought her hand down between her legs, and when she pulled it back up, as she suspected, it was covered in blood.

She was losing the baby.

Her baby.

Rex's baby.

Grant reached into the pocket of her vest and pulled out her keys, hitting the fob. She barely registered the fact that he was gently guiding her out of the store and into the parking lot, steering the cart with Maeve in it. The flash of her vehicle's taillights blinked out of the corner of her eye, but she wasn't really paying attention.

"All right, sweetheart," Grant said, hoisting Maeve out of the cart and fastening her back into her car seat. "Let's get you settled, hmm?"

Then Grant helped Lydia into the front passenger seat, reclining the chair as far back as it could go. That helped a bit with the pain in her stomach but did nothing for the agony in her heart.

He climbed in behind the steering wheel and engaged the engine. "Hand me your phone."

She did as she was told, and he put it into the holder on the dash. "Call Rex."

The phone did as it was told.

"He's working in Sooke all day. We just got off the phone, and reception was really spotty," she said, squeezing her eyes shut as a tear slid down her cheek and into her ear.

"Rex Hart, for Plumbtastic Plumbing and Harty Boys Security and Surveillance. Leave a message, and I'll call you back."

Yeah, she figured he wouldn't pick up.

Grant glanced at her as they approached a red light. "Do you want to put this on a voicemail?"

No. But she was going to have to.

Beep.

"Rex," she said, fighting the tears and the searing burn in her throat. "I'm on my way to the hospital. I ... I think I'm losing the baby."

Saying it out loud made more tears rush forward, and she turned her head, covering her mouth with her hand.

Grant ended the call. "Call Joy."

It rang twice before Joy picked up. "Lydia, my darling, how are you doing?"

"It's me," Grant said.

"Grant?"

"Ran into Lydia at the grocery store. We're on our way to the hospital. There is ... something wrong with the baby."

"With Maeve?"

His response was quiet. "No."

Joy's gasp on the other end only made the ache in Lydia's chest intensify.

"I'll meet you there."

"We'll need you to take Maeve," Grant said.

"Yes, yes. Of course. I'll leave right now."

The call disconnected.

"Doctor or midwife?" Grant asked her as he took the on-ramp for the highway that would take them to Victoria General Hospital.

"Doctor," she whimpered.

"In your phone?"

She nodded. "Call Doctor Aaronson."

It rang six times before the receptionist in the office finally answered. "Dr. Aaronson and Dr. Gurpreet's office."

"Hello, I have Dr. Aaronson's patient Lydia Hart with me, and we believe she may be having a miscarriage."

"How many weeks is she?"

"Ten," Grant confirmed. "We're on our way to Victoria General now."

"Dr. Gurpreet is on call there today. I will call and let her know to expect you. She will meet you at the entrance to Emergency. How far away are you?"

"Just turned off McKenzie onto the highway. Five, ten minutes tops," Grant said.

"Very well. I'll call her right now."

"Thank you." He ended the call and glanced at Lydia. She was staring straight ahead out the window, trying to calm her breathing. To calm the baby inside her and her racing pulse. Maybe if she slowed her heart rate, the blood wouldn't flow out of her so fast.

A few minutes later, he took the exit ramp off the highway onto Helmcken, which was right next to the hospital. "How are you doing?"

She glanced at him. The man had kind eyes. Empathic eyes. The creases around them spoke of wisdom and experience but also of well-known pain. His mouth was a slash, and when she caught his gaze drift back down to the V of her pants, she held her breath.

It was bad.

He tried hard to steel his expression, but it was impossible.

It was really bad.

Reaching for her hand, Grant gave it a gentle squeeze. "We'll get through this. I promise."

He was so calm. So reassuring.

He knew just what to do. Just what to say.

He'd mentioned on the weekend when Lydia and Pasha bumped into him in the clothing store that he and his wife had experienced miscarriages. But how many?

Even through her own agony, Lydia's heart went out to the man. Nobody should be a *pro* at dealing with a woman who was in the middle of a miscarriage, and yet something told her that Grant was.

He swung into the unloading zone next to the ER, and thankfully, Dr. Gurpreet was standing outside waiting for them.

Dr. Gurpreet opened the door, her brown eyes full of concern as she took in Lydia's pants. She stepped back up to the curb and wheeled down a wheelchair. "Let's take a look at what's going on," she said calmly. Her gaze flicked up to Grant. "You'll have to meet us inside after you park in the lot."

Grant nodded. "Yes, I know the drill. Maeve is asleep in the back. Her grandmother is on the way."

Dr. Gurpreet nodded and helped Lydia out of her SUV and into the wheelchair. Lydia turned back to Grant as Dr. Gurpreet wheeled her over the curb and toward the hospital entrance doors. "Thank you."

She barely caught it, but she did. A lone tear had slipped down his cheek, and he hastily wiped it away before nodding and jogging back around to the driver's side to go and park her vehicle and stay with her daughter until Joy arrived.

CHAPTER THIRTEEN
REX & LYDIA

REX DIDN'T BOTHER with the elevator. He raced up the stairs of the hospital, taking them two at a time. His chest ached from the way his heart violently shattered inside, sharp shards of it embedding in his lungs, making it difficult to breathe.

Lydia.

As soon as he heard her message, he'd violated all kinds of speed limits and traffic codes to get to her.

To get to *them.*

A message from his mother said that she had Maeve and that Grant was with Lydia.

What the fuck?

Why was Grant with his wife?

Why wasn't his mother with his wife? Or one of his sisters-in-law?

Why was his mother's boyfriend, or whatever the fuck Grant was, with Rex's wife as she possibly miscarried their baby?

This didn't make a lick of fucking sense, but all it did do was piss Rex off even more.

If Grant had done something, had upset Lydia in some way to

cause her to miscarry, Rex didn't give two shits if his mother was madly in love with the man. Rex would kick Grant's ass until the man had swollen eyes and broken kneecaps.

He arrived at the desk, not even out of breath but with his blood pumping because of the rage inside of him, and gave the nurse at the computer Lydia's name.

"Room Twelve-A," the nurse replied.

He thanked her, got his bearings, and headed off down the hallway. He saw the sign for Room Twelve-A, and the door was open.

Slowing his roll, he crept to the edge of the doorframe and just listened.

"This isn't your fault. This shouldn't have happened, and you are allowed to get and be as angry and sad as you absolutely need to be. This is all about you. About your family. You and your husband. You lost something today, a piece of yourselves that you can never get back, and if you want to scream or squeeze my hand until you think the bones will break, then you can. You can do whatever it is you *need* to do to ease the pain you feel inside your heart right now. To fill the sudden emptiness. Don't let anybody dictate how you get through this, okay?"

Lydia's "okay" was small and choked.

"None of this is right," Grant went on. "None of it. You did everything right. You are a wonderful mother and were a wonderful mother to that baby right up to the end. None of this is your fault. You understand me?"

"Yes," she choked out.

Right up to the end.

Fuck, that meant she miscarried.

The agony Rex felt in every one of his bones intensified to the point where he wanted to scream. But this wasn't about him. This was about Lydia. He'd bear his pain—and hers—in silence, because one of them needed to stay strong, to keep their little family standing.

"I need to hear you say it, Lydia," Grant went on. "Say, 'None of this is my fault.'"

"None of this is my ... fault," she whispered. The last word was forced out and followed quickly by harsh sobs and whimpers.

Rex peeked his head around the corner, hoping to remain out of view for just a moment longer, and what he saw made every ounce of anger and bloodlust he had disappear. Grant was in a chair, sitting beside Lydia, who was sitting up in a hospital bed. They were holding hands and had their foreheads pressed together as Lydia's body shook and she cried.

This man was there for Rex's wife when Rex wasn't, when he couldn't be, and by the way Lydia's chest began to rise and fall in even breaths and her eyes lay closed gently, Grant was also saying all the right things to ease the painful burden of grief inside her.

How was that possible?

Rex shouldn't feel like an intruder coming into his wife's hospital room, but at that moment, he did.

He also couldn't just loiter around the hallway like some weirdo, though, so even though his arms prickled with unease and uncertainty, he cleared his throat, rapped his knuckle against the doorjamb and stepped inside. "Sweetheart."

Lydia's eyes popped open, and she pulled her head away from Grant, untangling their hands and reaching out to Rex, her eyes instantly flooding with fresh tears.

Now he felt like he belonged. Only it was for all the wrong reasons.

Neither of them should be there.

This shouldn't have happened.

She didn't deserve this.

Neither of them did. But least of all Lydia. She'd already been through so much in her life. She deserved nothing but happiness and joy for the rest of her days.

He ate up the short distance between them, sat on the edge of the bed and scooped her into his arms, her body shaking with new wracking sobs as her tears drenched his long-sleeved shirt.

"I lost our baby," she kept saying.

"Shhhh," he murmured, stroking her back and kissing the side of her head. "We'll get through this. I'm so sorry, sweetheart. So sorry for what you have gone through and that I couldn't get here faster."

"I'm sorry," she wailed against his shoulder. "One minute I was picking sprouts. The next minute I was ..." She clutched him tighter. "Our baby!"

"Shhhh, sweetheart. We'll get through this. You did nothing wrong. You are the best mother in the entire world and took care of that baby."

"Not well enough."

Fuck, he was so lost right now.

She was blaming herself.

Even after Grant told her not to, that none of this was her fault, after Rex reiterated it all, she still believed that the reason she miscarried was *her* fault.

He hedged a glance at Grant, imploring him for direction. He seemed to know what to say, or at least it appeared that way.

Rex, on the other hand, was so freaking lost.

Normally, he had all the answers. He was the protector and the defender, but he had no answers here, no way of protecting his wife from her grief, from her self-deprecation and blame.

Grant's mouth dipped down into a frown and he was about to open his mouth when there was a gentle rap on the door.

"Is it okay if we come in?" Pasha's voice echoed softly through the hospital room.

Rex glanced up to see Krista, Pasha, and Stacey all standing in the doorway, waiting to be invited in.

Lydia pulled away from Rex's embrace and wiped her eyes, nodding at her sisters-in-law.

All three women entered wearing matching somber expressions.

Lydia sniffed. "One in four women, right?" Her lip trembled, and more tears sprang into her eyes.

"Oh, honey," Stacey crooned, nudging Rex out of the way and going in to hug Lydia. "That doesn't make it any less terrible."

Rex glanced at Grant again and tilted his head toward the door. Grant nodded, and the two men stepped outside the hospital room to give the women a moment.

Once the women's voices became no more than a murmur, shoving his hands in his jean pockets and studying the mottled tile floor, Rex looked up at Grant. "I need to thank you."

Grant shook his head. "I just did what I thought was right. I'm sorry if you think I overstepped."

Now it was Rex's turn to shake his head. "You didn't. You were there for my wife when I couldn't be. You took care of her, and you seem to be saying all the right things. So ... thank you." He held his hand out, waiting for Grant to take it.

Grant's hesitation only lasted a moment before he smiled grimly and shook Rex's hand, his grip firm and reassuring. "Wish there was a better way I could have proved to you that I'm not the monster you all think I am. That I'm just a lonely widower, looking for company and great conversation. And your mother provides me with heaps of both."

Rex's lips pinched, and he pulled his hand from Grant's. "How do you know what to say to her in this situation? I'm lost."

Grant's throat moved on a hard swallow, and his gaze turned sad. "My wife had ten miscarriages."

Ten?

Jesus Christ.

"Some were early, some a bit later. It was after we lost our daughter at nineteen weeks, Daphne called it quits. Said she wanted to get a hysterectomy because she didn't think she could survive another loss. But after everything she'd been through, losing ten babies and not ever getting one to hold and bring them home, I said she shouldn't have to go under the knife, so I got a vasectomy. She was always enough for me. The love of my life, but she desperately wanted a family. We fostered for a while, but that became too hard when we would have to say goodbye to children we'd grown attached to. We also considered adoption, but the day after we got the notification that we'd been selected to adopt, she got her cancer diagnosis, and it became a five-year battle that she eventually lost."

"Holy fuck."

"I know what to say ... or I should say, I *assume* that I know what to say because I've been down this road a few times. Both with the miscarriages and cancer. But every woman—every *person* —is different. And nobody knows your wife better than you, so just listen and be there. Let her pound her fists against your chest and scream if she needs to. Let her stay in bed and cry for days. Let her grieve the baby the way that feels right to her. She will come around, and each day it will get easier. But just give her time."

Rex nodded. "Okay. Thanks."

Grant's big palm landed on Rex's shoulder and squeezed. "And you're allowed to grieve, too. This is your loss, too. That was your baby, too. So don't bottle it all up inside until you feel like your head is going to explode because you think you have to be the last remaining pillar of strength for your family. Go a few rounds on a punching bag or drive out into the woods and scream. I know you think you're *her* protector, but who is protecting *you?*"

That last bit made Rex snort. "Lydia is *my* protector. Or at least she thinks she is. Protects me from myself."

"And she's currently out of commission to do the job. So you need to find somebody else. Or something else to help you." He released Rex's shoulder and took a half step back, shoving his hands into his pockets.

"How did you cope with the losses?"

"Various things. I would often go flying. Take the chopper up to a random mountain, stand on top of it and scream until I felt like my lungs were bleeding." Grant shrugged. "I also have a punching bag in my garage—*if* you need one."

Brock had one in his home gym, too, and Rex had gone more than one or two rounds with it over the years.

Footsteps behind Rex grew louder and Grant's expression perked up slightly as he focused on whoever was approaching.

"How is she doing?" Rex's mother asked, coming to stand between Rex and Grant and gaze up at them both curiously.

"Who's with Maeve?" Rex asked.

"I dropped her off with Chase. She's in good hands. But I needed to come to see how my darling was doing. How is Lydia?" His mother reached for Rex's hand and squeezed it before pulling him down to her for a hug.

Hugging his mother was always awkward given how short she was and how tall Rex was. But he sucked it up because the woman who'd raised him was also a saint and he loved her.

"I'm so sorry, honey," she whispered into his ear. "Let me know if there is *anything* I can do."

"Thanks, Mum," he said, though his words were growing more forced and jagged as he tried to cram them through his constricting throat.

"I hear the girls in there with her. That's good."

Rex nodded. Even though that was *his* wife in there and *his* baby, he wasn't sure he could give Lydia what she needed right now. Grant seemed to know what to say, and Lydia seemed to be speaking and not through sobs to her sisters-in-law, but what would happen when he walked back into that room?

Would she take one look at him and well up with tears again? Did she think he blamed her?

For the first time in a very long time in their relationship, he wasn't sure he was what Lydia needed right now, and the thought of that gutted him. He wanted to be there for her, to comfort her and help her through her pain. But the longer he stood there and listened to her talking to the other women, the more he worried he wasn't what—or *who*—she needed.

"I'm going to poke my head in and check on her," Joy said, stepping around Grant and Rex.

"We'll head down to Tim Hortons on the main floor and grab everyone some coffee," Grant said, stepping forward and patting Rex on the shoulder. "Come on, Rex. Everything makes more sense once we're caffeinated."

Rex snorted and fell in line with Grant. "Not gonna argue with you there."

————

THEY ARRIVED BACK at Lydia's hospital room a little while later with trays of coffees and boxes of pastries.

When they rounded the corner and approached Lydia's room, laughter could be heard coming through the open door.

"Well, at least she's not crying," Grant said with a lopsided smile, stepping to the side so Rex could enter first.

All the women, including Rex's mother, were crowded around Lydia's bed. Some were sitting in chairs, others standing.

But the most beautiful thing of all was Lydia's smile.

It wasn't huge, but it was real, and that made the shredded pieces of Rex's heart begin to fuse back together.

"What's so funny?" Grant asked, handing the coffees around.

"Krista was just regaling us with her most recent arrest," Pasha said with a giant grin. "You never told us you had a trespasser on your property, Grant. I hope you're okay?"

Grant glanced at Joy. "I didn't want to snitch. I figured his wife was dealing with him and there was no need to run and tattle to his mama."

"Oh, I dealt with him all right," Krista said, sipping her coffee coyly.

"Did you know your brother was going snooping?" Rex's mother asked, turning to him with pinched brows and that threatening look in her eye. Like she was one breath away from ripping off her slipper and throwing it at his head. Only she wasn't wearing slippers, she was wearing running shoes, and getting knocked in the brain with that would hurt.

Rex held up his hand in protest. "I did not. That was between Chase and Brock. I was at Heath's, and we were hanging out with the kids while our women shopped."

"Very convenient alibi if you ask me," Stacey said before turning to Krista. "I say we hook him up to a lie detector and put him under the bright light."

"Put electric probes on his nipples," Lydia added, then giggled. "Oh, wait, he might actually like that."

Rex glanced at his wife in shock. She was grinning at him, and a sparkle emerged in her eyes.

Thank fuck.

There was his strong, hilarious woman.

"Right, Rexwell. You got a penchant for pain."

"More than his mother needs to know, my dear," his mother teasingly lectured. "But I don't believe his plea of innocence for a minute either. I think they're all conspiring together."

Rex fixed his gaze on his mother for a moment, then Grant. "Not me anymore. I'm done. I'm out. I just want you to be happy, Mum. I happen to think Grant is not such a terrible guy."

Grant snorted. "That's the best endorsement I'm going to get, eh?"

Rex grinned. "Don't push it."

Everyone laughed.

"I'm dealing with Brock," Krista said. "He'll probably be the last to come around, but he'll get there. Just ... maybe invest in a security camera or borrow a rabid Doberman from someone for a couple of weeks. Just in the event he catches another case of stupid and tries to break into your house again."

Lydia snagged Rex's eye and reached for him. He went to his wife immediately and sat on the edge of the bed beside her. It creaked and groaned slightly beneath his weight.

She kissed his shoulder, and he kissed the top of her head as he wrapped his arm around her.

"Thank you for coming."

He could see it in her eyes, the determination to be strong battling it out with the pain and heartbreak that was so raw on the surface.

He squeezed her close. "Anything for you, sweetheart. You're in the driver's seat here. But just know, I'm here for whatever you need, whatever you want."

Fresh tears sprang up in her eyes, but she smiled through them. "I know you are, and I'm so glad that we're going through this together."

"I'm your rock, Lydia."

She nodded. "And I'm yours."

Fuck yeah, she was. And he'd never met anybody stronger.

CHAPTER FOURTEEN
GRANT & JOY

GRANT TURNED off the oven and, with a mitt on one hand, pulled out the steaming casserole dish of roasted squash. He'd gone back to The Root Cellar, but they were out of brussels sprouts, so he had to settle for squash.

Not a big deal.

He'd make his mother's famous truffle and Parmesan sprouts for Joy another day. But tonight, he was making a squash recipe he found online that had like a thousand five-star reviews. If a thousand people thought it was delicious, there was a good chance he and Joy would, too.

Soft rock played in the background and the fireplace had toned down its licking flames to a beautiful glowing ember.

Joy was set to arrive any minute, which was perfect because dinner was just about ready.

They'd been seeing each other for six months now, and he'd cooked for her many times, but tonight felt different.

Maybe it was because he had finally met all of her children and their families and was also getting to see another side of her—or perhaps it was because, after all this time, he was finally ready to tell another woman that he loved her.

He'd never said it to anybody else besides Daphne, and he knew Joy had never truly loved another man besides Zane, so for both of them, this was going to be a big step.

But he was ready—or so he kept telling himself.

He poured them each a glass of pinot noir that he had emptied into a decanter earlier, checked the steaks, which were resting, and brought the salad to the table.

He hadn't changed much in the way of décor after Daphne passed away.

Her taste had always been complementary to his—modern, clean and easy. She wasn't into knick-knacks or florals or even throw pillows. She liked clean lines, block colors, and lots of windows. He wouldn't call their home—correction, *his* home—sterile, because it had homey touches here and there, but it wasn't super kitschy or even what he would call cozy.

Unlike his wife. Daphne had been the warmest, most comforting, and caring person he'd ever met. So for her style to be on the colder side always made him laugh.

"What?" she would squeak. "My mother just had so many *things* and trinkets that would collect dust, and you know how bad my asthma was as a child. I don't need dust collectors. We have our few key pieces of art, our stylish furniture, this handsome, chic rug, and some plants. What more do we need?"

He would just laugh, shake his head, smile and say, "I need nothing else when I have you."

That would always make her blush and give him a smile that melted his insides.

"Such a charmer."

Then he'd scoop her up, carrying her over to their white leather couch, prop his feet up on the funky-cut burl coffee table, and they'd cuddle and watch television or make out like teenagers.

Because they'd met when they were teenagers.

She was his first love.

His first kiss.

His first ... everything.

The girl next door who loved to read her summers away in her family's backyard hammock, write poems in the spring and fall about the blooming flowers and changing leaves, and make pine cone and peanut butter bird feeders in the winter.

He'd loved her since he first laid eyes on her when her family moved in next door. He was fourteen. She was twelve.

She'd been shy, but her smile had made the entire world glow.

He waited until she was fourteen and "allowed to date" before he finally asked her out to the movies and ice cream. And when she said yes, he had fist-pumped and leaped into the air for joy.

They were together after that until she passed away.

He went to college in Calgary for two years, beginning his helicopter mechanics ticket while she finished up high school, then they traveled for a year together, and when they returned, she started college and he joined the air force.

They had a long-distance relationship while he was in basic training. Through it all, their love never wavered. It only intensified. Being away from Daphne for all those months made him realize that he was the luckiest son of bitch on the planet for a "swell gal like her," as he used to call her, to "fall for a schmuck like him."

When she finished her teaching degree, she followed him to Cold Lake, where she started teaching at the local elementary school, and he resumed his training and apprenticed to not only become a helicopter mechanic but a pilot as well.

He did his tours overseas, and she stayed teaching, their love withstanding the distance once again.

Then, when he finally returned to Canada, they lived blissfully for years, eventually relocating to Victoria when he was discharged from the air force and hired by a local helicopter company as their main mechanic.

He honestly thought he'd never find love again. That his one true soul mate had come and gone. In his life for thirty years but not nearly long enough. He and Daphne had been robbed of so much. Not only the family she desperately wanted but of time together, too. And with her death, he was certain, so had died his heart. And perhaps that was still true. Perhaps Daphne had been his soul mate and Zane had been Joy's, but that didn't mean that they couldn't find companionship and love while they lived.

Most of his heart had died with Daphne. And the way Joy spoke of Zane, most of her heart had died with him. But small fragments still beat within their chests, keeping them going, moving them forward and living the life their soulmates were denied.

He let out a long exhale and glanced at the picture of his wife that sat on the high, narrow wooden table she had along one wall. All that sat on it was a snake plant—hardy and nearly impossible to kill, as his wife had pointed out when she bought it—and a photo frame. Before she passed away, all that had sat on that table was the plant. But he put the frame there so that she was always with him.

More times than he cared to admit, he caught himself talking to her as he cooked or cleaned the house. Asked her if he was doing it up to her standards.

She only ever smiled at him.

Because that was what she always did.

She smiled.

Through the cancer treatments, the vomiting, the pain—Daphne smiled.

Sure, she cried, too. But his optimistic, bright and shiny wife always tried to put a positive spin on things no matter what.

He suspected it was to hide her fear and keep him from spiraling.

He liked to think that he was her rock through everything—

IVF, miscarriages, chemo, radiation, surgery, palliative care, but in reality, she was his rock.

And she knew it.

If it hadn't been for that smile, glowing at him every day, he knew he would have crumbled to dust more than once.

Even now, with her gone, that smile was what kept him getting up each morning and continuing with his life.

That smile ... and the woman who had just shut her car door outside and was making her way up the path to his house.

Joy.

Could she have been named any more perfectly?

Because she certainly sparked joy in him.

She rekindled flames inside him he'd thought had long been extinguished, had long turned to nothing more than cold, damp coal.

Smiling, he glanced at Daphne's photo. "You like her, don't you?"

Daphne just showed him those blinding white teeth, dimples, and rosy cheeks.

She would have liked Joy.

He reached the front door, opening it just as Joy was lifting her little fist to knock.

Her smile winded him, and her eyes twinkled. "I forget sometimes that you're one of *those kinds* of men."

"One of what kind?" he asked playfully, taking her overnight bag from her.

"Military trained with impeccable hearing, instincts, and senses. You probably knew I was in the neighborhood before I even parked my car."

They made their way into the living room and he released her bag to hand her one of the stemless wine glasses.

She immediately took a sip and made a sexy little humming sound in delight.

"Not quite, but I did hear you shut your car door." He set her bag down on the arm of the couch, took her wineglass from her, and set it on the table with his beside Daphne's photo. Then he wrapped his arms around her small frame, and she did the same to him.

He was over a foot taller than her, standing at six one—he'd been six three at his tallest, but age was causing him to shrink—and she was only four eleven, but her personality made her appear so much taller.

With twinkling blue eyes, her ballerina bun tucked up on her crown with not a hair out of place and fresh, glossy lipstick, she tilted her head up to look at him. "Smells good. And I don't just mean dinner."

His chuckle came out raspy since his throat had suddenly gone dry as he mentally prepared himself for what he wanted to say.

"You smell good, too," he said, ducking down and taking her mouth for a moment.

She hummed against his lips, parting hers so he could sweep his tongue inside. Her grip around his neck tightened, and she pulled him down, pressing her hips against his.

Joy Hart was a passionate woman. She also knew her way around a man's body and had taught Grant a thing or two about his own pleasure.

He'd been reluctant at first—even a little scared—but she was gentle and patient with him and showed him just how much more he could enjoy sex with a little bit of imagination.

He'd felt like a bit of a chump when they first got together. Although he'd had ample sex in his life with Daphne, he'd only ever had sex with one woman. Joy was a lot more experienced than he was, and the fact that she was a sex and relationship therapist—specializing in sexuality—meant she was a lot more comfortable discussing things than he or Daphne had ever been.

Joy had even ironically nicknamed him *Wild Man*, not only

because his last name was Wild but because he wasn't exactly "adventurous" or "worldly" in the bedroom.

The nickname had kind of stuck.

By the third time they'd had sex, she asked him if he'd ever had his prostate stroked and if he'd like her to show him. Then he was forced to let her in on the little secret that he no longer *had* a prostate—thanks, cancer. So she had nothing *to* stroke. That didn't seem to faze her though. She just seemed glad that he could still "rise to the occasion." That made two of them. The fear had been real when he found out he had the big C, but he crossed his fingers, said a few prayers or whatever to whoever might be listening, and thank the heavens, by a few months post-surgery, he was back letting his palm help him sleep.

And Joy, well, she seemed to take his lack of a prostate as a personal challenge. She wound up showing him all kinds of wicked and pleasurable things that had him not missing his prostate in the least.

The woman was a master in her craft. He was just going to leave it at that.

She knew *juuuust* what to do.

His erection was pressing hard against his jeans now, and his balls were telling him that cold, overcooked steak was fine and to take this to the bedroom, but he told his balls to shut the fuck up and broke their lip lock.

His balls—and Joy by the sound of her whimper—were none too pleased.

"Let me feed you first," he said, chuckling at her pouty face as she slid her hands down from his neck to his chest. "You'll need your strength. And these steaks are primo. I splurged." He grinned at her and went to step away, but her grip on the front of his shirt held him in place.

He stared down at her, mesmerized by the vibrant blue of her eyes and the softness of her skin. She didn't look sixty-six. He knew she took care of herself. Had a treadmill she used every morning, swam laps at the pool—which was where they met—and ate meals heavy on the veggies and low on carbs and sugar. She rarely ate red meat, but he knew she liked a good steak on special occasions. And the first time he'd spent the night at her place, he'd teased her about all the creams and serums on her bathroom counter.

But they worked because his woman was a looker.

Her throat rolled on a swallow, and she blinked up at him. A tendril of unease wormed through him as her eyes narrowed just a touch and she licked her lips. "I love you," she said after a few more heartbeats.

His mouth parted, and his eyes widened. His pulse also picked up tempo.

She shook her head and forced a smile. "You don't have to say it back. I know that Daphne was the love of your life. And Zane was mine. But ..." She glanced away for a moment before pinning her focus back on him. "What you did for Lydia today, the things you said to her. How you've treated my whole family since they ambushed us on Saturday ... and after Brock tried to break into your house ..." She shook her head again and forced a laugh. "And rather than tell me, you kept it quiet because you didn't want him to get in trouble." That made her laugh more and the corners of her eyes to crinkle. "I'm not done with that boy, by the way. He needs to learn some boundaries. But you never asked for any of this, and yet ... you're taking it all in your stride. You're stepping up in ways that I ... that you would never be expected to. And you haven't run for the hills. You ..." Tears welled up in her eyes, but her smile remained radiant. "You keep coming back for more. And, I ... love you."

He cupped her face in his palm and swept the single tear that broke free away from her cheek with his thumb. "I love you, too. And I keep coming back for more because this was all Daphne and I ever wanted. A big, noisy, crazy in-each-other's-business-just-a-little-too-much family. And I know that she would be happy for me.

I'm not going to try too hard or force things. And your sons don't have to like me. But they also need to know that I'm not going anywhere until *you* tell me to leave. They don't have a say in this. It's you and me in this relationship, and I'm in it until you say otherwise."

Another tear slid down her face, and he swept that one away, too. "I'm not telling you to go anywhere but to bed and to take me with you," she said, her voice rough but sultry. "I know Zane would be happy for me, too. He would have liked you. And if the roles were reversed and it was he who had raised the boys on his own, I wouldn't want him to live out his days without companionship or love. I'd want him to find comfort with someone. I'm not so selfish to wish that he pine away in grief for me for fifty or however many years I have left."

"Me, too," he said. "And I know Daphne would have liked you, too."

"I'm sorry you and Daphne weren't able to have the big family you always dreamed of."

His heart constricted, and an ache formed in the back of his throat. He clenched his molars and nodded. "Me, too."

"But you're more than welcome to join mine. And if Rex is any indication, I think the boys will come around. We just need to give them some time."

He nodded, bent his head low and brushed his lips over hers. "Time, I have. But our steaks don't, so let's eat, woman, then I'll take you to bed and *really* show you how much I love you."

Her giggle made him buoyant once again. "Sounds like a plan I can get on board with, Wild Man."

CHAPTER FIFTEEN
GRANT & JOY

THE FIRST THING he always did when they tumbled into bed was pull her hair free of her bun. He said it was like unwrapping a present. Taking the librarian from day to night. It made Joy wish she hadn't gotten LASIK ten years ago and still wore glasses, then she'd really give him a taste of the naughty librarian.

The steak had been mouth-watering, the squash divine, and Grant certainly knew his way around a vinaigrette, but none of that compared to how delicious the naked man spread out over the top of her was.

She still had to pinch herself from time to time—particularly when he got naked—that he was interested in her.

Sure, she wasn't some frumpy, dowdy old thing with one foot in the grave. She might be sixty-six, a mother and nana, but she wasn't dead, and she took care of herself. But Grant was out-of-this-world handsome. Now *he* really took care of himself. A sixty-year-old with abs like that? You rarely saw that unless it was in the gossip mags at the grocery store checkout and some celebrity she'd crushed on since she was a teenager was caught at the beach in just his shorts.

She'd always had a thing for Pierce Brosnan. The accent, the smolder. Even with a dad-bod, Joy would let Double-Oh-Seven take her to Pound Town if he ever asked her.

But alas, ol' Piercy was madly in love with his wife of decades and would never stray. That, of course, just made him all the sexier.

But she had her own Double-Oh-Seven candidate currently nibbling her neck and twiddling her nipple in a way he knew drove her gloriously mad.

They'd raced through dinner, or at least she had—determined to get on to dessert—and she didn't mean the raspberry sorbet he said he had in his freezer.

There were still dishes in the sink and counters to wipe, but that could all wait.

She wanted the man who had shown her she could love and be loved again to take her to his bed and pour that love all over her.

He placed one open palm on hers and splayed her fingers wide, locking their fingers together as his other hand made its merry way down her torso and between her legs.

She spread her thighs so he could settle between them, and her breath hitched as his fingers found her slickness. Of course, they used lube, since menopause and all that getting older crap.

His chuckle against her neck was warm and raspy.

"I'd say your oven is plenty preheated, hmm?"

"My oven is preheated before I even get in my car to drive over here, Wild Man," she said, sliding her hand between them to grab his shaft and stroke it. "All I have to do is think about *this* and you and the oven gets plenty hot—and fast."

She felt his smile against her jaw before he nipped, then peppered kisses across her cheek until he could claim her mouth.

Even though she couldn't get pregnant anymore—woot woot, menopause! STDs among the retired and boomer community were becoming a growing problem. A lot of their peers thought because pregnancy was a non-issue, so was protection.

But that was not how it worked.

So, they'd both gotten tested before they went condom-free.

It was only *after* that, that Grant revealed he had only ever been with Daphne and hadn't so much as kissed another woman since she passed away.

Joy couldn't say the same.

And she certainly wasn't ashamed that she couldn't say the same.

Sex was natural, sex was normal, and sex was wonderful.

Zane had passed away when she was in her thirties. She was still in the prime of her life. And most definitely in the sexual prime of her life. So even though she hadn't had any serious partners who she introduced to her children, she also hadn't denied herself something that she loved—which was sex.

She was discreet about it, keeping things casual and making sure her overprotective, nosy-ass sons didn't find out something they had no business knowing, and for a while, that had been all she needed.

She was in school for years getting her doctorate and raising four bull-headed boys. She had no time for romance.

But the sex was a necessary tension release. Her dresser drawer of vibrators could only do so much. Sometimes you just needed to feel the weight of a man on you. There really was no comparison for the rush of endorphins that skin-on-skin and the scent of sex in the air created as a talented man made you nearly get a concussion when your head slammed into the headboard.

Ah. Yeah.

But as her world settled down, the boys grew up and moved on with their lives and Joy's career became a manageable constant, she began to yearn for more.

Sex was great, but so was companionship.

She'd had a few beaus over the years, but nothing lasted more than a couple of months. She was always comparing them with

Zane, and none ever measured up, so she ended it. Then she'd revert back to her casual hookup ways, discouraged that her one true love had come and gone and she was destined to live the rest of her life alone, only seeking the temporary fulfillment of a hookup— or fuck buddy, as the kids were calling it these days.

Until she met Grant.

He asked her out. She said yes, and the rest was a beautiful, blurry memory she looked back on with fond bewilderment.

Since she had been with more people than Grant, to be on the safe side—even though she always was and got tested routinely— they both were tested so that they could go condom-free.

And oh, what a celebratory day that had been.

She'd called Grant with her test results, and not twenty minutes later he was on her doorstep, and then thirty seconds after that, they were both naked in bed.

And there they stayed for several hours.

He might not have had a lot of experience, but the man had enthusiasm and stamina, and those were two of her favorite qualities in a man. The experience they could easily fix—and they did.

A bead of precum emerged on his crown, and she swirled it around the top with the pad of her thumb, enjoying the tingly rush she felt through her body as he groaned in pleasure.

Heat bloomed like a spring rose inside her as he slid those fingers deeper between her legs and into her center.

He crooked them just right, and she moaned.

He broke their kiss. "You like that?" he asked, knowing very well that she did, given the way she lifted her hips and ground her clit against the heel of his palm.

"Silly men ask silly questions," she replied, releasing his cock and sliding her hand farther down to cup and gently squeeze his balls. "You like that?"

His grunt and the way his middle finger pressed up on her G-spot was all the answer she needed.

She tugged just a little, which made him grunt again.

"Wicked woman," he growled, scissoring his fingers inside her.

She grinned at the compliment and closed her eyes as he moved his face back down to her neck, burying his nose in her salt-and-pepper hair, which fanned across his pillow.

She'd embraced the gray when it happened, correcting anyone who mentioned it that it wasn't gray but, in fact, silver and she had earned it and valiantly so—raising four sons alone. Every single sparkly strand.

She took care of herself and was doing her best to age gracefully, but when those first threads of tinsel started to show up shortly after Zane died, she made the executive decision *not* to color her hair and try to smother the change but to rather embrace it.

It was freeing.

It was one less thing to stress about.

She had children to raise and school to finish. Worrying about coloring her hair was the least of her concerns.

And it quickly became no concern at all.

And she got compliments by the bucketload for her salt-and-pepper tresses.

His teeth found the shell of her ear and scraped. His tongue followed to soothe the sting, then he nibbled her earlobe and tugged.

"I'm all for foreplay—*believe me*—but I'm also really itching to get to the main course." She let go of his balls and gripped his cock again. Stroking once more and releasing their handhold, she used her other hand to tug at his arm until his fingers slipped free of her. "We've got all night."

"That we do," he said, lifting his head and staring down at her. "Seems to me we've got more than all night."

She blinked up at him, her throat growing tight as the impact of his words settled inside her. They'd said, "I love you." Both of them.

She hadn't been intending to say it tonight, but it just kind of came out.

Knowing what he did with Lydia that day, how he helped her. And how he just took everything with her wild and noisy family in his stride just proved to her more and more that Grant was somebody she could see herself growing older with.

She didn't even bother comparing him to Zane. Because she knew Zane would approve. She knew her husband would want her to be happy and that a man like Grant could make Joy happy.

And he did.

He made her so happy.

But the fact that he said that he loved her back only made her heart grow and heat and contentment unfurl inside her.

"Make love to me, Grant," she whispered, moving her hand from his arm to the back of his neck and pulling his mouth down to hers. "Because you love me."

"And you love me."

"I do," she said, before closing her mouth over his at the same moment he slid inside her.

He rocked into her, and she rocked back, lifting her hips so his lower belly grazed her clit, causing sparks to fly behind her closed eyelids and flames to flicker in her core.

Like she often did, she pictured what was happening with their bodies. Visualized it like she was floating above, a voyeur of her own romantic entanglement.

It was a technique she used with clients.

When one or both partners were finding their sex life lacking or unfulfilling, she would encourage them to remain engaged physically but disengage spiritually and float above. Watch in their mind what they thought and felt happening and try to gain pleasure from seeing it.

Her sex life was far from lacking, but that didn't matter. It was a technique she enjoyed because it turned her on. Visualizing

Grant's big body hovering over her. The wide expanse of his back, the narrowing of his hips. His thick thighs and the way his glutes bunched and flexed with each measured thrust.

And even though he was a strong man, the longer he held himself up, the more his arm muscles would pop, the more his back muscles would become defined.

Then she'd squeeze her eyes even tighter and move her floating self around the room to get other angles. The side view was one of her favorites. So was the end of the bed view. Watching as he disappeared inside her—nothing got her closer to the edge than that.

He still wasn't on board with the idea of filming them having sex, and he said he felt a little self-conscious when she suggested they do it in front of some mirrors—but he'd get there. For now, she was resigned to her own active and vivid imagination, along with the man who filled her up just right and made her body hum like an overpopulated beehive.

Grant's tongue stroked and tangled with hers—he really was an exceptional kisser—but as his tongue began to mimic the plunging motions of his cock inside her, she had to tear her mouth away from his. She was close.

So. Damn. Close.

He brought her to the ledge of the cliff so fast when his tongue did that and his hips did their flexy thing.

She wanted this to last.

She wanted to savor every moment they had together.

Sure, they had all night—and hopefully the rest of their lives— but he wasn't twenty anymore, and it would take some time for him to refuel and be able to go again.

So she wanted this time, the first time they made love after they said they loved each other, to last.

She opened her eyes for a moment, and he was staring down at her, one brow lifted slightly and a lopsided smile on his face. He was still moving that pelvis though.

Still grazing his lower belly over her clit until her breath snagged in her throat and she felt like she might pass out from pleasure.

"Problem?" he asked, his grin morphing into a cocky one.

She wrinkled her nose and glared up at him.

He knew she was having a hard time hanging on.

He knew her tells, and she knew his.

He could keep going, or he could come right this second. The man had stamina and uncanny control of his body.

"Silly men ask silly questions," she repeated, squeezing her muscles around him.

"And I'm a silly man?"

"I'm ... just trying to make it last," she said, knowing that if he kept doing that little hip swivel move at the end, her train of thought would derail and she'd start to come.

He did the hip swivel again.

Fireworks went off in her brain.

Damn him.

His grin widened. "But we have all night."

"But this is the first time we ... since we ..."

Damn him. Damn him. She was struggling to finish thoughts and sentences.

Him and those hips.

But understanding dawned on him, and he eased up; his grin faded, and sincerity filled his eyes. "Gotcha. Gonna let this one last."

"Thank you."

He took her mouth again, the kiss slow and lazy this time. There was no rhythmic plunging of his tongue in tandem with his cock. He simply explored her mouth. He nibbled her lips, broke the kiss to press a small one to her cheek.

He cherished her. He made love to her.

Slowly, the pressure in her belly began to build, and the prickling along her arms intensified.

She wasn't in her voyeur position anymore, watching them together from above, but rather, she was back in her own body, experiencing in person and with the person she loved.

She never thought she could love again, and yet here, against all odds, she did. And it was wonderful and magical and made her feel like her and Grant's love could do anything.

Her hips lifted up, and when his belly grazed her clit, she knew she was close again. He could sense it, too.

He broke their kiss and looked down at her. Asking if it was okay for them to climb to the summit together now.

She nodded and smiled, loving everything about this man and relishing the fact that he loved her back.

His cadence picked up. He dropped his head and took a nipple between his teeth, tugging just hard enough to make her gasp.

She raked her nails down his back, digging them into his butt cheeks, feeling them clench and release with each plunge.

His mouth moved over to her other breast, and he sucked hard. Pain and pleasure mixed inside her, and warmth spread down through her belly, settling in her core.

She was close.

He was close.

Releasing her nipple, he lifted up onto his arms and stared down at her.

His smile warmed her heart and sparked nothing but hope and clarity inside her. Then he leaned forward, took her mouth, and they found their release together.

CHAPTER SIXTEEN
BROCK & KRISTA

It was Thursday night, and Brock glared at the big, black thirty-passenger van that pulled up along the curb in front of his mother's house.

He could hear the jovial Christmas tunes playing inside the cab, and by the way his children and his nieces and nephews started bouncing on their toes, he could tell he was going to hate every fucking minute of tonight.

The way they'd done it for the last few years had been fine.

He and his brothers piled their families into their trucks, everyone had walkie-talkies, and they convoyed around Victoria, following a map to all the best decorated houses.

Why mess with a good thing?

Why did Grant have to show them all up with his access to the big old-person-mobile?

Just because the man didn't have any traffic violations or tickets didn't mean he was a good driver. Brock knew plenty of crappy-ass drivers who had never gotten a ticket—but definitely should have.

Anger prickled along his arms beneath his black leather jacket. He hated the idea of this. Even when it wasn't some poser who was dating his mother, driving his children around. The only time he felt even remotely calm when his children were in a vehicle was when he or Krista was behind the wheel. And if he was being completely honest, he only felt completely calm when *he* was the one driving. When *he* was the one in control.

Even the best of drivers can be hit by the worst of drivers. Nobody is one hundred percent safe on the road.

His mother's words came back to him.

His father—an incredible driver—had died in a car accident. Brock had been in the car with him—a police cruiser—and when a call came in about a speeding vehicle, even though Brock's father was off duty, he was still in his police cruiser and figured the presence of a black-and-white would make the driver slow down. It didn't, and Brock's father's vehicle was sticking out just a little too far into the road and the speeding truck hit them.

Brock remained pinned in the vehicle with his dead father until the jaws of life could get them both out.

He'd never forget the last time—the last *way*—he saw his dad. The best man he knew, the best driver he knew, taken out by some low-life scumbag who was drunk behind the wheel and going ninety kilometers an hour in a forty zone.

But even after all of that, Brock knew that a good driver, a defensive driver who was aware of his surroundings on the road, stood a better chance at survival than an idiot who'd barely passed their driver's test.

And he made sure to keep his children rear-facing and in their five-point harness car seats until they maxed out in weight and height. Zoe had maxed out—only recently—but Zane was still strapped in like a fighter pilot.

But even with the five-point five-hundred-dollar metal-framed car seats he bought for his children, Brock wanted to be the one in control of the multi-ton vehicle his babies rode in.

But nooooo, not tonight.

Everyone had voted against him. Including his own wife.

They all thought Grant's suggestion of going together in one vehicle was "great" and "generous" and "sure to be super fun."

Screw them all.

It wasn't super generous. It was Grant showing Brock up. It was Grant trying to carry favor with Joy's children and grandchildren so that he could come to Christmas dinner. It was Grant weaseling his way into the family—a family he had no business belonging to, let alone leading.

Well, the rest of them may have slurped down the Grant Kool-Aid and not minded the flavor, but Brock was having none of it. He had an allergy to the toxic sludge, and he didn't need to try it out to know that that shit would give him hives.

"All aboard," Grant called, having tugged the lever to open the big bifold door to the bus while still sitting behind the steering wheel.

Brock groaned.

A pointy elbow made contact with his ribs, and he let out a grunt of pain.

"Be *fucking* nice," Krista said through gritted teeth.

He glared at her.

She glared back.

"I hope you guys don't mind, but I swung by Tim Hortons on my way and loaded up on hot chocolate and Tim Bits for the journey," Grant said, which made the kids all squeal.

"Tim Bits!" Zane cheered, glancing up at Krista. "Mama, can we have some?"

At least they weren't full-size donuts. Tim Bits, or the more generic term, donut holes, were just round little balls of donut deliciousness. But since Tim Hortons was a Canadian staple, they coined their own term for the little balls of sugar.

And kids—and grownups—went apeshit for them.

"You can have a few," Krista said, tugging Zane's light blue knit cap tighter over his unruly red hair.

"Dibs on the powdered sugar ones," Connor said, being the first one to step onto the bus.

"There's plenty of powdered sugar ones to go around," Grant replied with a chuckle.

The rest of the children who could walk on their own boarded the bus.

Heath carried Eve in her bucket car seat and would strap the baby in with a seat belt once inside. The same went for Rex with Maeve.

Lydia had decided to stay home since she was still recovering from her D and C after the miscarriage, and as Rex put it, she just wanted to sleep and cry. Which she was totally allowed to do.

So, they were down one person tonight.

But unfortunately, it wasn't the person Brock was hoping would call in sick.

He loved Lydia and her dry, thin-filtered sense of humor. Grant, on the other hand—Brock wasn't sure he'd piss on the man if his gums were on fire.

A red Kia Rondo pulled up behind the bus and shut its lights off. They all knew who it was.

"Wait for the life of the party," Rayma called out, slamming her car door. The crunch of gravel under her boots grew louder as she jogged toward them, caramel-colored hair trailing behind her beneath her dark red beret-style hat.

"What, no date this time?" Heath teased as his sister-in-law sidled up next to him and Pasha.

"I'm in the middle of a dry spell," Rayma said with a pout. "Exams are a real cockblocker. And just when I could use the stress release the most."

"Don't have kids until you're ready for constant cockblocking then," Stacey said under her breath as she smiled and waved at her two little cockblockers. Both Connor and Thea were already on the bus with Zoe and Zane, and all four of them had powdered sugar around their mouths, smiles on their faces, and that crazy Christmas look in their eyes.

Rayma chuckled. "At least you *have* cock to be blocked. It's at your disposal if you can find a moment to get unblocked. I don't even have it *to* be blocked."

Chase cleared his throat and shot Rayma a look.

The one-liner queen and baby sister of Pasha just grinned at him and shrugged. "What? It's not like I commented *about* your cock. I just stated that Stacey *had* one on hand."

"You reduced me to nothing more than my genitalia," Chase retorted. His sense of humor had gotten dryer over the years. It was actually something Brock was really happy about. There were a few years there when Chase hardly ever smiled and rarely if ever cracked a joke. The trauma he'd been through had done a number on him, giving him fears and hang-ups that none of them truly understood, as hard as they tried.

But Stacey and the kids had brought Brock's brother to life, and although Brock knew Chase still had bad days, he also knew he had way more good days.

"How does it feel?" Rayma replied. "Now you know what women go through on the regular. Reduced to nothing more than a pair of tits, an ass, or a set of holes to fill."

Brock and his brothers made noises of discomfort in their throats.

"Ooooh, touché," Krista said. "Good one."

"Seriously, though," Rayma went on, "the ratio of women to men at UVic is ridiculous. One guy for every three chicks. No thanks. I've done that shit before, and it's not my jam."

Eyes widened in surprise, including Brock's.

Did she mean she'd been with one guy and two other women …

at the same time ... intimately? Or had she shared one man with two other women as in lack of exclusivity but one at a time?

He was afraid to ask for more details, but after the shock wore off, Krista and Pasha leaned in toward Rayma and demanded more details later.

Rayma did nothing more than smile like a sly fox.

With a throaty chuckle that always made his temperature increase, Krista stepped onto the bus, and Brock took the opportunity to ogle his wife's ass just a little. The woman really could fill out a pair of yoga pants like nobody's business. His cock did a little twitch in his jeans, and he hoped the kids didn't get too hyped-up on sugar that they couldn't sleep when bedtime finally came.

Brock had plans tonight, and they most definitely involved peeling his wife out of those pants that taunted him so.

"Stop drooling," Rayma teased him, elbowing him in the side, though much more gently than Krista had elbowed him.

"She's my wife. I'll drool all I damn well want." He stepped back so that everyone else could board, but he made sure to keep a close eye on Grant. He didn't trust the man an inch and wanted to make sure he wasn't casting his male gaze on any of the women.

So far, he'd only smiled and kept his eyes on people's faces.

Brock was as equally pleased as he was pissed.

"Where's Joy?" Grant asked, directing his question to Heath, who was last to board before Brock.

"Mum's just inside the house. She had the kids come over early and bake cookies with her for the tour, and they weren't quite ready."

At that, the door to their mother's house creaked open, then closed. "I'm coming, I'm coming," Brock's mother called as she jogged down the path, then the driveway, and toward them on the sidewalk. She was carrying a big red-lidded Tupperware container in one hand and her coat in the other. "Sorry, everyone. The cookies took forever to cool and then ice."

"You *iced* them?" Brock asked, giving his mother a look.

She gave him a *look* right back. "Yes, you buffoon. I *iced* them. My grandbabies can't have gingerbread cookies without icing, faces, and buttons. What kind of sadist do you think I am?"

Brock rolled his eyes.

His mother responded with her own eye roll and a mini sneer, but when she turned to face Grant, her eyes lit up and her smile went wide enough to nearly touch her ears. "Thanks for waiting for me," she said with a slight giggle to her voice.

Who the hell was this woman?

Brock had never heard his mother add a giggle to her voice or speak in that girlie tone before in his life.

"I'll wait for you for as long as you need," Grant said, which only made Brock's mother giggle and smile even more.

What the fuck was going on?

Brock glanced between Grant and his mother. They were looking at each other and smiling like ... well ... *buffoons*.

Had he slipped on some ice, bashed his head on the sidewalk, and was now in the hospital in a coma? Because this woman was not his mother. Joy Hart did not swoon. She did not giggle like a teenager, and she most certainly didn't get all moony-eyed over ... *anyone*.

"All right, little lady," Grant said, which only made Brock's mother giggle *again*, "find yourself a seat so we can get this party wagon on the road and see some Christmas lights."

"Christmas lights! Christmas lights!" the children chanted.

Brock still hadn't boarded the bus.

"You comin'?" Grant asked, eyeing Brock, his hand on the lever to close the door.

Brock glanced into the bus through the windows and saw all the happy smiling people he loved.

He didn't want to miss this tradition with his kids, even though

Grant was hijacking the way they did it and putting his own stupid spin on it.

He only had so many Christmases with his kids where their wide-eyed wonder and excitement was so real it was practically tangible. And since he'd missed out on a lot of Christmases with his own dad, he wanted to make up for it all with his kids.

With a grumble, a grunt and a glare at Grant, Brock climbed the three steps up into the bus.

Everyone stared up at him, including his wife and children.

"Daddy, you can sit up at the front," Zoe said, beautifully innocent and unaware of the stick of dynamite she'd just tossed into the raging wildfire. "There is a seat behind Grant."

Brock glanced down at the empty seat.

Motherfucker.

Why wasn't his mother sitting there if she was *so* infatuated with *Grant?*

Because his mother was sitting next to Zoe, that was why. Zoe had announced to everyone very early on that evening that *she* was sitting with Nana and nobody was allowed to argue with her.

Nobody dared argue with Brock's redheaded women. Not Krista or Zoe. They all knew better. Battles were picked sparingly and wisely, and this was one hill nobody wanted to die on.

Even though there were empty seats way at the back, he wasn't keen on being stuck there, away from his kids. If he sat behind Grant, at least he'd be close to Zane and Zoe and get to see the excitement on their faces. At the back of the bus like a reject, he wouldn't see any of it.

"Daddy, sit down so we can get going. People will start turning off their lights soon," Zoe ordered.

"No, they won't," Brock countered, immediately regretting arguing with his tiny ginger tyrant. Oh well, he was on the battlefield now. "It's six-thirty, ZoZo. We have several hours before people turn out their lights for the night."

Zoe's brows pinched, and she plopped her hands on her hips, staring him down like her mother so often did. "Sit, Daddy."

Guffaws and snorts of laughter echoed around the bus.

Zoe wasn't blinking.

Rolling his eyes, Brock eased himself down into the cramped single seat behind Grant. The rest of them were in two-person bench seats facing forward, while Brock was forced to squeeze his frame into a one-person sideways-facing seat directly behind the driver.

"Everybody buckled in?" Grant asked.

"Aye-aye, Captain Driver Man Grant," Zoe said, giving Grant a salute.

"I like your enthusiasm, Zoe," Grant said, putting the bus in gear, throwing on his indicator light, then pulling out into traffic. "And away we go!"

CHAPTER SEVENTEEN
BROCK & KRISTA

"... *DOWN IN HIIIIISSSSTOOOOOOOORYYYYYYYYY!*" The children sang at the top of their lungs, competing with the music Grant was playing at a reasonable level over the bus stereo.

"No more Tim Bits for you kids," Krista said, glancing at Stacey with an eye roll. Her sister-in-law was already using a baby wipe from her purse to tidy up Thea's face.

"Cookies, then!" Connor said, shoving his index finger into the air like he'd just reinvented the wheel.

"No. More. Sugar," Chase said before ducking behind the seat to pop another Tim Bit in his mouth.

"Hey, pass those back," Heath said. "I think I saw some Old Fashioneds in there. Those are my fave."

"Why eat a donut when you can have a fresh gingerbread man?" Rayma added. She dramatically took a bite right between her gingerbread man's legs. "And that's about as much action as I'll be getting from what dangles between a man's legs this holiday season."

Pasha snorted and glanced at her sister. "Impressionable ears."

Rayma rolled her gold-flecked brown eyes and took another

bite of her cookie, speaking through her chews. "Those ears are crammed full of sugar and Christmas music. They didn't hear a thing."

Krista accepted the package of baby wipes from Stacey and handed one to Joy. "Please wipe my daughter's face and hands. And no more sweets, Nana. Unless *you'd* like to be the one to put them to bed."

Joy glanced behind her at Krista and accepted the baby wipe. "I—"

"Have other plans that I'm *sure* you don't want cockblocked by sugar-demon children." Krista's mouth stretched into a teasing smile.

Joy's complexion went the color of a holly berry, and a playful smile tugged one corner of her mouth.

Oh yeah, Nana Joy was getting her groove back and then some.

Krista smiled knowingly at her mother-in-law. "That's what I thought."

"What's cockblocked, Mama?" Zoe asked as she allowed Joy to wipe her face and hands. Krista was sitting with Zane and was busy wiping his hands and face. How the kid managed to get donut jelly up his nose, Krista would never know.

"Yeah, *Mama*, what's cockblocked?" Joy repeated, turning back around to look at Krista, a twinkle of mischief in her blue eyes.

"Uhhh." Krista glanced at her husband for help. He was staring at his phone with a scowl on his face.

"Cock is a boy chicken, right, Mama?" Zoe asked. "So does it mean that a big boy chicken is blocking your path? Like he won't let the lady chickens get into the coop. He's cockblocking."

Out of the mouths of brilliant-brained babes.

"That's pretty much what it means, honey," Krista said quickly. "Yep."

Zoe seemed pleased with herself for figuring it out, but that glee didn't last long. Her nose wrinkled, and her brow furrowed.

"But we don't have any chickens. Neither does Nana. How can she get cockblocked if she doesn't have any chickens? Do you mean like the chicken meat we eat? Is there a bunch of chicken boobs blocking her path?"

"Chicken *breasts*, honey. *Breasts*. We use the proper terminology for things, remember?"

Zoe merely shrugged.

Snorts and titters emanated from the back of the bus.

"Walked into that one there, Krista," Heath said with a chuckle. "You might need to buy some chickens and have ol' Brocky build you a coop now."

"I'll buy eggs," Stacey said. "Farm-fresh and free-range are always better than store-bought."

"Me too," Rayma added. "And can I just point out how happy I am that it wasn't *me* who instigated this brilliant explanation to the kids by saying *cockblock* around impressionable ears?"

"Could very well have been *you*," Pasha admonished. "Last time it *was* you. And Krista and Brock had to explain to their children that there is no such thing as a 'beast with two backs' that will come scare them in the middle of the night."

Rayma bit her lip to keep herself from smiling. "That was during a *non*-dry spell. A ... wet spell?" She snorted. "Yeah, that's what that was. A wet spell." She sighed and glanced up wistfully. "And what a blissfully *damp* semester that had been."

"Can we get back to the chickens, please?" Zoe asked. "I know there is no 'beast with two backs.' That's just Aunt Rayma's way of saying she wants to hug boys. That when you hug someone it looks like you're one person but you have two backs. I don't know why you need to call it a *beast*, though. That just makes it sound scary for no reason. But I'm glad Aunt Rayma likes making the beast with two backs with people. So do I. I made the beast with two backs with like three of my friends at school today, Anna, Rachel, and Emmie."

The reactions in the bus were a mixture of chuckles, groans, and various murmured curses.

"Back to the chickens," Zoe said innocently, not realizing the things she'd just said and how she'd said them.

God, Krista loved her daughter, but sometimes Zoe was too curious and observant for her own good. She'd be one hell of an adult, but as a child, she was a lot to deal with. "Yes, honey, back to the chickens."

"How about Nana takes a stab at explaining this one?" Joy asked, offering Krista an olive branch with a knowing smile. "I think I can figure out how to explain it so you're no longer confused."

Zoe rolled her eyes and slammed the backs of her hands down on the bench seat. "Please, Nana, yes. Someone explain to me how you're going to get cockblocked when you don't have any chickens."

As Krista's mother-in-law attempted to explain the term "cockblocked" to Krista's impressionable, brilliant child, the rest of the bus erupted into a chorus of *oohs* and *aahs* as Grant pulled the bus over to the curb beside a brilliantly bedazzled house.

It was closing in on burn-your-retinas bright, but it was beautiful—as long as you didn't look directly at it, of course.

"Look!" Connor shouted and pointed, sitting up on his knees in his seat. "They have a giant blow-up dinosaur on the roof. The T. rex is in the sleigh, and he has a bunch of little triceratops pulling the sleigh. Like he's Santa and the triceratops are his reindeer. That's so cool."

"Not sure how he'd effectively steer the sleigh and hold the reins with those puny arms," Heath said with a chuckle as he ruffled Connor's hair with his big, meaty palm.

Connor rolled his eyes and glanced behind him at his uncle. "It's pretend, Uncle Heath. And dinosaurs are extinct."

Heath's lip twitched as he made eye contact with several of the adults. He fixed his gaze back on Connor. "You're right, little man. My bad."

"I like the cute display of Santa and Mrs. Claus sneaking a kiss behind the snowman," Stacey said, glancing back at Chase with love in her eyes.

Two small robotic statues, one of Santa himself and the other one of his better half, stood slightly behind a big, fake, grinning snowman. The robots would bend at the hips and make it look like they were sneaking a smooch behind Frosty.

Krista glanced at her husband.

But Brock wasn't paying attention to the light display outside or his children's admiration and wonder over it. He was watching his mother and Grant whisper.

And if looks could kill, Grant would be six feet under and worm food by now.

Rolling her eyes, Krista leaned and pushed forward on one foot. She swatted her husband's knee to get her attention. "Don't ruin this," she said with a hiss. "For them *or* your children."

Brock barely glanced at her.

Joy had stepped away from where she was sitting with Zoe for a moment and was currently crouched down next to the driver's seat where Grant was. The two had sparkles and love in their eyes and big smiles on their faces.

It warmed Krista's heart no end to see her mother-in-law happy and in love. She deserved it. Joy had spent way too many years doting on her children and grandchildren to not have something else in her life. Something just for her. Or in this case *someone*.

"Let's go to the next one!" Zoe cheered. "Nana, come back and sit with me."

Joy glanced back at Zoe. "All right, honey, just a sec." She turned back to Grant and said something under her breath that nobody else in the bus could hear—well, maybe Brock.

Oh shit, yes, definitely Brock.

A dark, stormy expression fell across Krista's husband's face—well, stormier than it already was—and his nostrils flared, reminding her of a bull in the ring, getting ready to impale the stupid fucking matador with his horns. But in this case—and *only* this case—she was actually rooting for the matador. She wanted Grant to get away unscathed by whatever verbal horns and hooves Brock was planning to impale and trample the man with.

Joy stood up, and Krista noticed that her fingers were laced with Grant's.

Krista fought the urge to swoon over the sweetness.

Their fingers untangled, and Grant's hand grazed Joy's butt.

The air inside the bus grew warmer, and Krista knew it was because her husband was getting ready to explode like a volcano.

Joy moved back to her seat.

Brock's lips parted like he was about to say something, but Krista cleared her throat loud enough to draw his attention.

She hoped her expression was fierce enough to convey what she was thinking. In no way was he to comment on Grant touching Joy's butt.

It was none of Brock's business, and his mother was happy. That should be the end of it.

Brock's gaze flicked to Krista, his cheeks a ruddy color, steam practically billowing out of his ears.

She shook her head and mouthed, "Don't you dare."

She wasn't sure how it was possible, but his expression grew even more threatening.

Joy settled back down in the seat next to Zoe and glanced back at Krista, a curious expression on her face. "Everything okay?" she asked. Her gaze bounced between Krista and Brock, and her brows slowly furrowed.

"Drive, please," Zoe said. "We still have more to see."

"Yes, ma'am, Miss Zoe," Grant said with an exaggerated salute before putting the bus back into gear and pulling away from the curb when the road was clear.

"Is he angry Grant and I were talking?" Joy asked Krista, bringing her voice down to a whisper.

Krista shrugged. "I have no idea. He's just being a miserable party pooper, and it's starting to piss me off."

Joy grunted and glanced back at her son. "Not anything really new, but the reasoning behind it is." Eventually she sighed, and her shoulders slumped. "Grant's not going anywhere, and it would make it a whole lot easier on all of us if Brock just accepted that fact."

"Agreed," Krista said, matching Joy's sigh. "He just always seems to *need* to have something to fret and be angry over. Like if he's not pissed off, he will cease to exist."

"He's placed all our safety and happiness on his shoulders. Made them his responsibility. So in his mind, he doesn't have time for his own happiness and to relax. Because when you relax, you let your guard down."

Krista rested her hand on her mother-in-law's that was gripping the back of the bus seat. "I know. I just wish there was something we could do to help take more of that burden from him."

Joy linked their fingers together and gave Krista's hand a squeeze. "Me too, honey. Me too."

―――――

ANOTHER HOUR of driving around town to look at Christmas light displays and they were all yawning and eager to get into their own beds. Maeve, Zane and Raze had all fallen asleep, while little Eve had been in and out of naps the whole trip.

"But I want to see *mooooooooore*," Thea whined as Grant pulled the bus up to the curb in front of Joy's house. "I know there are more."

"We can go do a small drive around town as a family, just us four, tomorrow night to hit the ones we missed," Stacey said to her precocious daughter as she smoothed some hair off Thea's face. "But it's getting late. Several of your cousins are already asleep. And it's past your bedtime."

Thea scrunched her face into a pout, crossed her arms over her chest and sat back into her seat with a huff.

Stacey merely rolled her eyes.

Grant turned off the engine. "End of the line, folks," he said with a chuckle to his voice. He pulled the lever so the door opened before glancing back at Brock. "Hopefully you were able to enjoy at least some of the tour. Figured with me driving you'd be able to spend more time with your kiddos and not worry about traffic and parking."

Krista held her breath as she focused on her husband and Grant.

It appeared Joy was also holding her breath.

"Worked just fine the way we've done it for years," Brock said gruffly. "Don't need to change it. 'Specially for a guy who's just using our mother."

Grant's eyebrows pinched, and he cocked his head. "Excuse me?"

Shit.

"Brock ..." Krista warned.

But he ignored her.

The tension in the bus was thick, and everyone shifted uncomfortably in their seats. It also appeared that the children who had fallen asleep were now awake, staring wide-eyed at Brock and Grant, as if even they knew what was going down.

Or about to go down.

Fuck, Krista really hoped nothing was about to go down.

"You don't think we're buying this, do you?" Brock went on with an asshole scoff of derision. "That you're actually interested in our mother? You've gotta have some other angle. Are you some hired assassin out to finally take out all the Hart brothers? Got a beef with us or something? Did the Petralias hire you from prison? Or the Rodriguezes in Mexico?"

Grant's eyes widened, and his mouth dropped open.

"Dude," Rex whispered. Even he knew Brock had overstepped. They all knew Brock had overstepped.

Silence hung heavy in the bus. Even the kids were quiet.

"Nobody's hired me, Brock. I have no *beef* with anybody. Though if I did, it would be with you for attempting to break into my house. But I don't. I'm also not *using* your mother. Not for anything. Not to get to you, your brothers, or anybody else. I have no *angle*. I love her, and that's all there is to it."

Brock's expression said he wasn't convinced. He sneered and scoffed again, shaking his head.

In front of Krista in her seat next to Zoe, Joy surged to her feet, coming to stand directly in front of Brock. Though her son was still taller than her even when he sat down, at the moment, Krista's fierce mother-in-law looked ten feet tall. "Are you saying that the only reason a man might show interest in me is to get to one of *you*? Are you saying that I'm not someone a man like Grant would find attractive, let alone sleep with? That the only reason he's even giving me the time of day is to get close to my sons and their families? A revenge plot so convoluted and calculated that he's willing to 'take one for the team,' close his eyes and sleep with me just to get inside this fortress of a family?"

Brock cringed at the mention of his mother sleeping with someone, but the color of his complexion was slowly draining of color.

Good.

Krista was not happy with her husband at the moment. She was furious, in fact.

If it wasn't almost below zero outside, she'd consider making the man sleep in his truck for this godawful behavior. Particularly because he was doing it all in front of their children.

Joy plopped her fists on her hips and hinged forward to glare at her son. "I'll have you know, Brock Lionel Hart, that I've had *loads* of sex since your father died. And I had *loads* of sex before I even met your father." As if smacked in the back of the head with a rubber chicken, she glanced abruptly at Grant. "I mean not *loads* of sex. I can tell you the name of every man I've ever slept with. I can even count them on two hands. So not *loads*. But I have been with men since Zane died. I wasn't even forty when he passed. I—"

Grant's lip twitched, and he held up two hands, cutting her off. "I know you have. We have no secrets. No judgment."

Joy appeared to relax a bit, then rounded on her son again, but this time she made sure to hit each and every one of her boys with a look. "Just because Grant is the first man you've met doesn't mean there haven't been others. I'm still a woman. I'm not dead, and just like you four overgrown rabbits, I also enjoy sex, and I'm not ashamed to admit it."

Groans from all four men echoed around the bus.

Stacey smacked Chase's chest, and Pasha smacked Heath's. Then, because Lydia wasn't there, Rayma smacked Rex's chest. Brock was too far away for Krista to hit him in the chest, but she figured he was getting enough of a verbal beating anyway that he'd be bruised black and blue by the time his mother was done with him.

"Mum ..." Rex started to protest.

"Did Nana just call Daddy a rabbit?" Zoe asked, turning around in her seat to look at Krista.

Krista petted her daughter's head. "Shh, honey. And yes." *Because he is.*

"If you can't accept the fact that I am in a caring relationship with a man who treats me well, and who I enjoy spending time with, then fine. I haven't liked all of the women you four man-whores have brought home either. Just like assholes, everyone has an opinion."

Rayma snorted.

Joy hit Rayma with a look that had the young college co-ed blushing. "But also, just like assholes, we don't need to hear everyone's opinions. So keep it to yourself—all of you. Grow up and accept the fact that Grant is in my life, that we love each other and he makes me happy." She leveled her viper stare on her oldest son again, and at long last, the man actually looked a touch remorseful. "Or so help me God, Brock, you will *not* be invited to Christmas dinner. I will choose Grant at my dinner table over you."

Gasps filled the bus.

But it appeared that Joy's lecture was done, because she lifted her chin at Grant, thanked him for the ride and stepped down the stairs to her driveway.

She also didn't stop. She headed toward her front door, unlocked it, stepped inside, and closed it.

A moment later, lights came on, and they could see her tiny shadow milling around inside behind the drawn drapes.

Everyone stared at Brock, but he wasn't looking at any of them. His head was down, his eyes on the floor.

"All right, folks," Grant said, breaking the awkward, thick silence. "You don't gotta go home, but you can't stay here." He paused for a moment, then looked back at all of them. "No, seriously. I told the retirement home I'd have the bus back to them by nine."

CHAPTER EIGHTEEN
GRANT & JOY

"THE BLOODY NERVE OF HIM," Joy said into the phone Friday morning as she applied her makeup in her bathroom mirror. Grant had spent the night, but after morning sex, a quick breakfast, and coffee, he said he needed to head out and finish up some Christmas shopping. Then he winked at her, cupped her butt, kissed the side of her head, and was gone.

Lydia sighed on the other end of the phone, which Joy had on speaker. "I know. Rex filled me in. And then Krista did. And Pasha. And Stacey. I've heard it from everyone. Even Rayma texted me to say that Brock has been uninvited to Christmas and Nana's got bigger balls than a prize bull."

Joy snorted. "She's only right on one of those. He hasn't been uninvited ... yet."

"Have you heard from him since?"

Joy shook her head and put her mascara away, then took a sip of her coffee. "From that buffoon?" She snorted. "No. He's *the* most stubborn man on the planet. And I thought I'd married the most stubborn man on the planet until I gave birth to my first child. Little did I know how much of a pushover Zane really was."

"Oh lordy," Lydia said.

"On another note, how are you doing, my darling? We missed you terribly last night, but of course, we all understood why you chose not to come." Joy opened up her blush compact and dabbed a bit of rouge to her cheeks.

"I've been better," Lydia replied, her voice sounding so far away, even though she was right there on the phone. "Just keep going over everything in my head, you know. What could I have done differently? What did I do to cause it? Was it something I ate? Something I did?"

"None of the above, angel. None."

Lydia let out another sigh. "I know. But at the same time ..."

"I know." Joy wished she could see her daughter-in-law. Hold her. Rub her back and provide the sorely needed comfort Lydia seemed to be crying out for. Lydia's mother was a delightful woman and actually planned to move to Victoria from her home in Hope in the spring. But at the moment, she was on a Caribbean cruise with her sister. "Have you told your mother?"

"No," Lydia said in a whisper. "I don't want to ruin her trip."

Yeah, Joy understood that, too.

Grabbing the phone, she took it with her as she wandered through the house turning off lights as she went. When she approached her office, which was an additional room off the kitchen and had an outside access door for clients, she paused with her free hand on the knob. "I'm going to tell you something I've never told anyone else, okay?"

Lydia's own "Okay" was drawn out and quiet, but there was also an upward tilt to the word. Curiosity.

"Not even the boys know this. And right now, I'd prefer to keep it that way. Given the tension among them right now—particularly Brock—it's just easier for this secret to remain between us."

Lydia's okay was a touch shakier.

"A few years after Zane died, I started seeing a man. It was casual. He was divorced, had kids. I was a widow and had kids. Our lives were too messy to try to make anything work beyond afternoon sex when the kids were in school a couple of times a week. But after about four months, I became pregnant."

Turning the knob to her office, she flicked on a few lights and adjusted the blinds to let in the muted gray morning light from outside.

"And you lost the baby?" Lydia asked. Her words were breathy and almost frightened.

There were really only three logical outcomes to Joy's predicament. Either she lost the baby, had an abortion, or had the baby and gave it up because obviously she only had four children, so Lydia was clearly wondering where that fifth baby went.

Settling behind her desk in her comfy office chair, Joy opened up her laptop. "I did. A little girl at sixteen weeks."

"Oh Joy, I'm *so* sorry." Now Lydia was blubbering. "I had no idea."

"Nobody does, sweetheart. We never told anybody. The boys were young, and I hid it. Neither Calvin nor I were really wanting any more children, but at the same time, neither of us wanted to terminate or give up the baby. However, I will say, and please don't take this the wrong way, I did feel a small sense of relief when we lost the baby. I still mourned her, however. Still cried for days over the daughter that would never be. But after a time, I picked myself up, brushed off the dust, and kept moving forward. The lives of the living trump the lives of the dead. I had four other children that needed me, that needed their mother present and not wallowing in grief. I needed to live my best life for *all* my children. The living and the non."

Hiccupped sobs echoed on the other end.

"But the point of my story, honey, is that no matter the timing, on a trip or not on a trip, the people who love you the most would want to know what you're going through and be there for you. Let people be there for you. Let them help you. *Tell* them how they can help you. Don't assume you're bothering them or 'ruining their trip.' I think you should call your mother. I called mine, and I'm very grateful that I did. She was a busy lawyer in Vancouver and shouldn't have taken time off from her job. But she did. Because she was my mother and her daughter needed her.

"She is the only other person who knew about the baby, besides the father. There was no judgment from her. She just hopped on the ferry from Vancouver and helped me with the boys as I recovered. And you know that you have an enormous family here willing to drop everything and anything to be there for you. But don't exclude your mother. Just because you're a Hart doesn't mean you're not still a Sullivan. I've been a Hart more than half my life, but I'm also still a Miller, and I always will be."

The headlights of her first clients' car cast a beam on the hedge next to her window.

"I'm really sorry for your loss, Joy. For your daughter." Lydia was still sobbing quite hard, but there was a new touch of clarity and resolution to her voice.

It would be hard, but Joy knew without a doubt that Lydia would get through this and come out on the other end stronger than ever.

"Where's that handsome husband of yours today?" Joy asked, changing the subject. She had about twenty more seconds before her clients knocked.

She hated having to give her daughter-in-law the bum's rush, particularly given Lydia's fragile state, but Joy also had a job to do and clients to see. Christmas was always a challenging time for families, and her clients tended to book more appointments than normal the further into December they got. And since Joy always took off the week between Christmas and New Year's, her clients had been booking sessions left, right and center. She was completely booked up right until her final session at one o'clock on Christmas Eve.

"Brock had some big assignment for all of them on the west coast. Last minute. Came in late last night. Apparently, there's a big movie being filmed in Tofino, and the security crew couldn't make it. Big A-list actors in the film and the production company asked for as many men as Brock could spare. It was a big-money gig with little to no notice and hardly any real danger, so they all headed out at like four in the morning. Rumor is they'll be there at least three days, but it might not be until the twenty-fourth that they're all back."

"And how do you feel about that?" She wasn't particularly happy with her son and the fact that he abandoned his wife so quickly after she'd just had a miscarriage. She'd have to have a chat with Rex. This was not like him at all.

"I told him to go."

Oh?

"He was smothering me. Plus, the money is good. I wouldn't let him pass it up, even though he said he would in a heartbeat."

Ah, there was her son. He probably fought Lydia tooth and nail to *not* go, but the woman knows how to dig her heels in. Rex probably just gave up, growled at his wife, and went on the job wearing a big scowl.

"Well, whatever you need, honey. Do you and Maeve want to come to stay here while Rex is gone? That way you're not doing it all by yourself? You're more than welcome. You know I have the space." She checked her watch. It was exactly nine o'clock. She couldn't make her clients wait outside in the cold any longer.

"Thanks. But Rayma has actually offered to come stay with us while Rex is gone. Her roommate went home for Christmas and she's feeling lonely, so it works out for everyone."

"That's my family, taking care of each other." Joy stood up from her desk and went to the door and unlocked it. "But you know that if you need anything, and I mean *anything*, just call, okay, angel?"

"I know, Joy, and thank you. I will."

"Always a pleasure talking to you, sweetheart. And make sure you give sleepyhead Maeve a big sloppy smooch from her Nana."

As if on cue, or perhaps hearing her name, a "Mama!" bellowed over the phone from Lydia's end.

"I definitely will," Lydia said. "Love you."

"Love you, too," Joy replied before disconnecting the call.

She turned to return to her desk and was about to sit down in her super comfy chair when the doorknob to the outside turned and the door flung open.

But it wasn't the McGilverys like she expected, a young married couple who could not get on the same page in the bedroom and worried that their entire marriage was going to collapse if they couldn't.

It was Krista, and she looked like she'd just witnessed a horrific car crash.

Joy bolted up in her seat. "What is it, honey? Are the kids okay? Is Brock okay?'

The McGilverys were sitting in their car in Joy's driveway talking, but they were eyeing Krista suspiciously.

"The kids are fine. Brock's ... well, he's fine. But we have a *big* problem."

Joy's mind raced in a million different directions. What on Earth could cause her tough-as-nails cop daughter-in-law to look so worried?

"It's the last day of school, the kids' big Christmas assembly, and ... Santa is missing."

———

WHAT DO you get the woman who appears to have it all together, has everything she needs but told you last night after she showed you just how much of a gag reflex she *didn't* have to "surprise her" for Christmas?

Why couldn't Joy be as direct and bossy in the gift-giving department as she was in the bedroom?

She had no problem telling him to move his finger up an inch, close his legs just a touch, or add another finger. She gave him cues between the sheets like a stylist at a photo shoot. But then when he asked her what she wanted for Christmas, she'd gotten all sparkly-eyed and said, "Surprise me."

Seriously?

So now, it was four days until Christmas and he was sitting in the mall parking lot waiting for the place to open at ten o'clock so that he could wander through the throng of people in search of the "perfect gift" that he could "surprise" her with.

Was edible underwear still a thing?

A candle?

Bath bombs?

What about a coupon book for all the sex and massages she could dream of? He'd overheard Lydia and Pasha last weekend complaining about their husbands and that Heath just wanted coupons for blow jobs and butt sex.

To be perfectly honest, Grant would be over the fucking moon if he found a coupon book like that in the toe of his stocking come Christmas morning. However, unless they were post-dated, there would also be a big possibility he'd blow through those coupons before Valentine's Day, hell, possibly before New Year's Day.

A new bathing suit maybe? They had met at the pool.

But she wasn't a showy or frilly kind of woman. Her suit was a one-piece and black. Practical for swimming laps. Another black one-piece wasn't very romantic. And he also had no idea her size. For all he knew, she could buy the majority of her clothes in the youth section, given how tiny she was. And if he actually *bought* something in the youth section and she found out, and then informed him that she didn't buy her clothes in the youth section but was insulted that he would think such a thing ...

This was a nightmare.

An absolute fucking nightmare.

It was a drizzly day with harsh gusts of wind that rattled his SUV. Mall workers in the various stores covered their heads and battled with their umbrellas as they parked their vehicles and ran for the entrance doors. Soon enough, that would be him too. Pulling up his collar, zipping up his coat, and beelining it for the door with the hope that not too many icy raindrops made their way into his ears or down the back of his neck.

Jewelry?

Again, Joy's bling was pretty minimal. She wore her wedding band and small diamond stud earrings. That was it. So if he got her something else, would she ever wear it? Or only wear it when he was around just to make him happy but then immediately take it off because she hated feeling like a frosted dignitary encrusted in gemstones?

A gift certificate?

Fuck no.

That was the ultimate in laziness. He might as well just hand her a wad of cash and be like, "Merry First Christmas together, Joy. I really, really love you. Now here's a bunch of cash. Go buy yourself something purty."

Grant raked his fingers through his hair, then dragged his hand down his face, pulling at the two-day-old scruff.

He was going to waste his entire day in that mall. Going from shop to shop staring at shit with absolutely no idea what the fuck he should buy.

The clock on his dash said one minute to ten.

He did NOT want to be one of those eager beaver assholes who milled around outside the store before the place had even opened. No, he'd finish his coffee, then he'd go in.

The clock dash rolled over to ten o'clock, and as if she knew how stressed he was about buying her the perfect gift, his phone rang and Joy's beautiful face popped up.

He set his coffee mug down in the cupholder and punched the green button on his screen. "Hey, gorgeous, miss me already?"

"Always, Wild Man. But that's not why I'm calling. Do you still have your Santa costume from when you would dress up for the fire hall back when you were a volunteer firefighter?"

"I do," he said slowly. "Why?" Oh man, did she want to role-play tonight? She'd suggested it a few times, but every time he tried, he just felt silly and broke character.

"Because the Santa who was supposed to go to the kids' school was run off the road last night and is in the hospital in ICU. And he was wearing his Santa costume to boot. Apparently, he was at some office Christmas party as a hired-out Santa and was sideswiped by a drunk driver. A hit and run."

Phew.

"Jesus, poor Santa."

"Yeah, they say he'll pull through, but it's going to be a long road. But meanwhile, the kids at Connor and Zoe's school are going to be without a Santa for their holiday assembly. For the past month, they've all been fundraising and donating for the Help Feed Families Foundation, and Santa was supposed to come and thank them and accept the donation check."

"And you're hoping your boyfriend can squeeze his massive beer belly into his mothball-scented Santa suit?"

"I'm hoping my extremely handsome *man*friend can put a pillow over his six-pack, spray the suit with Febreze and make some elementary school kids really, really happy."

Grinning, because how could he not when she flattered him so, he glanced at the dash clock again. "What time do I have to be there?"

"One o'clock. I'll text you the address."

Okay, that gave him a few hours to wander aimlessly like a lost puppy around the mall. Hopefully, in that time he would get even a sliver of an idea of what to buy her.

"You don't happen to have like a sleigh or something stashed along with your suit, do you?" she asked.

"A sleigh? Uh, no."

"Crap. The other guy had a whole big schtick. He parks his vehicle up the road and has this little chariot-like thing that he rides onto the school grounds and then into the gym. No reindeer, but the kids love it." She sighed. "Oh well. At least we have a Santa. Beggars can't be choosers at the eleventh hour. Thank you for doing this. I'll let Krista and Stacey know that they can end their search. We have our Santa." She blew kisses over the phone, then disconnected the call.

Moments later, an address popped up on his phone for the kids' school.

Just as he was googling the school and punching the address into his map app, Grant got an awesome idea. Yes, Grant got a wonderful, *awesome* idea.

But first, he needed to call the principal and make sure it was okay and that the field was big enough.

CHAPTER NINETEEN
CHASE & STACEY

STACEY NIBBLED on her bottom lip as she watched all the school-children file into the gymnasium for the December assembly and winter celebration pageant. Once the assembly was over, parents would be free to take their children home and officially start the holidays.

Along with Krista, Stacey had joined the PAC or Parent Advisory Council, known as the PTA at some schools, and along with the Friday hot lunch program, she helped put together the Christmas—sorry, *Winter*—fundraiser and Santa's visit.

Needless to say, when she got the phone call earlier that morning about the devastating accident their Santa Claus had been in, she'd called Krista immediately for advice.

This was her first year running the Winter Assembly or December Assembly. She'd called it the "Christmas Pageant" a few times and had been quickly corrected by a few parents and teachers. It was *not* the Christmas Pageant. It was the Winter Assembly. There was no singing Rudolph the Red-Nosed Reindeer, no bells jingling, and yet, they brought in Santa Claus. She couldn't figure it out.

But it also wasn't her place to figure it out. It was her place to organize the whole thing and make sure the third graders did their little "How the Snowy Owl Saved the Winter Solstice" skit and pass out snowflake-shaped gluten-free cookies to all the parents and grandparents who came to take part in the assembly and watch their children do skits and read poems about snow.

She'd booked the Santa Claus the school always hired back in October, thinking that that part of her job had been easy peasy lemon squeezy. But when she got the call from the school secretary at the butt-crack of dawn that their beloved Santa Claus aka Larry Grimes had been in a horrible accident, her heart had sunk to the box spring of her bed.

Not only did she feel for poor Larry, holed up in the hospital so close to Christmas and fighting for his life, but now she was on the hook to find another Santa last minute.

Her first call, of course, had been Krista.

Zoe went to the same school as Connor, but because of her shift work, Krista wasn't able to volunteer as much as Stacey could. She did a lot for the school in other ways, though. And since Krista had also lived in Victoria longer than Stacey and worked as a public servant, Stacey figured her super resourceful sister-in-law would have no problems finding a last-minute Santa Claus.

Boy, had she been wrong.

Krista's panic mode had gone from zero to sixty when Stacey called her. Which, of course, only escalated Stacey's own panic.

She could not, she would not be *that* mom at school who failed to produce Santa for their weird sort-of-Christmas-but-mostly-not-Christmas school assembly.

Thankfully, though, Krista had said, "I know who to call," then hung up on Stacey before Stacey even had a chance to ask *who*.

Roughly two hours later, Krista was calling Stacey with the good news that Grant of all people not only had a costume, but he would play the rotund immortal elf in a red jumper for all the children.

Stacey wasn't sure how such a handsome, *fit* man like Grant could pull off a transformation like that, but she also no longer cared.

Someone dressed like Santa was going to be at the school at one o'clock. She wasn't a failure. She wasn't *that* mom.

But that didn't stop her from gnawing away on her lip as the gymnasium continued to fill up.

Chase had been pretty upset that he was going to miss Connor's performance as "Reginald the snowflake elf" in his class's five-minute skit about global warming and climate change.

Yeah, it was a real hodgepodge kind of performance, but that had nothing to do with her. She just had to book Santa Claus, make sure the cookies were gluten-free and that they also had dairy-free and soy-free options, set up the chairs, and order the big ostentatious donation check for four selected children to present to Santa, which he would then take—in his sleigh—to the non-profit they were raising money for.

"It's going to all work out," said a familiar voice beside her before someone bumped her shoulder.

Stacey glanced down at her mother-in-law and wrapped her arm around Joy. "Thank you for having a boyfriend who just so happens to have a Santa suit and is willing to play Santa."

Joy chuckled. "You're welcome, dear. It's really the whole reason I'm seeing him. That Santa suit ..." Her smile and the twinkle of love in her dark blue eyes said otherwise.

Stacey hadn't been a member of the Hart family for long—only a few years—but she'd never, ever seen Joy look as in love or twitterpated as she did when she thought or spoke of Grant. The woman was in full-on swoon mode, and she had no plans of getting out of it. That was easy enough to see.

Stacey spotted Krista at the far end of the gym and waved her over. Her sister-in-law weaved her way through the heavily dressed guests, saying hi to various parents and staff before finally coming to stand in front of Stacey and Joy.

"Brock's pissed he's missing this," Krista said.

Joy lifted her shoulder. "Brock's pissed about everything."

Stacey and Krista exchanged looks, and both snorted.

"I said I would videotape it for Chase, so I'll just send a copy along to Brock, too," Stacey said, tucking a strand of her strawberry-blonde bob behind her ear.

Things were beginning to settle down inside the gym. People had found seats and were quietly chatting among themselves.

The stage in front of them all was decorated with sparkly snowflakes, fake snow, twinkly lights, and lots of fake green trees. A few real logs and stumps were organized into a semicircle facing the audience.

This was where each class would come up onto the stage and sit before they did whatever it was their teacher planned for them to do for the performance piece.

Some classes were doing skits, others reading poems, while she was pretty sure the kindergarteners were doing some kind of inter-pretive dance—their teacher was a bit out there.

The commotion behind them drew their attention.

It was the sixth graders.

Stacey, Krista, and Joy shuffled out of the way to let the hormonal youths pass. They took their seats right in front of the guests.

Next came the fifth graders, and the fourth, then the third.

She waited with anticipation to see her son. And when he spotted her, boy, he did not disappoint. His wave was crazy and his smile bright and carefree. As it should be. Her son had been through enough in his first few years on Earth that the rest of his life should be nothing but smooth sailing.

She waved back, wanting desperately to step forward and

brush his unruly dirty-blond locks off his forehead. But he'd probably make a face, growl, then gently swat her away.

Her little boy was growing up so fast. He didn't need his mama nearly as much as he used to, and he seemed to be deferring to Chase a lot more than Stacey lately, which both warmed her heart and frustrated her.

Yes, Chase was Connor's father and a man, so he could help Connor with things and in ways that Stacey wasn't well-versed. But for a long time, she had been all her son needed—all her son had. She could answer all his questions, fix all his problems. She was mom *and* dad.

And not that she would give up having a father for her children or the love of her life by her side, but when Connor would clam up about things and not talk to her but then talk to Chase, she couldn't control the tightness she experienced in her chest.

"Hi, Mummy!" came a squeaky little girl voice.

Stacey, Joy and Krista all turned around to find Zoe standing behind them with a big smile. She was also missing one of her front top teeth, which was in her hand and being held up in front of Krista's face. "Look what happened!"

Krista's eyes widened. "I didn't even know that was loose."

Zoe shrugged. "It wasn't. Some boys were picking on my friend Kayla on the playground at recess, so I went to defend her. Nico shoved Kayla. I shoved Nico. Nico took a swing at me, missed, but I didn't miss when I took a swing at him." She smiled big, wide, and gap-toothy. But the frown that followed hit Stacey hard in the solar plexus. "But then Nico *didn't* miss the next time he punched me. And he made my tooth fall out."

At this point, Krista's mouth was hanging open like a wide-mouth bass, Joy was covering her mouth with her hand, and Stacey had to blink a few times because she hadn't been and her eyes were starting to dry out.

"Honey," Krista said, crouching down in front of her daughter and taking the tooth, "we do *not* hit."

"Yeah, but you and Daddy have taught me to stand up for myself. And to defend the weak. And Kayla is weaker than me. She's going through chemo for her ... leukemia. Nico was just being a big meanie, so I told him to stop and to just be kind, then he shoved me into the mud and told me to mind my own business. I told him taking care of my friends and standing up for what's right *is* my business. Then he shoved Kayla in the mud, so I jumped up and shoved him into the mud. Then he tried to punch me, but he missed because Daddy taught me how to duck. Then I punched him and made him cry." Her lips twisted. "I actually feel really bad about that. Then he punched me again, and my tooth fell out. It fell into the mud, and we had to go digging for it."

Krista was quiet for a very long moment.

Stacey would have been, too.

They were all so freaking proud of Zoe for standing up for her friend, defending herself and doing what was right. Buuuuttt ... hitting wasn't right, no matter how warranted it might be in some cases.

Any physical violence on school grounds was call for suspension. Which on the last day of school before winter break was kind of silly. But still, Stacey could tell by Krista's reaction that she most certainly had not received a call from the school about this incident.

Stacey's sister-in-law took a deep breath before speaking. "How come I didn't get a phone call about this from the office, Mrs. Goyer, or one of the recess duty teachers?"

Zoe grinned again. "Because we decided to keep it all a secret. Nico said sorry, I said sorry, then he helped me look for my tooth in the mud. I told him picking on sick kids, or any kid, isn't nice and that Santa would skip his house if he continued to be a bully. He found my tooth in the mud, and we shook hands, agreeing not to tell the duties so that nobody got in trouble. But I also told him that if he picks on Kayla again, I'll call my dad and he'll come to *have a little chat* with Nico."

Joy snorted, covered her mouth even more and turned her head so Zoe couldn't see her laughing. But her small frame shook with amusement at her precocious and strong-willed granddaughter.

"So no teachers know about this?" Krista asked.

Zoe shook her head and placed the tooth in Krista's palm. "Nope. I just told them I ran into something and it fell out. Nico and I both said we slipped in the mud. I'm wearing my backup clothes."

"ZoZo, we don't lie," Krista warned.

"But it wasn't really a lie, Mama. It was just a ... truth stretch. I kind of sort of ran into Nico's fist ... right?" Zoe's blue gaze bounced between her mother, aunt, and grandmother. "And we *did* both *slip* into the mud when we got hit with the other person's fist." She nibbled awkwardly on her lip. "You're not going to get me in trouble with Mrs. Goyer, are you? It's the last day of school. Nico says he'll be better. And Daddy told me I could use that promise on people. That if they were meanies, he would come and *have a little chat* with them."

"Oh lord," Krista said on a groan. "He can't say that kind of stuff."

Zoe seemed confused. "Can I tell them my mom is a cop and will come and arrest them if they're mean?"

"No!" Krista exclaimed. "You need to tell your teacher or one of the recess duty teachers."

Zoe rolled her eyes.

Krista's brows rose, and Zoe immediately apologized.

Krista's expression softened, and she pulled her daughter in for a hug. "I'm glad you defended your friend and that you're not hurt. But you *know* that violence is not the answer. Please, no more hitting. And no more threatening your friends with a *chat* from your father."

Zoe nodded and pulled free of her mother's arms. "I need to go find my class."

Krista nodded.

But before Zoe walked away, Joy piped up. "Any idea what the big front teeth are going for these days with the tooth fairy?"

Zoe's holey smile was back. "Mila Richards got a whole five bucks for each of her top front teeth."

Krista groaned. "Mila Richards' parents must have ticked the box at the hospital for the *deluxe* tooth fairy. Your dad and I just ticked the box for the *basic* tooth fairy. I think that means she brings a buck a tooth, no matter the size."

Zoe's face scrunched up, and she made an adorably perturbed face. "I hope you ticked the *basic* box for Zane, too, then."

Krista smiled at her daughter and ran her hand over her head. "We definitely did. Now go find your class."

"Don't lose that tooth," Zoe instructed as she headed off to go and sit with the rest of the second graders.

When she was out of earshot, Krista blew out a big breath and turned to face Stacey and Joy. "That's a lot to unpack."

"And you handled it perfectly, darling," Joy said, still chuckling. "I've said it before, that little girl came into this world fighting for her life, and she hasn't stopped. She defends the weak because she was once weak. And now that she's not, she feels it is a sense of duty to defend those who cannot defend themselves." Joy wiped a tear from the corner of her eye, and Stacey felt herself getting emotional as well. "She gets those traits from both her parents. Gets her stubbornness, too."

"I'm just glad they all made up. But she needs to stop threatening kids with a *chat* from Brock. He's not going to be allowed on the school grounds if people start to deem him as a true threat." Krista held the tooth out on her palm. "What the heck am I supposed to do with this thing until we get home?"

Joy reached into her purse and pulled out a metal tin meant for mints.

She opened it to reveal only three small white mints left. They each took one, then Krista placed the tooth inside and shoved the tin in her purse, thanking her mother-in-law.

Glancing back out into the gym, Stacey soon realized that everyone was there and the festivities were about to begin.

"Better go find a seat," Joy said, resting her hand on Krista's arm.

They both glanced at Stacey, who had to remain standing and on alert for Grant's arrival, waved and smiled before wandering off toward two empty seats near the back.

Studying her phone like it held all the answers to the universe and not just a bunch of fingerprints and makeup smudges, Stacey listened to the school principal prattle on about winter, family, and giving back to the community.

And even though she was literally looking at her phone screen, waiting for Grant's message, she still jumped when a text popped up and made her phone vibrate.

But the text wasn't from Grant.

It was from Chase.

And it was followed up by a picture.

These two need a home. Deal with new families fell through last minute. I know you've been talking about getting the kids a puppy. Thoughts?

Every single cell in her body began to tingle as she took in the sweet faces of two chocolate lab puppies.

But they couldn't have two ... could they?

The thought of separating them though ...

They had been talking about getting the kids a dog. Their place on Prospect Lake was fully fenced and perfect for a dog. Plus, the kids had been begging for a dog for well over a year. Everyone loved

Rex and Lydia's pit bull, Diesel. He was a big, slobbery bundle of muscly love.

Rex and Lydia also had their cat Pia, which was mostly indifferent to people, but on occasion, she'd jump into your lap for a pet.

And Krista and Brock had just had Krista's cat Penelope put down late last year after cancer had taken over her poor old body. The kids had been devastated, but they'd also asked when they were going to get another pet.

She glanced at the picture again. They were really freaking cute.

A text from her husband followed. *Girl and boy. Brock has texted the pic to Krista, as they've been talking about getting one, too.*

At the mention of Krista, Stacey's head snapped up from her phone to find her sister-in-law looking at her with a big smile.

Stacey nodded.

Krista nodded.

Then they both put their heads back down and replied to their men.

A Christmas puppy. Was there anything more wonderful?

———

As WONDERFUL AS THE SKITS, poems, and dances from each grade were, Stacey was having a hard time concentrating on the children's performances. Well, she focused completely on Connor and Zoe's classes and videotaped both for their fathers, but she couldn't be bothered to watch the rest. She was too busy worrying about Grant.

It was five minutes to one o'clock.

Where was he?

She glanced at Joy and mouthed, "Where is he?"

But Joy just shrugged and shook her head.

Thunderous applause nearly shook the building as the sixth graders finished their ensemble story-reading and bowed.

She definitely didn't hear the alert to the text on her phone, but she felt the vibration.

Thank God.

It was Grant. *Three minutes away. Please open the westside doors of the gymnasium. The ones that face the soccer field.*

Huh?

It was like two degrees Celsius outside and he wanted her to open the doors?

She was about to text him *Why* when his text of *Just trust me* popped up.

All right then, she would do as Santa Claus instructed.

As the sixth graders filed off the stage via the side stairs, Stacey made her way around the crowd to the double side doors of the gymnasium. She caught Principal Payne's gaze, but he didn't appear to be questioning her.

Had Grant found a chariot that he was going to ride in on?

A few parents gave her the stink eye, and some made a dramatic show of shivering, but she ignored them. *Put your coat back on, then.*

"Can you close the doors, please?" one woman asked. "It's cold."

"Santa asked me to open them," Stacey said, loud enough for the children in the front to hear. "And what Santa wants, Santa gets."

"Yay, Santa!" a few children cheered, but their excitement was quickly drowned out by the *whomp whomp whomp* of a low-flying helicopter.

A *really* low-flying helicopter.

A dangerously low-flying helicopter.

Icy wind rushed in through the open door, but nobody seemed

upset by it when they all looked out onto the field to see none other than Santa Claus himself landing the helicopter.

"Santa flies a helicopter!" one child screamed. "This is SO cool."

Stacey's smile hurt her face as she found Joy and Krista in the crowd. They all grinned at each other.

The helicopter settled onto the damp grass, and the propellors started to slow down. A moment later, the door to the cockpit opened and a man with a big belly, white hair, and a velour jump-suit the shade of a candy apple hopped out.

"Santa! Santa! Santa!" the children all chanted as Grant aka Santa Claus made his way across the field toward the doors. He made eye contact with Stacey and winked.

The moment he stepped over the threshold into the gym, the entire audience erupted into applause. Kids stood up, and the older students did whistles and hoots. You'd think the man was a real Hollywood celebrity and not just Kris Kringle.

Eventually, the warm welcome died down. Grant waved, shook his belly, and laughed the perfect *ho, ho, ho.* It was like he had been born for the role.

"Hello, parents, grandparents, aunts, uncles, guardians, fami-lies, teachers, and students of Fern Valley Elementary."

"Hello, Santa!" everyone replied.

"Now I don't think I even need to ask, because you've *alllll* been extra good this year, right?"

"Yes, Santa!" more of the little kids responded than the older students or adults, but it was still pretty impressive for the number of people in the space.

"That's wonderful to hear. I know you normally see me in my sleigh, but you know what ... it's in the shop. I need my sleigh in tip-top shape for Christmas Eve, so I have my elves working on it, which is why I decided to fly my helicopter instead."

"Why don't you just fly your helicopter to all the houses all the time?" one little boy asked, making a bunch of the parents in the audience muffle their chuckles.

Grant stroked his beard. "Excellent question, young man. I can tell you're a real thinker, but—"

"Helicopters are too noisy and windy and big for some houses. You can't land them on triangle roofs."

Stacey knew whose voice that was without even needing to see her. Her speech was slightly impeded now by the lack of a tooth in her mouth.

Oh, Zoe!

"That's right, young lady. You're a real thinker, too. We have the great minds of the future in this room, I can tell," Grant went on, chuckling and making sure to give each child a little bit of one-on-one eye contact.

Stacey grabbed the big check for their raised funds and stepped up toward Grant. They'd already randomly selected four children from various grades who would present Santa Claus with the check, and those kids knew that the moment they saw Stacey walk toward Santa with the check, they were to get up and join her.

A journalist from a local online newsfeed and one from an actual newspaper were both there to take pictures for articles—any publicity the school could get, the better. Or at least that was what Principal Payne said.

"Ho-ho-ho, what do we have here?" Santa asked, turning to Stacey and the children as they walked toward Grant, all holding on to a piece of the check.

The fourth-grader who was picked to help give Santa the check cleared her throat to speak her lines. "On behalf of Fern Valley Elementary School, we would like to donate this money to the Help Feed Families Foundation." She smiled for the camera, then stepped back.

Then the second-grader stepped forward. He cleared his throat, glanced up at Santa, then back out into the crowd.

"SANTA, CAN YOU PLEASE TAKE THIS MONEY TO THE HELP FEED FAMILIES PLACE IN YOUR HELICOPTER OR SLEIGH. THANK YOU." Poor kid yelled it all like the helicopter was *inside* the building and the rotors were still going.

A few people chuckled in the crowd as he stepped back in line with his schoolmates.

The first-grader and kindergartener stepped forward together. "Thank you, Santa, for coming here today and helping us help others." They reminded Stacey of those twins from *The Shining*, the way they spoke in sync.

But all in all, everyone did wonderfully.

Santa accepted the check, and the children went back to their seats all smiles and twinkly-eyed.

"Thank you so much, families and students, teachers and staff of Fern Valley Elementary, for your selfless and caring hearts. Your donation will feed many families this Christmas. Many children who normally wouldn't have toys will wake up to toys—besides from me—this year."

Oh, good catch, Santa.

Stacey could practically see the children squirming, ready to call Santa out on that, but he caught himself. He made sure to say that he'd leave toys regardless.

Grant really was born for the role.

"Thank you for inviting me to your Winter Assembly, and I apologize for the wind from my helicopter, but I must get this money where it needs to go so it can help lots of people. I also need to go and feed the reindeer." Grant headed toward the door, but Stacey watched as his eyes snagged Joy's. Santa's face lit up. Joy's face lit up.

Santa winked.

Joy bit her lip but kept smiling.

It was freaking adorable.

Grant exited the door, continuing to wave.

A few children, despite their teachers telling them to get back to their seats, crowded the doorframe to watch St. Nick climb into his chopper and turn over the engine.

Once again, the wind whipped through the open doors, but the children didn't seem to mind. Their arms waved frantically as they all yelled, "Bye, Santa," and their heads tilted, following the copter lifting into the air.

Grant hovered the aircraft there for a moment, looked out the window and waved at all the children, which only caused another uproar of cheers and whoops.

"Thank God they're all going home with their parents after this," Principal Payne said, sidling up next to Stacey. He hit her with his brown gaze. "Good work, Mrs. Hart. Thank you."

She grinned at him before glancing back out the door to where the helicopter was no more than a speck in the gray sky. "Don't thank me. Thank Santa."

CHAPTER TWENTY
CHASE & STACEY

IT WAS the morning of December twenty-fourth, and despite the whispers that the crew would be done filming by now, they weren't, and the rumor around the movie set was, because of weather, they might not be done filming until after the new year.

Needless to say, Chase and his brothers were pissed.

This was not what they signed up for.

They did not sign up to be away from their families on Christmas. No amount of money was worth that.

But it seemed like there was no way around it.

They'd signed agreements, and to make matters one million times worse, a huge storm from the Pacific had rolled in two nights ago and caused major damage to the road. The ONLY road.

Because there was only one way in and one way out of Tofino, it was along a windy highway, rock bluffs, lakes, and through old-growth forests.

According to the news, a giant rock and mudslide had washed away a large chunk of the road, and then on another section, big trees fell, blocking the passage.

So even if the filming had ended, they were stuck.

Merry fucking Christmas.

Rex was beyond pissed and had spent a large portion of last night pacing the hotel room he and Chase shared, trying to figure out a way to get home to Lydia and Maeve. He'd cursed out the film crew, the road workers, and when none of that worked, he drove out to where one of the trees had fallen and tried to lift and remove it himself.

Now he was complaining about back pain, was hopped up on pain meds, and passed out in his bed snoring.

Chase was waiting for it to hit seven o'clock so that he could call Stacey.

He didn't want to wake her, but his children rose at seven sharp without an alarm clock, so Stacey would be up with them and getting them dressed and fed.

He was already dressed in gray sweatpants, a white T-shirt, and a hoodie, so when his phone said six fifty-five, he quietly opened the hotel door, careful not to wake his brother, and stepped out into the hotel hallway.

He took the stairs down the three flights to the lobby, where he'd grab a cup of complimentary coffee from the Keurig machine, then flop into one of the chairs by the fireplace.

He was just getting situated in his chair, his tongue scalded because he'd stupidly taken a sip of his coffee too soon when his phone started to vibrate.

His wife's gorgeous smiling face popped up, which immediately made Chase smile, the pain on his tongue forgotten.

He hit the green button and put the phone to his ear. "I was just about to call you."

"Great minds," she said sleepily.

"How are the kiddos?"

"Missing their father. They keep asking if Santa is going to bring you back, wrap you up and shove you under the tree."

Chase's heart tightened another painful degree. He would love nothing more.

"Any news about getting home?" she asked hopefully, but he couldn't mistake the somber undertone there. She already knew his answer but was asking anyway just in case things changed from last night.

He was quiet for a moment. "Roads are blocked. They also say that the storms have set back filming, so they might not resume until the new year."

Now it was Stacey's turn to be quiet. "I figured as much."

The thought of not getting to be there with his kids and wife on Christmas tore at his insides. He hadn't been Connor and Thea's dad for very long, but since becoming their father, he hadn't missed a Christmas, Easter, birthday, or Halloween.

Their biological father had been a wife-hoarding, deceitful bastard who'd gotten tangled up with the mob, despite being a cop, but ultimately ended up dying in a car accident. He died before Thea was born, but even Connor was having a hard time remembering much of him now.

It was for the best.

From what Stacey had said, there were few redeeming qualities about Ted anyway, and if the only father Connor remembered having was Chase, all the better.

"We can just have another Christmas when you get home," she said, her words coming out choked like she was crying.

Fuck. Fuck. Fuck.

His own throat grew tight.

If there was one thing that made Chase get close to tears himself, it was his wife crying. Stacey had been through SO much in her life. Her shitty parents, shittier husband, dealing with the aftermath of that husband's betrayal to the mob and the threat it meant to her family, Connor's abduction, Chase's abduction. She'd been through hell and back more times than anyone deserved.

Some might say he'd also been through hell and back more times than anyone deserved, and he wouldn't necessarily disagree with that statement, but he also felt like he'd been through all that hell to earn the heaven his life was now.

Because Stacey and the children were his heaven.

They picked him up when he was in the darkest pits of his own mental hell and brought him into the light.

And now, that heaven was going to celebrate Christmas without him.

Hopelessness swirled with anger inside him, and he leaned forward to take a sip of his coffee, this time hoping that it burned.

"I mean ... military families and stuff do this all the time, right?" she said, her voice now soft and sad. "And families where the parents work in hotels or airports or other places that *don't* close on Christmas. Even movie theaters. And I bet your dad had to work the odd Christmas, right? So it's not like we're unique. We're just going to have to adapt a little. Maybe the kids will be excited about two Christmases."

Even though everything she said was true, that didn't make it sting any less. Since becoming fathers, he and his brothers had made sure they were never away on assignment for any of their kids' birthdays or any other holiday kids went ape-shit for. Particularly since their children were all so little still, and the hope and wonder in their eyes on Christmas morning were enough to get drunk on for another three hundred and sixty-five days.

And yeah, his dad had worked on Christmas several times, and each time he did, it sucked.

He was just in a pissed-off, woe-is-me, pouty mood because he was going to miss Christmas with his kids and there was literally nothing he could do about it.

"Poor Heath and Rex, they're going to miss Eve and Maeve's *first* Christmases," Stacey said, no longer bothering to hide her sniffles.

Fuck, he forgot that this was Rex's first Christmas as a dad. And the fact that Lydia had just miscarried, no wonder the big buffoon had gone out in the freezing rain and tried to lift soggy logs off the highway. Chase would have done the exact same thing. Fuck, he probably would have climbed over the logs, braved the mud and rockslide, and run the nearly two hundred miles home to his family.

He'd been tortured and locked naked in a pine box in preparation to be sold like a steer at auction. He could handle a two-hundred-mile run in the icy rain. Child's play.

"We can FaceTime or Skype or something when we open presents and are at your mum's tomorrow," she offered, still sniffling. "Is the hotel at least putting on a Christmas dinner?"

He didn't know what the hotel was doing, and he didn't care.

Yes, the movie producer had put Chase and his brothers up at a pretty swanky hotel, and the halls of that hotel were decked to the nines. But he didn't give a flying fuck about the garland on the banister or the big tree in the foyer. And he sure as fuck didn't care if the chef was preparing turkey six ways or whatever. He'd take cold pizza in front of a modest tree with a bald patch in the back with his wife and children given the choice any time and every time.

"The kids up?" he asked, having to sip more coffee to clear the strain in his throat.

She made an "mhmm" noise in her throat. "They're watching Bluey in the living room and eating Cheerios."

That made him smile. Even when it was Christmas Eve, his kids were little creatures of habit.

"Do you have to work today?" she asked.

"Don't know. Filming is weather-dependent. And right now, the movie stars are holed up in their hotel rooms, so they don't really need security. They're in a separate wing, and the hotel staff seems to be pretty educated on discretion."

"So basically, you probably *could* come home if it wasn't for the road blockage? Then when filming started, you guys could just go back."

"Theoretically, I suppose ..." What was she getting at?

"What's the weather like right now?"

With a grunt and groan fit for a man twenty years his senior, Chase pried himself out of his chair and walked toward the enormous picture windows of the hotel that looked out over the Pacific Ocean. "Actually, pretty calm. Eye of the storm, maybe?"

She was quiet for a moment, but he could hear her tapping away on her laptop. "Weather Network says that the next storm isn't set to come through until the twenty-eighth. That winds won't be much more than a small-craft warning for a bit."

Great?

Either way, they were all stuck in Tofino until the roads were cleared.

"So filming could resume, or they could wait until the next storm passes."

Now it just felt like she was talking to herself.

"So you'd need to be back either the twenty-sixth but definitely before the twenty-eighth. Or in the new year if they decide to hold off filming until then."

"Care to fill me in where that gorgeous head of yours is going?" he asked with a slight chuckle as he moved back toward his seat by the fire.

The hotel was starting to wake up, and guests were making their way downstairs to the dining room for breakfast.

"Just thinking," she said with a bit of pep to her voice.

"Care to share?"

"Not yet. But I will if it works."

He shrugged and finished his coffee, his attention caught by Brock's big frame making its way down the stairs. They gave each other a chin lift, then Brock went over to get coffee.

"About the puppy," she started. "The breeder is happy to keep them until you and Brock come home."

They'd already discussed this, and the answer was yes. He and Brock had paid their deposits and would bring the puppies home with them when they returned to Victoria.

What was going on with his wife?

With his coffee, Brock came to sit in the chair across from Chase, lifting a brow in curiosity, which was probably in response to the twisted expression on Chase's face.

"Okay," Stacey said, sounding even more chipper. "I can't wait to see the looks on the kids' faces."

"Me too."

"But listen, babe, I've gotta run and get the kids dressed and stuff. We're meeting Krista and the kids in a little bit to go pick up the pottery they painted last week. Then we're grabbing lunch and checking out all the Christmas trees at the Bay Center. We can chat tonight, okay?"

Why did he feel like he was getting the brush-off? One minute she was all weepy and sniffly on the phone, crying about not getting to see him on Christmas, and now she was happy and giggly and saying goodbye because she had things to do.

He knew that life must go on and all that shit, but a little less joy in her tone would be appreciated.

"I love you," he said, rubbing his hand over his bald head. "Kiss the kids for me."

"I will, and I love you, too." Then she hung up.

"Everything okay?" Brock asked, gingerly taking a sip of his coffee.

Chase blinked a few times. "Woman was crying about me missing Christmas one minute, then happy as a pig in shit the next talking about the puppy and heading with Krista and the kids to see the trees at the Bay Center. It was almost like the crying was for show."

"Or was the glee for show?" Brock asked, cocking his head to the side. "She's fielding a lot of questions and dealing with some pretty disappointed kids right now. Maybe they were within earshot?"

He hadn't thought of that.

His confusion and hurt started to dissipate, but he cocked his head and leveled his gaze on his brother. "How come you're all full of wisdom and reason about this kind of shit, but when it comes to Mum and Grant, you can't see past the stick up your ass?"

Brock grunted and shifted in his seat.

"He saved the Winter Assembly at the kids' school. He was there for Lydia when she miscarried, helping her and being what she needed, and you have to admit the bus for the Christmas lights tour was pretty cool. He also shoved Thea out of the way from getting hit by a car." Chase shrugged. "Do I *want* to think about Mum having sex? Fuck no. Is it weird to think of Mum with anybody but Dad? Fuck yes. But Dad's been dead for thirty years. She deserves happiness, just like we all do. She's been through her own kind of hell. Burying the man she loves, raising four sons, going through all the turmoil and worry whenever one of us is in danger. She deserves to have someone to lean on."

"She has us," Brock said with another grunt.

"We're not enough. And we shouldn't have to be. You're being a selfish ass. Expecting her to have nobody and just watch us with our families. That's not fair to her, and you know it."

"You saying you're *okay* with Grant?"

Chase nodded. "I am. I'm not going to stand in their way, and I'm not going to help you take him down."

"The same goes for me." Rex joined them, holding coffee.

"And me," said Heath, chiming in and sidling up next to Rex with his own mug of java. "Grant's proven he's not an ass, and he's not using Mum to get to us. He's also not trying too hard, which I respect. I like him, and I support his and Mum's relationship."

Rex's head bobbed. "I'm grateful to him for how he helped Lydia. I've got no beef with the man."

Brock's green eyes flitted back and forth between all his brothers. His cheeks turned ruddy.

Heath and Rex both rolled their eyes.

A text message popped up on Chase's phone. It was from the puppy breeders. "Anybody want to go snuggle with some puppies?"

Heath and Rex's faces lit up.

Even Brock's frosty exterior seemed to thaw a bit, and he stood up when Chase stood up.

Heath smacked their eldest brother on the back. "Not even the Grinch can say no to getting mauled by puppies. Now if only your heart could grow a few more sizes and you stop being such a jerk to the man boning Mum."

"It'd be a fucking Christmas miracle for that to happen," Rex replied with a dimpled grin.

All Brock did was grunt.

CHAPTER TWENTY-ONE
HEATH & PASHA

"I'M GOING to need to have another shower or at the very least wash my face," Heath said with a giant smile as they walked back toward the hotel lobby after getting mauled by puppies. "Puppy breath is great, and their kisses are right up there with kisses from my wife and my kids, but still, I can feel the saliva hardening on my cheeks."

His brother snorted and chortled.

Rex opened the door for them, and they all stepped into the lobby, making their way to the front desk.

"Any messages for Harty Boys Security?" Brock asked the woman behind the desk in the holly-red red blazer and matching pencil skirt.

Heath loved a good pencil skirt on a woman.

His wife in particular could rock a pencil skirt like no tomorrow. That perfect ass of hers tucked up in the tight fabric. He could bounce a coin off that gift from God.

It was even better when he pushed the fabric up her thighs until it rumpled around her waist as he fucked her.

He stifled his groan, glad that he was wearing loose sweatpants that wouldn't reveal the half-chub he was sporting at the thought of taking Pasha on her home office desk with her skirt around her waist.

Not that he would ever pressure her for sex, but fuck, it'd been a long time since he'd felt the hot silk of his wife around his cock.

And more than have sex with her, he wanted to fucking eat her.

Heath's ultimate happy place was with his head between his wife's thighs and her squeezing him until he couldn't hear a damn thing.

But she'd just had Eve a little over a month ago, and even though she didn't say it, he knew she was self-conscious about her body.

If he could give his woman one thing for Christmas—even for a day, fuck an hour—it would be for her to see herself the way he saw her. Goddamn beautiful. Fucking perfect. The stretch marks, the widened hips, even that dark line down the front of her belly turned him the fuck on.

She'd given him children, carried them inside her body for nine months. Children made out of their insatiable passion and soul-rocking love for each other. If she didn't lose an ounce of the baby weight, he'd still consider her the most exquisite creature on the planet.

"The what now?" Chase asked, leaning forward and asking the front desk employee to repeat herself.

Heath shook his shaggy blond head to dislodge his thoughts of his wife.

He was going to miss Eve's first Christmas, and that was gut-wrenching enough. He didn't need to torture himself with the fact that he also wouldn't be getting to eat Pasha's Christmas *pudding* either.

"All I was told was that you needed to pack your belongings, go back and get the puppies—the breeders have been notified and have given the go-ahead—then you are to head out to the helipad.

Your chopper will be here within forty-five minutes," the woman said with a single shoulder lift.

Heath and his brothers all exchanged looks.

They'd heard about Grant aka Santa Claus flying to the rescue at the kids' school, but was he also coming to get them and take them home for Christmas?

None of them had to say anything. They were all thinking it.

Rex snorted and nudged Brock. "You can't hold a grudge against the dude now. Not if he's taking you to your kids for Christmas. He's literally *saving* Christmas."

Brock grunted, then thanked the woman behind the desk and punched a few buttons on his phone with his big meaty finger. He put his phone to his ear a second later.

But nobody picked up, and with a growl, he shoved his phone into the pocket of his black leather jacket.

"Try Mum?" Heath asked, knowing full well that Brock had called Krista. Brock and their mother hadn't spoken since the night of the Christmas lights tour. And since both of them were as stubborn as they came, it was anybody's guess who would be the first to break the seal of silence.

Heath had twenty bucks on their mother, simply because Rex had thrown twenty bucks on Brock breaking his silence first, and Heath needed to counter if he was going to make any money.

It was really anybody's game who held out the longest through.

And if it really was true that Grant was on his way to pick them up and take them home for Christmas, then they were all in for one hell of an awkward day tomorrow if Brock and their mother did make amends.

With a shrug, Heath broke free of their tight foursome and headed for the stairs. "I don't know about you guys, but I'm itching to see family, so I'm going to go pack." Then, not waiting for his roomie Brock to join him, he took the steps two at a time up to their room, whistling "Jingle Bells" while he went.

Forty-five minutes later, all packed up and shivering in the wind with the puppies hiding in their coats, the four Harty Boys stood and watched as the chopper hovered and then dropped down to the pad.

As they all expected, Grant was in the cockpit.

Shielding their faces—and the puppies' faces—from the extra wind from the rotors, they waited until the propellers completely stopped until they moved.

Grant swung the door open and hopped down, all smiles, his gray eyes bright. "Howdy, fellas. Need a lift?"

Heath was the first to rush forward and shake Grant's hand. "Grant, thank you so much. This means the world to me, getting to be there for my baby girl's first Christmas ... thank you." Then before he could stop himself, because he was just that over-whelmed with gratitude, Heath pulled Grant in for a hug.

Grant didn't seem to mind and gave Heath a swift back pat in return as he chuckled. "Happy to do it. Just glad the weather is cooperating for us."

Heath released Grant's hand and body and looked skyward. "Yeah, no kidding, eh? Been brutal the last few days and projected to get worse next week."

"Winter storms are part of Tofino's charm, but if you ask me, Mother Nature got a bit too carried away this time." Grant lifted his chin when Rex and Chase approached as well, offering him their hands in thanks.

"You just keep saving the day, man," Rex said, opening up the rear door of the chopper and tossing his duffle bag inside. "I'm starting to think you really *might* be Santa Claus. Saving Christmas and all."

Grant's cheeks turned a little redder than would be expected from the wind, and he smiled and glanced away. "If it makes Joy smile, I'll do pretty much anything."

"And that's why I'm on your team now," Chase said. "Anybody

who would do all the things you've done just to make our mother happy is okay in my books."

Grant nodded and stretched his hand forward to let the nosy puppy sniff his hand. The dog did, then licked it. "They're both cuties. This one's a male?"

Chase nodded. "Brock's got the female."

Happy and ready to go and see their families, Heath, Rex, and Chase piled into the helicopter. Heath rode shotgun, while the two bald beasts climbed into the back.

All the while, Brock just stood there watching it all with a sour expression on his face.

Heath glanced back into the helicopter at his brothers, and both Rex and Chase rolled their eyes.

"You comin'?" Grant asked. "There's room for one more."

Heath saw his oldest brother's body stiffen and his gaze turn steely.

He didn't have to see Grant's face to know the man was probably rolling his eyes just like the rest of them.

Sure, when they all met Grant, they were skeptical about the man. Did their due diligence and dug around to uncover any skeletons lurking in his closet, any nefarious deeds in his past. But the man was clean.

And more than that, he was actually really fucking nice.

He wasn't trying too hard to get Heath and his brothers to like him. He didn't seem to care whether they did or not. And in all honesty, that made Heath respect Grant even more.

Now Heath, Rex, Chase and all their wives and kids really did like Grant. He'd proven himself to be a likable guy, even without all the extra things he did to make their mother smile. But the fact that he *did* make her smile as much as they'd all witnessed lately was just a big bonus.

"Gonna let the pup catch a chill?" Grant asked Brock.

Brock's bottom jaw jutted out.

Grant's shoulders slumped slightly. "Look, Brock, you can hate me. I really don't care. You can think I'm the scum of the fucking Earth. I. Do. Not. Care. What I *do* care about is your mother, and she wants her sons home for Christmas. This is one of *my* gifts to her—particularly since she's an impossible woman to buy for. *But* you're not getting in this chopper until you promise me you'll apologize to your mother. I don't give a flying fuck what you say to me or about me, and you're more than welcome to break into my house and lift up my mattress or dig through my sock drawer—you won't find anything. But the things you said to your mother were unacceptable. I'll take the dog to your family, and you can stay here with your anger, but those are my conditions. I'm happy to fly you home for Christmas, but you owe your mother an apology."

Heath glanced back at Rex and Chase again. They all nodded and shrugged.

Points to Grant.

Not too many people had the balls to call Brock out like that.

And Grant was proving to have grapes the size of grapefruits.

Brock tightened his hold on the puppy in his jacket. But his nod was there. It was tight and it was curt, but it was there.

That seemed to be enough for Grant, because he clapped his hands once, nodded, and spun to open up the door to the cockpit. "Well, that's settled then. Let's get this bird off the ground and get home."

Grant climbed up into the pilot's seat, and Rex closed the rear door once Brock was in his seat.

"All right, puppies and Harty Boys, I'll have you back with your families in no time. I'd like to thank you for choosing Wild Ride Helitours today. We pride ourselves on our safety, attention to detail, and customer service. Please let your friends know about us and receive ten percent off your next booking."

Heath put the aviation headset on his head and grinned wide at Grant.

"Time for a dust-off!" Rex cheered, following it up with a hoot.

"Ho ho ho!" Grant laughed as he turned over the engine for the chopper and, after she was all warmed up, gently lifted her into the sky. "And away ... we ... go!"

―――――

BOTH KIDS WERE NAPPING.

Honestly, it was a rarity.

For Pasha, it seemed like if Raze was down, Eve was up, and if Eve was down, Raze was up. Even at night—particularly over the last ten days—the kids seemed to tag-team her. She rarely got more than sixty minutes of uninterrupted sleep before one of her wonderful, beautiful crotch fruits was stirring and calling for her.

Raze, of course, wanted snuggles, since he was off the boob. But Eve just wanted to eat.

Even if Eve was only asleep for twenty minutes, when she woke back up, it was like she was starving and hadn't eaten in twenty hours. The way she latched on and sucked at first was like a vacuum in space, and Pasha had to pop the baby off and readjust her for fear of broken blood vessels on her areola.

And now, that baby was cluster-feeding. Which meant, if Pasha got twenty minutes of free, uninterrupted time, be that sleep or a shower alone, she was freaking lucky.

She knew women did this on their own and had done so on their own for eons when their mates would go off hunting mastodons or moose for days, sometimes weeks.

But she didn't live in that era, and she missed her husband.

Those women probably missed their husbands too. And it was probably really hard on them, too.

She empathized with them.

She missed how hands-on Heath was with the kids.

How much Raze just adored his daddy and even the biggest of crocodile tears could be cleared up with a bear hug from Dad.

A tear slipped down Pasha's cheek as she stood at the kitchen sink washing baby bottles.

God, how she missed Heath.

Rayma and Joy were doing their best, bouncing between Lydia's house and Pasha's to help with the kids and help Lydia walk Diesel, but eventually, they left. And Pasha was once again alone with her offspring.

Rayma had expressed how truly bad she felt for abandoning her sister, but Pasha wouldn't hear anything of it. Rayma was Lydia's sister, too, even if not biologically. Pasha was part of the Hart family and sisters-in-law with Lydia, and because Rayma was so enmeshed in the family as well, and had been a, for lack of a better term, ward of Joy's for a while, she was Lydia's sister, too. And besides, Lydia needed the help more. She was recovering not only from a procedure, but her heart was healing, too.

"Your mother had five children. You can handle two," Pasha kept reminding herself.

But then she'd also remind herself that her father was home a lot, not off on missions, and her mother also had her children further apart in age than Pasha did.

So it wasn't the same.

Deep in her pit of pity, she wiped away another tear.

It wasn't just that she missed her husband; it was that *he* was going to miss Christmas. Eve's *first* Christmas. Raze's second Christmas.

She could tell by the sound of Heath's voice last time they spoke that he was just as torn up about the whole thing as she was.

It also seriously sucked because they only had Mother Nature to blame. And she wasn't as easy of a bitch to get mad at as a real, breathing person.

Tomorrow was going to be weird.

Tomorrow, as hard as she would try to make it not suck, was going to suck. There was no way around it.

Placing the last clean bottle on the drying tray, she dried her hands on the dish towel and took a deep breath.

She could do this.

Christmas was just another day.

Easter changed dates all the time. Sometimes it was in March, sometimes April. Why did Christmas *have* to be on the twenty-fifth?

Tiptoeing around her house, she reached for the mug of luke-warm tea she had sitting on the kitchen island and gingerly took a sip. Even the sound of softly slurping could wake the beasts that slumbered within their home. She needed to be silent.

Truth be told, she should be sleeping, too.

Sleep when the baby sleeps.

Did that apply to everything else, too?

Fold laundry when the baby folded laundry.

Unload the dishwasher when the baby unloaded the dishwasher.

Order groceries when the baby ordered groceries.

Feed the toddler when the baby fed the toddler.

She snorted silently.

Whoever came up with that bit of wisdom obviously had a houseful of butlers.

But alas, Pasha had no butlers, not even one. She was forced to surrender her sleep time to take care of domestic necessities.

The giant pile of clean, unfolded laundry on the couch crooked a finger at her, and with an eye roll, she went to it.

She reached for her earbuds and put in one, then with her phone, she turned on her new favorite guilty pleasure: romance books on tape. Since she hardly had time to read anymore, she had taken to listening to audiobooks. It didn't quite allow her to flip to the back of the book and read the final few pages like she normally did, but she found she enjoyed being read aloud to. And when the male narrator's voice was deep and gritty like the one she was listening to now, her lady parts got all tingly.

She had both baby monitors set up on video mode, and if either child made so much as a fart, it would register on the voice meter and little red lines would go up on the side of the screen. But just in case the power went out, she only allowed herself one earbud so she could still hear if her loin spawn awoke.

She reached for the first clean cloth diaper off the stack, then sifted through the pile for the insert. On days like today, when the laundry pile nearly touched the ceiling, she regretted cloth diapers.

But then she thought of Mother Earth and the environment and how long it takes for a disposable diaper to decompose in the landfill, and she rolled her eyes, bit her tongue, and sucked up the hour it took to fold laundry and single-handedly save the environment.

The book was just getting to a steamy bit ... Raphe had stumbled upon Delilah in the stream, bathing naked beneath the waterfall. Her hair covered her breasts perfectly. But through the strands, dark, dusky nipples, hard as diamonds, peeked through. Beads of water hung from those nipples, glistening in the midday sun. Twinkling as if she had two piercings of crystal gemstones.

"Pardon my intrusion, Delilah, but ..." the narrator's molasses-coated gravel voice began.

Pasha felt her nipples pebble beneath her T-shirt.

Big, strong, warm hands gripped Pasha by the waist, causing her to scream and leap nearly a foot off the floor.

"What the hell?"

An elbow to the gut of her attacker was her first instinct. She made contact with a wall of hard abs, then broke free of his grasp and spun around, reaching for the first weapon she could find—the TV remote.

What are you going to do? Mute him?

Heath was holding his abdomen and slightly hinged over, a pained expression on his face.

Two sets of cries emerged from down the hallway and echoed loudly on the baby monitors.

Without saying a word to each other, they both took off toward the bedrooms.

Heath grabbed Raze and Pasha grabbed Eve, all four of them returning moments later to the living room.

As she settled into the recliner with a grunting and famished Eve, she had to pinch her wrist to make sure she wasn't dreaming.

He was here.

He was home.

Heath was home for Christmas.

Raze was snuggled in tight to Heath's chest, his favorite stuffed animal tucked under one arm, while his cheek was pressed over his father's heart.

"How did you ..." Pasha started before emotion caught in her throat like a fishhook and tears flooded her eyes. "The road was closed. A rockslide. A tree. How?"

Her gorgeous husband smiled and glanced down at Raze, brushing their son's unruly blond hair off his forehead. "Santa Claus. Though, for speed, and because the sleigh is currently being loaded with toys, he brought his helicopter to pick us up." His grin grew. "You can thank Stacey for the idea. She thought of it and called Grant to set it up."

Oh, she would be hugging the bejesus out of her sister-in-law when she saw her tomorrow. Hugging her and not letting her go for a very, very long time.

All the tears spilled forward, and a few even landed on Eve's cheeks.

The baby didn't seem to give a crap ... but she did crap her pants. Pasha felt it.

But at the moment, she didn't give a crap about the crap.

Her husband was home, and that was all that mattered.

"Do you have to go back soon?" she asked, mentally chastising herself for asking a question that could potentially ruin her impeccable mood.

Heath shrugged. "Probably, but hopefully not until the new year and for not as long. They only have like two more days of filming left, and when we spoke with the film crew, the director didn't think the ideal day was in the forecast until at least the second of January."

She breathed out a deep sigh of relief and let her smile break free.

"I hated the idea of not being here for Evie's first Christmas. Of not being here for you. I know you're struggling having two on your own."

Brushing a hand over Eve's platinum-blonde hair, Pasha smiled again, but this time it wasn't as big. She could never hide her true feelings from her husband, not even when she tried. He read her like a book. She was a house made entirely out of windows, he liked to say.

"It's been hard," she finally said. "I won't lie. But it also just makes me appreciate everything you do around here and for me all the more."

A whimper by the front door drew her attention away from Heath's face.

Her husband followed her gaze. "I didn't get a dog. I know that we're not in that place in our lives right now. But Brock and Krista and Chase and Stacey *did* get their kids dogs for Christmas, so I offered to hang on to the pups until tomorrow when we all go to my mum's."

"*Pups.* As in plural? You have both?" she asked. The *thwack thwack* of tails against a crate echoed through the house.

He nodded. "Chocolate labs. Male and female. The kids are going to be so excited. Grant offered to hold on to the pups, but

Brock got his tighty-whiteys in a twist, so I just said I would. It's only one night."

Eve popped off Pasha's breast, looking far happier than she did a moment ago. Pasha switched her to the other side but had to pop the baby off and readjust her when Eve went all Hoover on her nipple. "Have things between Grant and Brock gotten any better?"

Kissing the top of Raze's head, Heath shrugged, then shook his head. "I don't think so. I mean, Grant demanded that the only way Brock was getting in the helicopter was if he promised to apologize to Mum. Grant said he really doesn't give two shits if Brock likes him or not. He does, however, care about our mum and that the way Brock spoke to her was wrong and she deserves an apology."

Pasha's brows narrowed, and she nodded. "Damn straight he owes your mother an apology. He was really freaking rude."

"Agreed. Rex, Chase, and I have no beef with Grant. We're on his side now, so it's just Brock that is digging in his heels. He's being a stubborn ass, and he better not ruin Christmas because he can't get over his own ego. Dad's been dead for thirty fucking years. Mum could have remarried ages ago, but she didn't. And maybe that's because she was worried about how we would react, or maybe she just wasn't ready. But whatever. That's her thing to deal with. But I like Grant, and he takes care of Mum and makes her happy, and that's all that matters."

Raze shifted in his father's arms and turned to face Pasha. Her little boy always ran hot, so he often woke up from his naps sweaty, and today was no different. Damp hair clung to his forehead, and his cheeks were flushed.

"Are you hungry?" she asked him.

Raze nodded.

It was only just after lunchtime, and she did have his lunch all prepared for him at his highchair.

Without even asking, because they were just that in sync,

Heath stood up and plopped Raze into his chair, then brought Pasha a glass of water.

"I've missed you," she said as Heath bent down and pressed a kiss to their daughter's cheek and then to Pasha's lips.

"I've missed you so fucking much," he murmured against her mouth. "Every part of you."

Their eyes locked. Midnight blue to her brown.

Her earbud had fallen out when he startled her, so it wasn't the narrator's voice getting her all tingly in her yoga pants.

A smile broke free across her mouth.

She knew *exactly* what she was going to give Heath ... and have Heath give her for Christmas.

At long last, her bells were finally ready to get jingled again.

CHAPTER TWENTY-TWO
REX & LYDIA

WITH HER HUSBAND wrapped around her from behind, holding her tight into his hard chest and warmth, Lydia woke Christmas morning and smiled.

It was the first morning since she'd lost the baby that she didn't immediately think about what was no longer in her belly.

Would she forever think about the child she and Rex lost? Of course, but today it wasn't the first thing on her mind, and tears didn't spring into her eyes before she had a chance to rub the sleep from them.

This was a good sign.

Her heart was on the mend.

And she knew, beyond a shadow of a doubt, it was because her Hart was home.

When Rex came through the door last night, Lydia had ugly-cried tears of joy. She had sobbed in his arms, clutched him so tight, the man might have bruises.

She'd been lying in bed crying over their baby, over the fact that Rex wouldn't be there for Maeve's first Christmas, over not having her own mother there to hold her as she wept. She cried for all the things she didn't have. Because as Joy put it, she was allowed.

At first, Lydia had tried putting on a brave face. Tried looking for all the silver linings. Tried thinking about all of those people who had it worse than her. Whose grass wasn't as green as hers.

Then she started to think: Maybe there was something wrong with the baby and this was nature's way of not putting the child through pain and discomfort. She should be happy that Maeve was healthy and happy. At least she had one baby and didn't struggle with infertility. Some women couldn't have any, were unable to get pregnant or carry a baby to term—like Grant's wife. At least Lydia *could* get pregnant and had carried Maeve to term. Maybe she should stop feeling so sorry for herself and just get over it. Be thankful for what she did have rather than be sad about what she didn't.

But Joy had knocked her upside the head—verbally, not physically—and told her to throw those thoughts "out the fucking window."

Just because other people have it worse off did not diminish the pain or loss that Lydia was feeling. She had a right to experience her loss and handle it however felt right to her.

So, what felt right was to lie in her bed and cry. To cry about all the things she didn't have. The things she wouldn't have.

And then, strong, warm arms wrapped around her middle and a big body tucked in behind her and just held her.

She knew it was him.

Neither of them said a word.

Because they didn't have to.

Rex held her until she fell asleep.

Then she woke up. He drew her a bath, massaged her back with a delicious-smelling oil, and washed her hair. After that, they had dinner as a family. All three of them.

Rayma left to give them some alone time, just their little family.

Rex kissed the back of her neck. "Merry Christmas," he murmured groggily, linking their fingers together over the still slight swell of her belly.

"Merry Christmas," she replied, squeezing his fingers.

"How'd you sleep?" he asked, now nuzzling her neck.

She unlinked their fingers and slowly spun around in his arms to face him, cupping his cheek and bringing her lips to his. When the kiss ended, they both smiled. "I always sleep better when you're in the bed with me."

Blue eyes blinked, and those devilish dimples came out to play. "Ditto, baby."

"Think we got Maeve too many toys?"

His nose wrinkled, and he shook his head. "It's my baby's first Christmas. I'm going to spoil that little girl rotten. Not that she could *ever* be rotten. She's Daddy's perfect angel. As sweet as a lollipop. Would melt in the rain."

Lydia rolled her eyes and chuckled. "You keep that mentality between us. If she figures out how tight she has you wrapped around her pinky finger, we're going to have hell on wheels in no time. If we don't already."

"Do you want to exchange gifts here first or wait until we get to my mum's?"

A quick glance at the analog clock on Rex's nightstand said it was just past seven in the morning. Hopefully, since Maeve had been excited to have her daddy home and put up a stink at bedtime, she would sleep in for a bit and Rex and Lydia could have a little more time together, just the two of them.

She pressed her lips to his once more, then rolled over and stood up on the floor. "Let's exchange our gifts to each other here together. I'll go make coffee."

She honestly hadn't made coffee since the morning she lost the baby.

This was a really good sign.

She wasn't over her grief and probably never would be fully, but she wasn't letting it consume her anymore.

Throwing on her white bathrobe and sliding into her slippers, she headed out of the bedroom and down to the kitchen.

She wasn't in the kitchen two minutes before the sound of footsteps on the stairs and Rex chatting away with Maeve filled her ears and made her smile.

"There's Mummy," he said in the soft, gentle voice he used with Maeve.

Lydia abandoned the bag of coffee beans and went to her daughter. She kissed Maeve several times. "Merry Christmas, my sweet, sweet girl."

Rex smiled down at Lydia. "You seem better."

"I am better. I'm not *over* it—"

"And you have every right never *to* be."

She smiled. "Thank you. And yes, I know. Your mother made sure I was aware of that. But having you home has just ..." She sighed. "It's just made me be a lot more grateful for what I do have, and I'm going to focus on that."

With Maeve still on his hip, he cupped the back of Lydia's head and bent down until their foreheads were pressed together. "I live for your happiness, Lydia. Truly. Whatever you want to do, however you want to handle this, I'll follow your lead."

She blinked and pressed her forehead a little harder against his. "I know. And thank you. Eventually, when the time is right, I would like to try for another baby. But I'm not in any rush. Let's just enjoy the child we do have and the wonderful life she's made even richer."

He removed his head from her forehead and kissed it. "You're the strongest woman I know."

With a wink, she turned back to finish making the coffee. "I'll finish that sentence for you. *But I'm also the bossiest.* Now please make your daughter her bottle and go turn on the lights and the tree in the living room."

"For you, my wife, anything."

———

Rex's face lit up as he opened the gift bag. "Sweatpants!"

Lydia chuckled and took a sip of her coffee. "Full disclosure, those might be more for me than you."

"Like when I buy *you* lingerie?"

She nodded. "Yeah."

He chuckled and continued into the bag. "And shirts. I love shirts."

She snorted. "I'm almost buying this enthusiasm as real. You could quit being the bodyguard on these movie shoots and start being the actor."

He made a wounded face. "I actually really like my gifts. No acting here. You know how much I hate shopping for clothes. And—" He shoved his hand down his sweatpants, located the hole near his crotch and stuck his big index finger through. "I need new sweatpants."

She rolled her eyes. "We can keep the holey ones for the bedroom. But they're not suitable for the public."

"Agreed." He sipped his coffee. His wily wife had added eggnog instead of creamer and then a splash of Bailey's. He needed to pace himself if he intended to drive to his mother's for dinner. He could drink that coffee like water if he wasn't careful and have a holly jolly buzz going before noon.

Below the T-shirts was a bevy of charcuterie. Long, thick hunks of cured meats. "Oh mama," he said, the saliva filling his mouth. "Meat. A way to a man's heart, or at least this Hart's heart, is through meat. Damn, woman, you hit the jackpot."

He pulled out all the different kinds.

They were cold, since she'd obviously had them in the fridge until the moment they decided to exchange gifts.

Blueberry bison salami, fig and port salami, dried chorizo, prosciutto, candied pancetta, and more. It was enough cured meat to last him several months. As well as the meat, there were also a few different kinds of cheeses that would probably pair well, some olives, pickled asparagus, spicy pickled beans, and four tall cans of beer from four different microbreweries.

It was, honestly, the most perfect gift ever. He would drink and eat all of it with a smile on his face.

"You can thank Grant for the suggestion of all the food. Pasha and I bumped into him when we were shopping last weekend, and he said that he and his wife always struggled with what to get each other for Christmas. So they started buying only consumables. Nothing that would forever take up space. He said it made it way easier and it also helped them find new foods they enjoyed and cool little local gourmet shops."

He was reading the back of one of the lengths of salami but looked up at her. "That's a great idea. I love it. What kind of consumables would you like? For future reference, of course."

She tapped her finger to her chin in a cute way. "Ummm, wine. Obviously. Cheese. Chocolate. Maybe some cool dips for crackers. Like cauliflower asiago dip or something. I saw that at the store the other day and thought it looked good."

Rex committed her list to memory and nodded. "Dips, wine, chocolate, and cheese. Got it."

Maeve finished her bottle where she was sitting on the floor in front of the tree and tossed it to the side before lunging forward and grabbing a branch of the tree that held a small red bulb.

Fuck, his baby had brute strength. The whole tree started to lean. Rex and Lydia were up off their seats and prying the limbs from Maeve's chubby vice grip before the whole thing toppled over on her.

"Need to secure it with tie-downs next year," he said, moving a few tempting ornaments from his daughter's level to branches higher up and out of her reach.

Pia stretched from her spot beneath the tree, completely unaffected by the fact that she was nearly buried in needles, trunk, and ornaments. As Rex went about righting the tree, Lydia picked up Maeve before she snatched the cat by her tail and caught a paw to the cheek as a form of feline discipline.

Rex had taken Diesel out for a pee and a crap once Maeve had her bottle and while Lydia was making coffee. Now his happy pupper was chewing voraciously in front of the gas fireplace on the new piece of antler Rex bought him.

"Is it charcuterie for breakfast?" Lydia asked with a laugh, bringing a grunting and frustrated Maeve over with her to the couch.

"Got no qualms with that," Rex said, having resecured the tree and snagged Lydia's gift from under it in the process. He placed it on her lap, then sat back in his chair. Diesel abandoned his antler and came to stand in front of Rex, resting his big, chunky head on Rex's thigh. Rex gave D's ears a scratch, and the dog's tail began to wag against the floor. "Open your gift," he urged, lifting his chin toward the bag on her lap.

Making sure that Maeve wasn't going to abandon ship and head back over to tear down the tree, Lydia pulled the tissue paper out of the bag and set it beside Maeve.

Immediately, their baby began shredding the flimsy red paper. Whatever. At least she wasn't trying to make the Christmas tree horizontal anymore.

Lydia's hand went into the bag, and she peered inside. A gasp fled her throat before she pulled the gift out.

Rex sat there pretending to be calm on the outside, but inside he was a nervous wreck.

Crafting was NOT his forte.

Puzzles, he liked.

But glue, glitter, paint, and all that shit—no thanks. His fingers were too big for intricate detailed things like beading or crochet. And he didn't have the patience to wait for the glue or paint to dry.

But for Lydia, he'd wait for paint, glue, or whatever else to dry. He'd wait forever if he had to just to see the look on her face when she opened her gift.

Fresh tears welled up in her eyes as she pulled out the vase that had his and Maeve's handprints on it.

He'd done some googling, and there was this technique that involved little to no skill—which was exactly what he needed. All you had to do was buy a clear glass vase, pour paint inside the vase, swirl it around, and if you used two colors, as he did—white and turquoise—it created a cool marbled effect once dried.

Then, using more paint of whatever shade you desired—he'd used peach for his hand and black for Maeve's—you could make handprints on the outside.

So, he'd done his giant ham of a hand, then over the top, he did Maeve's little one. Then, for good measure, he covered their hand-prints in glitter, because he really wanted to find glitter everywhere for the rest of his life, including his pubes.

Seriously, what the fuck had he been thinking?

Well, it was done now. At the moment he saw glitter on his arm and a few pieces on the coffee table.

As his wife spun the vase around in her hand, he got up from his spot on the couch and headed to the garage. He was back in seconds with a bouquet of flowers for the vase.

Lydia blinked up at him, her smile brighter than the sun shining on the snow. "This is the best present I've ever received."

He snorted. "Now whose enthusiasm is put on?" But he was just teasing her. He knew she was being truthful and how much the gift meant to her. She loved all that handmade stuff. She loved anything crafty. She gushed over every scribble and plastic spoon glued to a pipe cleaner her students brought her at the preschool. She acted like every piece was by Picasso himself. But he could tell right now she wasn't faking it.

He lifted a shoulder. "I mean, that's not *all* we got you, right, Maevy?"

Maeve was now eating the tissue paper.

Lydia pulled the paper out of her daughter's mouth and moved the shredded bits to the other side of her so Maeve couldn't eat anymore. Her shit was probably going to have red pieces in it now.

Lydia reached down into the bag and pulled out an envelope.

Rex cleared his throat. "Now, I should say, I bought this before … when I thought we would need a weekend alone before … so we don't have to go. But …"

Her eyes closed. "A babymoon? A weekend away before the baby was born?"

He nodded. "I'm sorry. I just thought—"

Her eyes opened. She shook her head and smiled. Her hazel eyes were wet with tears, but they weren't sad. There was hope there. Hope for them. For their family. For their future. "Well, maybe we can use this when we're ready to try and make a baby. Sort of … full circle."

"When you're ready."

Her throat bobbed on a swallow, and she pulled Maeve into her lap and kissed her head. "When *we're* ready. Because we're in this together. We lost together, and we'll get through this together."

With a final scratch to Diesel's ears, he sat up from his chair and moved over to the couch to sit with his girls. Lydia pushed the tissue paper to the floor and made room for him. He wrapped his arm around his wife and kissed his daughter.

As if they knew that now was the time for the whole family to be together, Pia leaped up gracefully onto the couch, careful to avoid Maeve's wandering eyes and grabby fingers, and sat behind Lydia's neck. Diesel came to stand between Rex's legs.

"We are rich," Lydia said, her words hoarse and strained. Her eyes grew wet, and he could see the tight corners of her mouth as she tried to force the smile.

"We are," he said softly, kissing her on the side of the head. "But we also know loss. And together, as a family, we'll get through it. You don't have to suffer alone."

She turned to him. "And neither do you." She leaned the side of her head against his and turned Maeve in her lap so they could see her. So their daughter's beautiful face was right before them. "Merry Christmas, Rex."

He pulled her closer to him, turned his head, and kissed her crown. "Merry Christmas, Lydia."

CHAPTER TWENTY-THREE
HEATH & PASHA

Not bothering to knock because people were already in the house and there was zero risk of him walking in on his mother in a compromising naked position this time, Heath opened the door to his childhood home. "Cerry Mistmas!" he shouted, holding the door open for a slow-moving Raze and Pasha with the bucket car seat and diaper bag.

"It's *Merry Christmas*, Uncle Heath," Thea corrected him, coming to greet them all at the door, dressed in a cute little red dress with a small white bow in the middle of her neckline.

"Is it?" Heath asked teasingly. "Well, thanks for correcting me, small fry. And don't you look ravishing!"

Thea wrinkled her nose. "What does that mean?"

"Pretty, honey. It means pretty," Pasha said with a bit of exasperation to her tone. "Less chitchat and more moving *into* the house." With a grunt, she put down the bucket seat. Eve was wide-eyed and awake inside. She'd screamed the entire drive over, so that was fun.

Heath set down the multiple bags of gifts he'd brought in, then

did a whistle that he and his brothers had used during covert opera-
tions before.

In seconds, Chase and Brock emerged.

"You got the stuff?" Chase asked with a cheeky smile that made
Heath's own face break out into a smile.

He would never grow tired of seeing Chase smile or hearing
him joke or laugh. Out of all of them, Chase had experienced the
worst in the field, and he carried a lot of that with him. So, for him
to joke, it meant he was relaxed. It meant his demons weren't with
him, and that was a big fucking deal, and a Christmas present in
itself.

Heath nodded. "Goods are in the cab of my truck. What's the
plan?"

"Sooner the better," Brock said. "Kids are growing antsy with
all the gifts under the tree and not getting to open them."

"It's teaching them impulse control and patience, or so says
Lydia the preschool teacher," Chase added.

"Just let me get Pasha all set up, then I'll come to help you,"
Heath said, not wanting to abandon his wife as she maneuvered her
way through the small foyer, tripping over all the shoes.

Raze had already stepped out of his boots and was off to find
his cousins.

Heath ditched his loafers for a moment, not wanting to track
mud and crap onto his mother's carpeted floors, then he brought
the bags of gifts into the warm, decorated, heavenly-smelling living
room.

He gave his sisters-in-law quick kisses and hugs, made sure his
wife and Eve were okay in the spot they'd found on the couch, then
he slid back into his shoes and accompanied his brothers out to the
truck.

"How'd they fare the night?" Chase asked, rubbing his hands
together to ward off the chilly wind that had come down from the
north.

"Really well. You've got two super chill pups on your hands, which will be great for the kids. Fed them, took them out, played with them a bit. Raze would just lie down and the puppies would climb all over him and lick him until he giggled so hard he peed."

Brock and Chase both snorted.

"Gonna have to get one yourself," Brock murmured, opening up the back of Heath's truck.

"Eventually," Heath agreed. "But with the new baby and stuff, we'll probably wait a couple more years until they're out of diapers and life isn't *so* chaotic. Your kids' ages are perfect."

Stacey and Krista had gone out and bought all the necessary stuff for puppies. Each house had a kennel, a bed, toys, food, food bowls, all of it. But since the puppies were still small and used to being together, they'd put them both in one for the night at Heath's, so that's where they were now.

Brock opened the metal grate door to the kennel, and one of the puppies stepped forward curiously. "There's my girl," Brock said in a tone of voice Heath didn't recognize. Brock had never even used that tone with Zoe. It was all cooey and gentle.

Who was this man?

He took the pup in his arms and kissed her head. "Ready to meet your new family?"

Chase and Heath exchanged curious looks as Chase reached inside and the male pup hesitantly stepped into his arms. "Hey, buddy."

They leashed the dogs and let them out into the yard for a quick pee.

Heath was the first to reenter the house.

Krista and Stacey had made sure that everyone was in the living room in a semicircle around the tree.

At the sound of the door closing, heads turned.

"Are we ready to start opening presents?" Heath asked, directing his question to the older children.

"Been ready for *ages*," Connor said. "We had to wait for you guys."

Stacey shot her son a look.

"And that was okay," Connor quickly followed up. "It wasn't that long. It just felt like ages. But you're here now." He glanced at his mother, his expression asking if he was forgiven and could still open his presents.

Stacey rolled her eyes and ruffled his hair.

Connor's *phew* shoulder shrug and look of relief was hilarious.

"Well, these presents don't really need to be *opened*, but they do need names and a whole lot of love," Chase said, being the first to round the corner with the little male puppy tugging away on his leash.

Connor and Thea's eyes went saucer-size, and they leaped up from their spots on the floor.

"A puppy!" Connor exclaimed, sliding back down to his knees in front of the puppy. Thea was right beside him.

The puppy wanted nothing to do with their pleasantries of holding out their hand to be sniffed. He pawed his way up their laps and started licking their faces.

Both of Chase's kids were giggling like crazy.

"Is he really our dog, Dad?" Connor asked. "We get to keep him?"

"Or is it a girl?" Thea asked. "If it's a girl, I want to name her Thumbelina Tinkerbell Cinderella Bader Ginsberg. Or Ginny for short."

Adult snorts and guffaws echoed around the living room.

"He's a little boy, I'm afraid, sweetheart," Chase said with a laugh.

Connor's eyes widened. "He looks like chocolate."

"He's a chocolate lab," Chase replied.

Connor turned to his sister and whispered something in her ear.

Thea enthusiastically nodded.

They both turned to Chase again.

"We're calling him *Fudge,*" Connor announced, so freaking pleased with himself.

Chase's face fell. "Fudge? Really?"

Both kids nodded until Heath thought their necks might snap.

Thea planted her hands on her hips. "Fudge ... *Bader Ginsberg.*"

"I kind of like it," Stacey said, chuckling. "Lots of nicknames. Fudgy. Fudgsicle. It's cute."

Chase rolled his eyes, then crouched down and scratched the dog's ears. "What do you think, boy? You want to be called *Fudge?*"

The dog's tail started to wag even more.

"I guess that's a yes," Grant noted.

Brock came into the living room next, and when Zoe and Zane spotted the little dog on the leash being held by their father, just like their cousins, they leapt up off the floor and slid down beside the door.

"Boy or girl?" Zoe asked, or more like demanded.

"A little girl," Brock said.

"Cocoa! We have to name her Cocoa!"

Zane started chanting, "Cocoa! Cocoa!"

Thea turned to Zoe. "Cocoa *Bader Ginsberg,* right? Because I think the puppies are related." She glanced at Brock. "Are they related?"

Brock nodded. "Brother and sister."

Thea seemed satisfied with that reply.

All the mothers, including Heath's, were very vocal in educating the children—boys and girls—about human rights, women's rights, and democracy. They all had copies of the children's book *I Dissent: Ruth Bader Ginsberg Makes Her Mark* in their households, and it was read to the kids multiple times a week.

Zoe nodded enthusiastically. "Yeah! Cocoa Bader Ginsberg!"

"I guess that's settled," Krista said, joining her husband and children as they all sat down on the floor and started petting the puppy.

"Well, that was a lot of excitement, wasn't it?" Heath's mother said, standing up from where she'd been sitting in her chair and bending down to grab a present from under the tree.

She began handing them out around the room until everyone had a present.

Rex had a hold on Diesel's collar just in case he got the inclination to run through the crowd to go introduce himself to the latest canines in the family.

Nobody was worried about how Diesel would be with the puppies, just that he was big and his tail had a mind of its own. Once the excitement wore down, they'd take the dogs into the backyard so they could meet each other properly.

"Everybody got a gift?" Heath's mother asked.

They all nodded.

"Okay, then ... and ... open," she announced.

Heath's gift was from his mother. It was a nice sweater. Each of his brothers got ones similar.

Heath murmured out of the side of his mouth to Rex. "Have Mum and Brock spoken yet today?"

Rex shook his head. "They got here after we did, and it's been awkward. They've just been avoiding each other. At least it's easy enough to do with a houseful of people, but still. It's Christmas."

Heath nodded and let his gaze wander over to where his big brother was rubbing Cocoa's belly and smiling as he did it. His wife lifted her head, and Brock and Krista exchanged looks, then she rested her hand on his bulky shoulder and squeezed.

What was all that about?

Slowly, but efficiently, they made their way through the heaping pile of gifts until only a few remained.

Heath and Pasha hadn't exchanged at home, but he also wasn't sure if he wanted her to open and explain her gift out loud.

Another gift was placed into his wife's lap—his gift.

She recognized his handwriting and lifted an eyebrow at him in curiosity.

He grinned back at her and mouthed, "Open it later."

She replied with a nod and then set the gift aside. He'd already opened his gift from her, which was sweatpants, T-shirts, and food. So, in other words, the best fucking present ever.

"Grant!" Heath's mother exclaimed, drawing all their attention. "What is the meaning of this?"

The room fell silent.

Grant, ever the calm, cool, and collected presence among their incessant chaos, actually appeared a little flustered. What on Earth had he given their mother?

"You said it's been forever since you went away on *vacation*, Joy. So this here is an all-inclusive of your choice. I'm not taking no for an answer. I'll fly us there. You just pick the place—within the continent, of course, because I can't fly a helicopter to Tahiti. But if you want to go to Tahiti, I'll book us a flight. No place is off-limits. But I can only fly us where I can fly a helicopter from Victoria."

Heath's mother's eyes welled up with tears. "You bringing my boys home for Christmas was my gift. That's all I wanted. This is too much."

A throat cleared behind them all. "No, it's not," Brock said quietly. He'd stood up and was standing toward the back of the room.

Their mother's gaze narrowed, and everyone turned to face Brock.

He glanced down at Krista, and she gave him an encouraging nod from her spot on the floor, reached for his hand and squeezed it.

"It's not too much, Mum, because you deserve it all. You

deserve happiness. You deserve love and companionship. You deserve to feel the kind of love that I feel for my wife. That we all feel for our spouses. You had that, and it was robbed from you too soon, and you shouldn't be punished and denied that love again because Dad died and your son is a jackass. You deserve to be treated the way Grant treats you and to be taken on a vacation. You gave up so much for us as kids. And you deserve to have the fun you sacrificed for all those years."

Heath's oldest brother stepped forward between all the adults, children, dogs, gifts, and wrapping paper scattered across the living-room floor. He held out his hand for Grant.

"I'm sorry I was such an asshole—to both of you. Grant, you *literally* saved Christmas, you make my mother happy, and because my brothers and I are here today with our families, you've made it impossible for me to hate you."

Tears streamed down their mother's face as she laughed at that last bit.

Grant stood up and took Brock's hand. "Joy's lucky to have such protective sons who love her as much as you four do."

"And she's lucky to have a man who loves her as much as you do," Brock said in his own grumbly way. "I'm sorry for the issues I've caused." He pinned his gaze on their mother. "I'm sorry for what I said, Mum. All of it. You know it wasn't true."

Brock and Grant released their hands just as their mother lunged from her chair, wrapped her arms around Brock's neck and tugged him down for a hug.

Several of the women were sniffling, but leave it to Heath's son Raze for comic relief. He walked up to Heath and very loudly exclaimed, "I go poop!"

———

PASHA CLOSED the bedroom door with the baby monitor in her hand. She'd just managed to get Eve down for a nap after nursing for what felt like forever. She was pretty sure the kid had drained both tanks well over forty minutes ago and was just using Pasha's tits as a pacifier.

But whatever.

The baby was napping, and that was all that mattered.

Raze was off with his cousins, getting up to holiday mischief, and Pasha was going to take this rare opportunity of being alone in a house full of people to open the gift from her husband. She wandered into one of the other empty bedrooms and sat down on the bed.

It wasn't a very big gift. About the size of a brick. It also wasn't very heavy.

He'd done a horrible job of wrapping it—like he always did with presents. The man could do a lot of skilled things with those fingers, but wrapping presents did not seem to be one of them. His tape was all twisted; his corners were bunchy and crinkly.

It made her giggle and smile at the thought of him trying to wrap the thing and the grunting and swearing that must have taken place.

Once she got the tape free, she ripped the paper and set it beside her on the bed.

It was a booklet.

A handmade, or better put, a professionally designed—by a graphic designer—coupon book. And she just so happened to be married to a man who moonlighted as a graphic designer.

In addition to fighting bad guys and guarding A-list celebrities, Heath had a graphic design side hustle. He mostly made book covers for romance authors, but the man could do anything if he put his mind to it.

And it appeared as though he had put his mind to a coupon book.

Was it for blowies and butt sex? Because if that was the case, he could go sleep in the garage.

For a moment, she allowed herself to appreciate the beauty of the book. Mandalas and lotuses, ornate sketched designs she knew he had probably done himself. He was so talented in so many different things.

The fact that he was complete shit at wrapping presents actually made her feel better. He wasn't perfect.

She knew he wasn't perfect already, but the fact that he was actually really terrible at something just humanized him all the more. Made her love him even harder.

She turned the first page of the book.

This coupon is good for: One back rub.

Page two. *This coupon is good for: One night where the sex is ALL about you. Sit on my face all night if you want.*

She giggled at that last bit. That coupon was as much for him as it was for her. He loved it when she sat on his face.

Page three. *This coupon is good for One sixty-minute foot massage.*

Oh, Mama. Yes, please. Where was this coupon three months ago when she was massively pregnant with Eve?

She flipped through the rest of the book. It was many more of the same, with a few more creative things thrown in. There were also a few girls' nights and weekends away where he had the kids. All just really thoughtful things that she knew she would never need a coupon for, she could just simply ask, but the fact that he knew she needed these things was what mattered.

The last page of the book was the big one though. *This coupon is good for: A weekend away with your husband. No kids. No distractions. Just us.*

A shiver ran through her at just how perfect the gift was. At just how perfectly perfect for her Heath was.

As hard as the wait had been for him, he never pressured her.

He waited until her body was ready.

Until her mind was ready.

Well, now they were both ready. They were both *more* than ready.

With the coupon book in her hand, she left the bedroom, found Krista, handed her the baby monitor, told her to make sure Raze stayed alive, then went on the hunt for her husband.

CHAPTER TWENTY-FOUR
HEATH & PASHA

HEATH WAS in the garage grabbing the gravy his mother had made yesterday. She had gotten in the habit of cooking the turkey, stuffing, and gravy the day before and then just reheating everything. That way, she wasn't stuck in the kitchen nonstop preparing the food, and the house didn't overheat with the oven on all day.

She was a smart woman, his mother.

One of the smartest.

Bent over and sifting through all the containers and covered bowls, he barely registered the garage door into the house being opened.

But he did hear the *snick* of the lock being set.

Normally, deadbolts were on the other side of garage doors. But for security purposes, Brock had installed a lock on the inside of the garage. In case an intruder entered the house, their mother could run to the garage, lock herself inside, then escape that way.

"I opened my present," came Pasha's voice.

He grinned and let go of the container, stood up to his full height, closed the fridge door, and turned to face her. "Yeah?"

She bit her lip and slowly, provocatively walked toward him.

Instantly, his cock twitched in his dress pants and his heart rate picked up speed.

"And?" he asked, knowing that look in her eyes and feeling a pang of melancholy over how long it'd been since he'd seen it.

She wanted him.

Finally.

She wanted them.

Together.

Finally.

She reached him and stopped when they were toe to toe. "Coupons didn't have an expiry date."

"Because neither does our marriage."

That made her grin.

And her grin made him hard.

Her smile faltered slightly, her gaze left his, and her hand slid to cover the slight swell of her belly. Her *fupa,* as she called it.

What a horrible fucking term.

If Heath wasn't preparing to give his wife her present right now, he'd go off and find the idiot that coined that term and given them a real ass-kicking.

But he had better things to do.

Better people, and a better woman to do.

"You have a lot of dirty one-liners collecting dust in the queue?" she asked, having seemed to slightly rally her mood and toss on another smile.

He nodded emphatically. "But I won't hit you with all of them."

She placed her hand on her hip and lifted a brow in a sassy challenge. "Gimme a few."

Giddy like he'd just been told he was going to have a threesome with his wife and his wife from another dimension, he nodded. "Knock knock?"

"Who's there?"

"Ice cream."

"Ice cream, who?"

"I'll scream your name all night long if you lick my cone."

She snorted and rolled her eyes. "Oh man. Lack of sex makes your jokes even cornier than normal."

He was inclined to disagree, but he didn't bother to say that out loud. "You're like the roads after a snowstorm."

"Slippery when wet?"

Heath threw his head back and barked out a laugh. "I was going to say, in need of a good plowing, but yours is better."

She merely grinned.

"Last one."

"Okay, make it good."

He stroked his chin for a moment, running through the long list of dirty one-line jokes he'd come up with in the last several months that just hadn't felt right saying out loud to Pasha. "Okay, I got it. If you were a pumpkin, I'd pick you."

A cute, sweet smile lifted one side of her mouth. But then her eyebrow lifted too. She knew this was too good to be true. "And?"

She knew him too well.

"And I don't have to cut you open to feel your soft, wet insides." He wiggled his finger in the air, stuck out his tongue, and bit it.

She lunged forward and swatted his arm. "That's gross."

But they were both laughing.

Fuck, he loved her laugh. Loved it so much.

"Which coupon would you like to redeem?" he asked as their chuckles ebbed. He took the coupon book from her hand and flipped through it. He held up the one where it said: *Good for one "snack" anytime anywhere.* "I am starving. I know that table of apples and snacks is loaded out there, but you *know* what my favorite meal is."

She bit her lip again.

He flipped through the coupon book some more and stopped at

another one. "How about this one? *Good for one dirty quickie, no questions asked. I don't even have to get off.*" His eyes widened. "You ready for *that?*"

Slowly, her head bobbed. "I'm ready for all of it. I want my husband. I want him to eat me to within an inch of my life, then fuck me until we both come. Then I want us to go home and do it again tonight."

Now it was his turn to smile wide. "Are you telling me you're stacking your coupons?"

She lifted a shoulder, causing the wide-necked, billowy black sweater she was wearing to slip off one shoulder and expose her black bra strap.

He didn't bother to hide his groan. Even his wife's creamy, soft shoulder got him going.

"Didn't say anywhere on there that I *couldn't* stack my coupons."

He glanced back down at the coupon book and made a "tsk-tsk" sound. "Whoever made this forgot to include some fine print."

With a giggle, she lunged forward, wrapped her arms around his neck, and kissed him.

He set the book on the workbench behind him and wrapped his arms around her waist, deepening the kiss, spreading her lips with his tongue to take full possession of her mouth.

She tasted like eggnog and gingerbread.

They kissed for a few minutes, but when she started to grind her pelvis against his very obvious erection and dropped her hands to his zipper, he pulled away, waggling his finger at her and saying, "Tut-tut."

Her brows furrowed, and her nose wrinkled.

He took her hand and walked them both around his mother's Corolla, stopping in front of the big full-length mirror on the wall. On warm summer days, his mother would pull her car out of the garage and do workouts in the shade and in front of the mirror. She had a treadmill in the basement and all her workout gear there, but she said she also liked the breeze and fresh air, so sometimes she worked out in the garage.

"Take off your clothes," Heath ordered. Both of them were standing and looking straight ahead into the mirror.

Still facing the mirror, she flicked her gaze up at him.

"Trust me," he said gently.

With her lips pinned tight and a slightly annoyed look on her face, she nodded and slid her dark gray pants over her thighs, removing her socks with them.

The garage floor was chilly, so he snagged a dark blue yoga mat he found in the corner, unrolled it, and folded it beneath her feet so she had some cushion and a barrier between her skin and hard concrete.

Her shirt was long enough that it covered the apex of her thighs.

He watched as she studied herself and her lips curled up in critical appraisal.

This would not do.

She needed to know how fucking gorgeous she was. How fucking gorgeous *he* thought she was. How badly he still wanted her.

"Now the shirt. And the panties and the bra. All of it."

Another glance at him by way of the mirror. "When I came in here, this wasn't what I was expecting, Heath. I just—"

"You've stacked your coupons. You're getting the VIP treatment. And if you read the invisible fine print, you'd see that the VIP treatment involves one-on-one attention from the CEO himself. And that's me. So just soak it up, woman." He wiggled his fingers in the mirror to indicate she needed to get a move on.

With a sigh, she lifted the shirt over her head. Her nose instantly wrinkled again, and her lips curled up as she criticized herself.

"I want you naked, Pash."

Her throat rolled on a swallow, but she complied.

First the panties, then finally her black maternity bra with the clip on the straps to bring the cup down so baby had easy access.

Once she was fully naked and standing in front of the mirror, he picked up her clothing, folded it all and set it on the hood of his mother's car. Then he wandered around to stand in front of her, but slightly to the side so that she could still see herself in the mirror. The garage wasn't cold, but she was naked, and he watched as gooseflesh raced across her arms and her chest until her body couldn't handle it anymore and shivered.

"Heath ..." she started to protest.

"Enough."

Her mouth snapped shut.

"Tell me all the places on your body that you don't like. Touch them."

She glared at him in the mirror and shook her head.

"Do it, Pasha."

Her nostrils flared, and her glare intensified. But she acquiesced, and her hand fell to her lower stomach. "I hate this. I hate that it makes my pants two sizes bigger than I need."

He fell to his knees and inched forward, removing her hand and kissing the swell of her stomach, twirling his tongue over the soft skin and round her belly button. "You mean here. Where you safely, lovingly carried our children?"

Her glare started to fade.

He continued to kiss her in a spot where she hated herself.

A spot he loved unconditionally.

"Where else?" he probed.

She touched her hips. "Here. They grew so much with Raze and now ..."

"They're perfect." He moved across her belly to her hipbone and kissed it. Swirled his tongue, then skimmed across her stomach to the other hipbone and did the same thing. "Your hips grew so you could safely give birth to our children. And now, they're more for me to hold on to. They add swish to your walk. I think they're sexy as fuck." He kissed the bone again. "Where else?"

"My thighs. They're huge."

They were not fucking huge.

But he didn't want to ruin the moment. He didn't want to get into a pissing match with his wife because we all saw ourselves differently than the way others saw us. Physically, emotionally, and intellectually.

Some people probably saw Heath as a goofy idiot with two hollow legs. That all he cared about was sex and food. And a part of him still was like that. But who he was also went deeper, and only those he trusted were allowed to see more.

And Pasha trusted him, which was why he was allowed to see more. Allowed to see all of her.

Twirling his tongue down over her hipbone to her thigh, he pressed kisses to the tops of each one. Then he gently encouraged her to spread her legs, and he planted kisses on her inner thighs as well.

Her breath hitched above, and he tilted his eyes to look at her.

One tear slid down her cheek as she watched him.

"Where else?"

She sucked in a rattling breath. "I'm worried I'm not going to be tight enough for you anymore."

"So here?" he asked, using one finger and slowly pushing it up into her warm, slick pussy.

She nodded.

His kisses had made her sopping wet, and a small trickle of arousal ran down her inner thigh. Leaning forward, he ran his tongue up from her knee and caught the drip, continuing on his journey to gather the full stream. He didn't stop until he reached her clit.

He sucked.

She gasped.

He pulled his finger free of her and licked it clean before shouldering her legs farther apart and wedging his tongue into her center. He kissed her soft folds, sucked on them, and pulled them into his mouth.

Taking half a step back, Pasha leaned against the hood of the white Corolla and tilted her pelvis forward so Heath had an easier time reaching her sweet center.

Alternating between licks and sucks, he had her bucking into his face in no time.

Her clit swelled beneath his lips, and the rush of her juices poured across his tongue. He struggled to lap them all up but managed because no way in hell was he going to waste a drop of that honey.

Pushing one finger, then two back into her slit, he pumped them, crooked his fingers against her wall, then scissored.

His wife ground against his face, making it so he couldn't breathe through his nose.

He fucking loved it.

More, please.

He could tell by the way she was moving, though, how plump her folds had gotten and, slippery as she was, that she wasn't going to last much longer.

He sucked on her labia, releasing it with a wet *pop* that made her croon, then he took her clit into his mouth, moved his tongue over it counter-clockwise and ...

BAM!

Her body stilled, her mouth parted and a breathy "Oh God" rattled at the back of her throat.

She pulsed around his fingers, filled his mouth with her sweetness.

He removed his tongue from her clit and lapped up everything that spilled over his fingers as she rode each wave of her climax like a pro surfer in Hawaii.

When her body finally went lax and her pussy no longer throbbed around his fingers, he kissed all of her once more as he gently pulled his finger free. Licking his fingers clean, he stood up.

Her eyes were slightly glazed over, but the relaxed, serene smile that crossed her face was the perfect fucking Christmas gift he could ever hope for.

"I know we all see ourselves differently from how others see us, Pash, but know that I wouldn't change an inch of you. Not a pound. You're fucking perfect, and I am still so attracted to you, so in love with you—more in love with your body since you gave me our beautiful children. Everything you are is everything that I want. Everything I could ever want."

Drawing in a breath through her mouth, she lifted her sleepy, satiated gaze to him. And even though the contentment was plain to see and a sloppy smile lifted one corner of her mouth, a tear fell.

She reached for him.

He went to her.

"I'm confused," she said.

He lifted one brow and cocked his head. "Hmm?"

"I thought happiness started with an *H*."

His brows pinched. What was she getting at?

"But all along, it started with *U*."

That had him smiling until his cheeks hurt. "That's the best one yet. You've got real talent.

Her expression sobered, and she held on to him tight by the shirt. "Make love to your wife, Heath," she murmured, pushing up onto her tiptoes and taking his mouth with hers while her hands went to work on the zipper and button of his pants.

She had his cock fished out in seconds. She leaped up onto his hips and guided him home.

And then he felt like shedding a tear.

Because inside Pasha, with his wife, was home.

Her heat surrounded him.

She was still tight enough for him. Abso-fucking-lutely. He felt every ridge, every squeeze of her walls, every soft, hot inch of silk that shrouded him. Hugged him like a warm, satin cocoon. She was made for him and he for her.

Nothing felt better than being seated inside his wife. Then being one with the woman who had shed a bright beacon of light on his darkened soul.

Gripping her by the butt, he backed her up against the car and they started to move. He loved that she was completely naked.

Everything he wanted, everything that he loved to suck and tug and play with was right there for him. No fabric was in the way.

Drawing a nipple into his mouth, he twirled his tongue around it, then gently tugged.

Since she was nursing, he wasn't sure how this would feel. But when she moaned and rested her head against the roof of the car, he knew she didn't mind.

He did again, and harder.

She moaned more.

Up and down she bounced on his cock, squeezing his waist with her hips, rubbing his lower stomach against her clit.

Her fingers made their way into his hair like they often did, and she pulled until his scalp tingled.

Fuck, yes.

His teeth found her neck, and he scraped along the delicate skin, up to her jaw. Her head against the door and roof of the Corolla gave him perfect access.

Her throat rolled on a swallow, and his tongue followed the bob until he found the hollow at the base and sucked.

Her sharp inhales of breath made him do it again.

All the while, neither of them stopped moving.

She bobbed up and down on him. He bucked into her.

Their movements weren't frantic, and they'd certainly had better rhythm in the past, but they were rusty, and this was fun.

He was just enjoying them being together again. At long last.

She squeezed herself around him.

"Jesus Christ, Pash, you keep doing that and I'm not going to last much longer."

She did it again.

He chuckled and nipped her jaw.

She did it again.

Heat spiraled in his lower belly, and his balls drew up tight.

Dropping his head again, he drew a nipple back into his mouth and tugged on the hard bud with his teeth.

Another moan burbled up the back of her throat, and she clenched her muscles around his cock again.

If she did that one more time, he'd blow his fucking load.

"So ... good," she panted, dragging her top teeth over her bottom lip. "God, I missed this."

"I missed you," he said, switching to her other breast. "I missed my wife."

Grabbing him by the ears, she hauled his head away from her breast and crushed their mouths together, at the same time clenching her muscles again.

He bucked up one more time, and because he knew she was close, too, he knew he wasn't rude when he let the dam break and the orgasm crash through him.

She let her dam break as well, and together, in the fluorescent-lit garage of his childhood home, with their entire family in the rest of the house, Heath and his wife came together, and it was a holly fucking jolly Christmas miracle.

CHAPTER TWENTY-FIVE
GRANT & JOY

BING BONG!

"I'll get the door," Grant called into the house as he made his way through Joy's dining room and living room to the front door.

It was six o'clock, and everyone was just sitting down to dinner. He already knew that it would be one of two people behind the door.

Both people had spent their entire day making the world a better place.

He opened the door to find Officer Jordan Lassiter—the other cop who had been with Krista when they apprehended Brock outside of Grant's home—standing on the front stoop. He was still in his police garb since he probably hadn't even bothered to go back to the precinct to change before coming for dinner.

"Merry Christmas," Jordan said with a slight shiver to his voice.

"Merry Christmas, Constable," Grant said with a smile, stepping out of the way so Jordan, or Lassie, as a lot of people called him, could step in.

"Hold the door! I'm here, I'm here!" Booted footsteps stomped up the driveway, and a frenzy of wild caramel-colored hair was caught up in the wind. Rayma's cheeks were flushed and her brown eyes bright. She had a big tote bag of gifts under her arm and a bouquet of flowers.

"Miss Rayma," Grant said with a nod and a smile that made the color in her cheeks intensify. "Glad you could make it."

"Wouldn't miss Nana Joy's turkey for anything." She stopped in her tracks and unashamedly let her gaze wander over Jordan. "Hi." She didn't bother to hide her appreciation for the young man's looks.

"Hi," Jordan replied. His smile grew wide as he let his green eyes take a thorough inspection of Rayma. "I'm Jordan. I work with Krista."

She blinked her long lashes at him a few times. "I can see that. I'm Rayma, Pasha's sister."

They gazed at each other for another moment, then Grant cleared his throat, and the spell was broken. Rayma turned her attention to him and thrust the flowers and tote bag into his arms. "It takes hands for me to get out of these boots."

Grant snorted and was about to close the door behind them with his foot when he noticed flurries falling from the sky and glanced up toward the dark gray clouds that hung low over the city.

"Yeah, it's starting to snow," Jordan said, removing his jacket. Grant could see the small flakes of snow in the young man's dark brown hair. It was also on Rayma's coat and in her hair as well.

"Christmas miracle," Grant said before finally closing the door.

Rayma hung up her coat, and once she was out of her boots, she followed Grant and Jordan into the house.

"In here," Grant said to Jordan as he put the tote bag on the coffee table.

Joy was just coming out of the kitchen, and her whole face lit up at the sight of the newcomers.

Like the firecracker that she was, Rayma was around the table and snatching the bouquet from Grant before he could even blink, then she tackled Joy in a gigantic hug. "Merry Christmas, Nana Joy!"

"Merry Christmas, my angel. Thank you." Joy pulled away and took the flowers from Rayma. "These are lovely."

"I, uh ... no grocery stores or florists are open today," Jordan said awkwardly, standing next to Brock's seat at the head of the table and shoving his hands deep into his pockets.

"So?" Joy asked, cocking her head.

"I ... I didn't bring anything," he went on.

Joy waved her hand. "Oh, pishposh. You don't need to bring anything here. Not to *my* house. I always have everything we need. That's what nanas do. And besides, you were off saving the world. I know how it is. I was married to a cop for many years."

Grant grinned at Jordan, but that seemed to just cause the man's cheeks to burn even brighter.

"Always room for one more at the Hart table," Joy went on. "Now, you two, grab the seats that are left and let's get eating. I know Heath must be *starving*."

Heath made a noise in his throat and caught his wife's eye for just the briefest of seconds. "Not starving, Mum. I've had a couple of snacks today."

Pasha rolled her lips inward to keep herself from smiling.

Rayma gasped, then smiled. "Oh, I know what *that* means. I've shared a wall with these two horndogs more than once."

"Sit down!" Heath and Pasha both ordered rather loudly.

Rayma took a seat.

Jordan took a seat.

They were next to each other.

Grant's gaze flicked to Joy, and she smiled at him and tapped her nose.

Oh, that matchmaking minx of a woman of his.

When Krista mentioned to Joy a few days ago that her rookie, Lassie, had nowhere to go for Christmas, Joy said that now he did and told Krista to invite him over and not to take no for an answer.

Grant didn't think the young guy would have put up much of a fight, and even if he did, Krista had a stubborn personality like her husband, so Jordan's attendance was inevitable.

"Is a horndog like a corndog?" Connor asked.

"It's gotta be," Zoe added. Her speech was a little funny now that she'd lost her tooth. "Like maybe it's curved so it's shaped like a rhino's horn." The big gap in her smile was adorable, but the little girl was certainly having a hard time keeping her fingers and tongue out of the newly empty space.

Connor nodded. "That makes sense."

Many of the adults around the table made faces of relief.

"I don't understand why Aunt Rayma would call Uncle Heath and Aunt Pasha horndogs, though," Connor said after a moment of thought.

"Because they're being silly. It's like when Zane calls us all little grubs or pudding heads. Horndog is just another way of calling someone a pudding head. I'm sure of it." Zoe seemed almost frustrated with Connor that he didn't see the rationale behind it all and they were still having this conversation.

Luckily, Connor finally seemed convinced, and he reached for a pickle.

"Now that that is settled," Joy started, catching Grant's eye and smiling, "I'd just like to thank all of you for coming today. This has truly been one of the most magical Christmases. Our family continues to grow. Our love continues to grow, and by this time next year ... Who knows how big we'll all be? How much more love will be in this room and at this table."

Everyone exchanged glances and smiled.

"We've also experienced some losses," she went on. "So I'd like to say an extra big thank you to Rex and Lydia for sharing their family, their love, and their Christmas with us today, despite what they're going through."

Rex dropped his hand from the table, and by the looks of things, he reached for his wife's hand. Lydia was trying to remain strong, but Grant could see the tension in her jaw and how her blinking intensified as she stared straight ahead at her empty plate. She'd have good days and bad days. Good moments and bad moments.

"And to our newest additions, Eve, Maeve and Jordan—"

Rayma snorted. "You're with the babies."

"Rayma," Pasha whisper-yelled.

Jordan's lip twitched.

Joy merely lifted a brow at Rayma before repeating. "And to the newest additions to our table, Eve, Maeve, and Jordan, we hope that this is one of many Christmases you grace us with your presence, your smiles, your hearts, and your time. And please know that no matter where your travels may take you, you'll always have a place at my dinner table."

A few of the adults murmured *well said* and *thank you*.

"Well, dig in, everyone. Don't let the food get cold." Joy dabbed at the corners of her eyes, and everyone leaned forward and was about to pick up a spoon or grab a piece of bread when Brock cleared his throat at the head of the table.

Every hand paused in midair.

He stood up.

Eyes followed.

"I think Grant can sit here if he wants. I'd like to sit next to my wife." His green eyes found Grant's, and he lifted a brow. "Only if you want. I'm not saying you're the patriarch or anything—"

That earned him snorts from his brothers and their wives, along with an even louder snort from his own wife.

"But I see my brothers sitting next to their wives, and I'd like to do the same. So if you'd like to sit here, you're welcome to." He shuffled awkwardly on his feet for a moment, then looked away, almost in what seemed like embarrassment.

Grant appreciated what Brock was doing, but in truth, he didn't want to be at the head of the table. This was all still really new to all of them, and it didn't feel right.

With a smile, he walked toward Brock and clasped him on the shoulder. "I appreciate the offer, Brock, but honestly, I'd rather sit next to Joy."

"Oh for crying out loud," Rayma said, standing up from her spot, which happened to be between Joy and Jordan. "Brock, you take Grant's seat. Grant, you take my seat, and *I* will sit at the head of the table. Just because I spent my entire day handing out turkey dinners to the homeless doesn't mean I ate any of them. I'm starving."

Grant and Brock locked eyes and smirked as they moved to sit next to their women.

Rayma sat down where Brock had been and let out a long sigh. "Ah, much better. Now, let's do these Christmas crackers, get the stupid hats on our heads so we can eat!"

"Always a wizard with words, sis," Pasha said sarcastically as she grabbed the Christmas cracker from her plate.

"Someone's gotta be," Rayma said.

A British tradition adopted by Canadians and Australians, Christmas crackers consist of a cardboard tube with bright colored paper wrapped around it and tied at each end. Running through the center of the cracker is a very small explosive mechanism called a snap, which is glued to either end of the cracker. When each end of the snap is pulled, it makes a small *crack* noise. The same sound as a cap gun going off. Inside there is usually a paper crown, a fortune, and generally a crappy plastic toy of some kind.

Cracks echoed around the table, and one by one, they all put on their stupid paper crowns.

"Pink is most definitely your color," Joy said with a little giggle next to Grant. She had landed a yellow crown, and it suited her perfectly.

Grant put his crown on proudly and puffed up his chest. "I'm man enough to pull off pig penis pink, right?" he asked under his breath.

"So manly," she cooed, leaning into him.

Quickly, because Rayma's huffs and sighs of starvation and impatience were loud enough for Grant and Joy to hear at the other end of the table, they all collected their treasures from inside the crackers, then tossed the scraps into the plastic bag that Zoe wandered from person to person with to take it all to the recycling bin in the kitchen.

"Now can we eat?" Connor asked. "I can only chew this pickle for so long before my mouth makes me swallow it."

"We can eat, honey," Joy said with a laugh. "We can all eat."

———

"You're quite the matchmaker," Grant said, making his way back into the living room after seeing the last of their guests to the door.

Rayma had had a few drinks, so Constable Lassiter offered to drive her home, which, if she was being honest, was Joy's plan all along.

She'd only met Lassie, as they called him, a couple of times before, but she liked him immediately and thought he was perfect for Rayma. Several steps up from the duds she normally chose to date. Pompous private school jerks with micro pricks and massive egos.

With a warm rum and eggnog in each hand, heavy on the rum, Joy used her elbow to turn off lights as she made her way from the kitchen to the living room. The only light in the room was from the softly glowing Christmas tree in the corner.

Grant sat on the couch, and she fell gracefully into his lap. He took his drink from her and sipped it.

"Mmm, woman, you make a damn stiff drink."

"I can make many things stiff. It's one of my many talents." She wiggled in his lap before leaning forward and licking the small bit of frothed milk off his upper lip, his stubble rough beneath her tongue. A tendril of arousal spun through her.

"Not much effort on your part there, darlin'." His tongue flicked out and caught her lip as she pulled away.

Smiling, she settled into his embrace. "This was a wonderful Christmas. You brought my boys home to me. You and Brock are no longer ..." Enemies was the wrong word. So was adversaries.

"At odds over the same thing?" he offered.

She glanced up at him. "Huh?"

"How much we love you. Because really, that was what we were at odds about."

Sighing, she kissed his jaw. "I'm one lucky woman."

"I'm glad he apologized to you. I wouldn't have cared if he continued to dislike me, but the way he spoke to you was unacceptable." He lifted his hand from where it rested on her thigh, clutching his drink, and took another sip.

"We spoke a little more later. He's still struggling with the feeling that I'm replacing his father, but he knows that's not true. But of all the boys, since Brock was the oldest, he had the strongest bond with his father. He knew him the best. And boy oh boy, did that kid idolize his dad. The sun rose, set, and shone blindingly bright on Zane when it came to Brock. He could do no wrong. In his eyes, you don't even have shoes to fill; the shoes just don't exist. His father is incomparable."

"And so he should be."

"But because Zane died when Brock was only a kid, he only remembers his father that way and in a childlike state. So to him, it feels like by me moving on, his dad is trying to be replaced."

"Is this your therapist's analysis?"

She shook her head, shrugged, then finally nodded. "No ... well, kind of. This is what Brock told me. Not in so many words, of course, because the man sometimes struggles to form many complete sentences in a row and would rather communicate entirely by grunts, but basically, yeah. And then I discerned some of it because I'm a professional and could read between the lines and the grunts."

He made a chortle in his throat that had her nipples pebbling. "Are you analyzing everyone all the time?"

"Yes," she said blandly.

Because it was the truth.

"It's like reading or speaking. Once you learn the skill, it's impossible to turn it off."

"Are you analyzing me right now?"

"Haven't stopped since the moment we met."

He kissed the top of her head. "Well, you're obviously not *too* scared about what you've deduced because you haven't dumped me."

"You're not a nut." She craned her head around to look at him. "And I'm a doctor, so I can legally make that diagnosis—or lack thereof." Turning back around, she brought her mug to her lips and let the warm, sweet, boozy holiday drink slide down her throat. "Brock will get there. He's already made huge strides today in accepting you. We just need to give him time."

"For you, I can do anything."

She turned her head and kissed his arm.

"Any thoughts on where you'd like to go for your vacation?" he asked.

She was grateful that he switched topics.

"My vote is somewhere where you're not wearing much clothing and the booze flows free and frequent. An adults-only resort somewhere, maybe?" He adjusted how he was sitting on the couch, and she felt his semi-hard cock beneath her butt.

A little wiggle by her had him groaning.

She giggled. "I'm definitely down for an adults-only resort and you with hardly any clothing on. Where did you have in mind?"

"There are some pretty great places in Mexico or Cuba. Or we could go to Grand Cayman or the Virgin Islands. Anywhere my Hart's heart desires, and I'll make it happen."

His Hart's heart. The words made her body temperature spike.

"And if I say I trust you to make the perfect choice for me, will you book it and surprise me?"

"Hmmm," he hummed, stroking his close-shaved beard. "You're going to put that kind of trust in me?"

Glancing back up at him for a moment, she cupped his face and brought his mouth down to hers, but she didn't kiss him. She spoke into his parted lips, allowed her breath to mingle with his. "I trust you, Grant. I trust all of you. With my family, my heart, and my soul. I think I can trust you to book the perfect vacation."

He smiled against her mouth. "What about your body? Do you trust me with that?" Without moving their heads, he deftly set his mug down on the windowsill behind him, took her mug and did the same. Then she was beneath him.

"Oh, I trust you with that," she said, glancing up in the beautiful stormy-gray of his eyes.

"How about a couple of Christmas orgasms?"

She grinned at him and spread her thighs so he could settle between them. "Is Santa going to—how did Rayma put it? *Stuff my stocking?*"

He grinned. "She's a pistol, that one."

"With a heart of gold."

"And yes, that's exactly what Santa intends to do." His lips fell to her neck.

She smacked his butt. "Then hop to it. Go put on the costume. Mrs. Claus wants the full getup."

Lifting his head, he stared down at her in wide-eyed shock. "You're serious?"

"As a heart attack. The costume is in the bedroom. Don't come out until it's on." She wedged her hands between them and pushed him off her.

He climbed out from between her legs, stood up and gave her a weird look. "You're an odd one, Joy Hart," he called as he headed down the hallway.

"And you love it," she hollered after him.

Sitting back up on the couch, she reached for her mug and took a long sip.

"What's taking so long? How long does it take to turn yourself into St. Nick?"

"Cool your raging libido, woman. I'm trying to get into character."

She giggled and sipped her drink. The rum was going to her head, and she loved it. She'd suggested they try some role-playing a few times, but Grant had never truly felt comfortable. He broke character, then just tore off all her clothes and made love to her. She never *really* complained. But she liked to have fun in the bedroom. Explore and expand her sexuality.

If the man stayed in his Santa costume and character for two minutes, that would be impressive.

Closing her eyes, she reflected on everything that had taken place that day.

Today—Christmas—had truly been magical.

Not only had Grant managed to bring her sons home to her for

Christmas, but she had her grandkids with her, her surrogate kid—Rayma—Lassie and now Grant. And his gift to her—it made her gift of a handmade mug that said "Wild Man" on it seem paltry. But he claimed to love it, and even though she wasn't the human lie detector like Rex, she was pretty sure he was telling the truth.

Crossing one leg over the other, she bounced the dangling foot and sipped her drink. She finished it, then, like the saucy minx she was currently feeling like, she reached for Grant's drink and started sipping that. "I hope you don't mind, but I'm too comfortable sitting here waiting to bother getting up and make myself another drink, so I started drinking yours."

"Don't mind at all."

Suddenly, loud music flooded the room, making her jump.

Oh, she knew this song.

She'd gone to see *Magic Mike XXL* with some girlfriends. She knew this song *well*.

"Pony," by that rapper who doesn't know how to properly spell the word *genuine,* started playing.

Was Grant about to do what she thought he was about to do?

The lights in the living room flicked off.

Yes, yes, he was.

Oh wow, was he ever stepping out of his comfort zone.

And he was stepping out of it for her.

Giddily, but with her heart soaring from just how much he loved her, she took another sip of her drink and sat back, ready for the show.

"Ho ho ho!"

A thrilling tendril zapped through her.

"Ho. Ho. Ho. Where my hos at?" And out he came, dressed like Kris Kringle himself with a swagger that was anything but innocent.

He grooved to the beat, set the pillowcase he was pretending to use as a sack down on the coffee table, then went about removing the buttons of his coat.

He didn't even make it to the fourth button before the pillow that had been *inside* the pillowcase fell out from the bottom of the coat.

"Have you been a good girl?" he asked in a rough, gritty voice. "Or a *bad* girl?"

Smiling, she bit the tip of her finger and shook her head. "So bad, Santa. So, so bad."

With a flourish like he might have actually done this once or twice before, he pulled open his jacket, revealing that luscious, lickable stomach.

But then he paused, and his face fell.

"What's wrong?" she asked, sitting up from the back of the couch. Did he feel foolish?

She hoped not. This was all harmless fun. And she loved it.

He shook his head. "The blinds are still open."

Whipping around, with her mouth open wide, Joy discovered it to be true. And of course, one of her nosy neighbors from down the block had stopped in her tracks, her spitz puppy Judo having a piss on Joy's hedge, while Wendy stared gape-mouthed at Grant.

"Is that Wendy from down the block?" Grant asked.

Joy snorted and nodded. "You want to put on a show for the neighborhood and charge for it, or is this the champagne room? VIP guests only?"

"Only one VIP I want to see this show," he said, appearing to have regained his mojo. "Besides, she couldn't afford the tickets to this gun show."

Damn straight she couldn't.

Joy snorted.

Grant waved at the woman still staring at them. "Oh hey, Wendy! Merry Christmas," he called out.

Joy quickly waved at Wendy as well, then pulled the blinds

closed before resuming her spot on her couch and sipping the eggnog. "You may proceed."

Grant's smile made her pussy clench, and when he started to gyrate, she figured with a few thigh squeezes, she might be able to get herself off.

He still had the beard and hat on but was working on getting his pants off.

When he finally freed himself of those, she was greeted with another surprise.

He was wearing bright red boxer briefs, and over his erection was the picture of mistletoe, and above it was written: "*Kiss me.*"

The corners of her mouth had minds of their own and tried to reach her ears, her smile was so big.

He made his way over to her, his torso moving like a stripper's, rippling and gyrating. He put one foot on the couch, putting his crotch right up in her face, then like the strippers on *Magic Mike* did, he bucked into her face.

She burst out laughing.

Oh man, she was breaking character first!

"You're really into this. Did you moonlight as a dancer somewhere to pay some hefty gambling debts?"

He shook his head, then straddled her, pressing his cock into her belly. He caged her in with his arms and dipped his head. "Just making it up as I go along."

"Well, you're quite the improviser."

"Is Mrs. Claus ready to have her stocking stuffed?"

Joy nodded. "More than ready. But first, kiss me, Santa." He went to pull the beard down from his mouth, but her hand to his chest stopped him. "Leave the beard."

He quirked an eyebrow up at him. "You are an odd one." Then he took her mouth and swept his tongue inside. The synthetic beard was no match for how good his real scruff felt against her skin. But the change was interesting. She kissed him back, wedging her hand between their bodies to feel his length.

He groaned into her mouth, brought his hand down to hers, and pulled it away, lacing their fingers together. "Come on, woman, let's go make this the best Christmas ever." Then he stood up and hauled her off to the bedroom, "Pony" still playing in the background as she drunkenly, happily skipped after him. Madly in love and with a gloriously full heart.

EPILOGUE

Two years later ...

"I THINK that's the last of the presents under the tree," Joy said, staring at the knee-deep piles of wrapping paper, gifts, and gift bags strewn about her living room. "And to think we drew names this year for the adults and only bought for the children."

"There *are* a lot of us now," Krista said, bouncing her new nephew, Von, on her knee. Rex and Lydia's son was three months old and absolutely beautiful. And as far as her sons and their wives were concerned, he was the last grandchild she was going to get. They were all done.

She had no problem with that. She had eight beautiful, healthy grandbabies who she spoiled rotten, so she considered herself incredibly lucky indeed.

"I dunno," Grant said, making his way back into the living room from where he'd been brewing more coffee in the kitchen, "I think there might be *one* more gift under there."

Joy gave him a poignant look and scrunched her face. "What color is the wrapping or bag?"

"Maybe check *inside* the tree. I think it's small. Green paper. Gold bow."

She did as she was told, looking within the tree among the branches and ornaments. It took some real Where's Waldo skill on her part, since nearly half the ornaments were green or gold, but eventually she found it. The box was about as big as a square tissue box. A little too big to be hiding in a tree, in her opinion, but it was light, so she didn't say anything.

"Who's it for, Nana?" Zoe asked, sitting next to Cocoa and petting the dog's head as she gnawed on a breath-freshening chewy stick.

Joy checked the tag. "It's for me."

"What is it?" Zane asked.

"I don't know. I guess I need to open it to find out."

"Need help, Nana?" Thea asked.

"I think I got this, sweetheart, but thank you." Carefully, she slid the gold bow off the box and set it down beside her. She could tell the box was professionally wrapped with minimal tape, so carefully, she was able to lift the tape off and unwrap the paper without ripping it.

"You can use that paper again," Thea said. "Reuse and recycle. That's what we learn at school."

"You are so right, my angel."

A few of the kids crowded around her, eager to see what was inside the plain white box.

The *From* portion of the tag was empty. All it said on it was *Joy.*

She let her gaze bounce from person to person inside the house, but everyone just smiled at her. Nobody gave off any suspicious vibes like they were harboring some big Christmas secret.

With a *harrumph,* she opened the box.

Inside was another box.

"Oh, for crying out loud, if this is some Russian nesting doll type game, I'm not having it." She pulled out the second box. This one was small, blue, and made of wood and leather. It was the kind of box a piece of jewelry would come in.

Her gaze flicked up to Grant.

His expression remained neutral.

"Open it, Nana," the kids all encouraged her.

"I bet it's earrings," Thea mused. "Or a necklace."

"Or a ring," Zoe added. "I bet it's a ring. I bet Grantpa is asking Nana to marry him."

Anticipation became a living entity inside Joy, and her pulse began to beat loudly inside her ears. She swallowed. Was he? Was that what this was?

"Nana, open it!" Maeve shouted in her tiny almost-three-year-old voice.

Nodding, with her heart in her throat, Joy opened it.

It was empty.

What the what?

She lifted her gaze to her family, but in her peripheral vision, motion caught her eye. Grant was getting down on one knee.

Her hand covered her mouth, and the box fell to her lap. He had a beautiful ring in his fingers.

"I was right!" Zoe cheered.

"Shh," Krista warned.

"Well, I was," Zoe murmured, giving her mother the stink eye.

"We've all given our blessing," Heath said.

"Not that you need it," Pasha added.

"Joy Hart," Grant started, "will you continue this wild ride of life with me? Marry me and be the missing piece of *my* heart."

A smile broke free on her face. "I see what you did there. Wild and heart."

He grinned back at her and winked. "I'll admit, I had some help."

Rayma waved her hand. "It was me. I helped him with the wording. Just because I switched majors from marketing to social work doesn't mean I still don't know how to sell people on a product."

Joy laughed through her nose. "Thank you, dear." Rayma smiled proudly and snuggled into her man's arms.

Joy turned back to Grant, tears stinging the back of her eyes. Tears of pure happiness, of course. She was sixty-eight years old, and her boyfriend—a younger man, no less—was proposing to her.

"So, Mum, what's your answer?" Rex asked.

Her head nodded so hard and so fast, she'd probably have to go see her chiropractor for an adjustment later in the week, but she didn't care. She slid off her chair to meet Grant on the floor, and he slid the simple but beautiful diamond onto her finger.

"I'm a little hard of hearing," Rayma said cheekily, cupping her ear. "I can't hear nods very well. What's your answer?"

"My answer is yes!" Joy said through a barrage of tears and a tight throat. "Very, very much yes."

Then out of nowhere, all the adults leaped up and loud *pops* echoed around the room as streamer cannons were set off and the room filled with long, thin strips of colorful paper.

Another *pop* sounded, and Heath came into the living room with a bottle of champagne. He must have been storing it in the snow.

"So many flower girls, Nana," Zoe said excitedly. "I can't wait to walk down the aisle in front of you."

Joy ran her hand over the back of her granddaughter's curly red head. "Me either, angel."

"This is the best Christmas ever!" Thea cheered, her little fists in bunches as she shook them.

Grant helped Joy to her feet, and they accepted their flutes of bubbly, then they gazed into each other's eyes. "Yeah, it really is the best Christmas ever."

He leaned in next to her ear so only she could hear. "It will be once Santa comes out to play tonight." Then he kissed her warm, most definitely blushing cheek and clinked glasses with his soon-to-be sons-in-law and their wives while Joy stared at the Wild Man she was madly in love with. He was now her fiancé and would, very soon, be her husband.

FOR A FULL HART BONUS EPILOGUE GO HERE:
https://whitleycox.com/bonus-material/

SNEAK PEEK - QUICK & SNOWY

Read on for a sneak peek of Chapter 1 from
Quick & Snowy
The Quick Billionaires, Book 5

QUICK & SNOWY - CHAPTER 1

"You're welcome to tickle my nuts and sniff my ass crack, but I know damn well I don't have to remove my leg." Barnes Wark leaned forward over the rolling belt in airport security and squinted at the name tag on the baby-faced TSA agent.

Oden.

He resisted the urge to sneer at the name since he too had an unusual name that often garnered some quirked eyebrows.

He felt half an ounce of sympathy for the kid.

But it wasn't enough sympathy to save him from Barnes's impatience.

No way.

The barely-legal kid's Adam's apple jogged and his brown eyes shifted from Barnes's to his supervisor who was standing in the corner.

"Don't look at her, look at me," Barnes continued. "I'm the person you're dealing with right now. You saw my prosthetic after I took off my shoes and thought, *hey, let's make the cripple remove his leg. I've never seen that before.*"

The kid's face was turning the shade of an overripe tomato. He shook his head as if Barnes hadn't just dived into his sick subconscious and read his mind.

Barnes ignored the man's silent, but colorful denial. "I'm going to give you a second chance to speak to me like a human being with the same rights as every other person in here. So tell me again exactly *what* I need to remove."

The kid's eyes found Barnes's once more, he swallowed again and nodded. "Belt, shoes, all electronics, all liquids and anything metal. But I *don't* need you to remove your prosthetic, sir. A pat-down will be necessary, though."

Barnes nodded and did as he was instructed, then waited for another TSA agent to wave him through the metal detector.

Of course, it beeped.

He always forgot his dog tags. They were an extension of who he was—just like his leg—so it skipped his mind that they would need to be removed before proceeding through the detector.

Stepping back through, he lifted his tags out from under his black T-shirt and tossed them in with his belt and wallet.

The moment they were off, he felt exposed.

Vulnerable.

A piece of himself was missing.

He needed them back.

He needed them back to feel whole. To feel like himself.

Calmly, with a hard swallow, he stepped back through the detector.

It beeped again.

He rolled his eyes.

It would beep until the day he died.

He'd been through this scenario hundreds of times. But once in a while, he encountered a wet-behind the ears greenhorn who had either skipped the page on amputees in the TSA training handbook, or had some overwhelming curiosity that made them break protocol.

He NEVER indulged them.

Sure, he didn't give two shits that his left leg was made of tita-nium. He'd come to terms with that part long ago. He'd rather be bionic and still alive, then not alive at all. But he did give two shits, probably more than just two about being made a spectacle or having his rights violated.

He was waved over to the side where two male TSA agents approached him.

He didn't say a word. Just spread his legs and let them do their thing.

They wouldn't find anything.

He was one of the good guys.

Or at least he tried to be.

The TSA agent who was sliding his hands up Barnes's thigh was busy explaining what he was doing and why. Barnes tuned him out. The other agent had Barnes's passport. He glanced into the bin of Barnes's stuff and his brows lifted.

Barnes waited.

Three ...

Two ...

One ...

"Thank you for your service, sir," the man said, suddenly standing a little straighter

As predictable as the tides.

"My father served as well. We appreciate everything you've done to keep our country safe."

Barnes nodded at the man and accepted his passport back. If only this thirty-something guy with the wedding band and baby spit up on his collar knew the kinds of things Barnes had done to keep this man and his family safe.

It would give the average person nightmares.

Fuck, from time to time it still gave Barnes nightmares.

"Thank you for your cooperation," the other man said, standing back up.

Barnes grunted, then continued on to gather his stuff.

He was almost home.

One more flight, Chicago to Portland and then he could hunker down until the new year.

With his dog tags securely back in place, he finished putting on his belt and shoes, slung his rucksack over his back and headed toward his gate.

His sister had offered for him to come and spend Christmas with her family in Maine. His nieces and nephew were dying to see their uncle Barney, but he just didn't have it in him to do the big family Christmas thing.

He wasn't ready to go back to Maine.

Not yet.

The memories were still too raw. Too painful.

Right now, all he wanted to do was sit home alone in his small beach front cottage in Seaside, Oregon, drink beer, listen to the waves crash and not see a soul for at least two weeks.

When was the last time he'd been home?

The last time he'd slept in his own goddamn bed?

He'd been on the hunt for nearly four months now, so at least four months.

Hired by the billionaire McAllister family to track down *another* long-lost sibling—yes, *another one*, meaning they'd had long-lost sister they found a few years ago, but now they found one more sibling—and he'd been hitting nothing but dead ends. He didn't even have a first name for this person. Or know if they were a man or woman. And if he or she or they didn't know that their father was the late millionaire deadbeat Randall McAllister, chances are they weren't even going by McAllister. Because so far, every McAllister he'd tracked down had been the wrong one.

He wasn't giving up, but he sure as shit wasn't happy that it was taking him this long to find the person.

He'd done enough jet-setting in his lifetime to write a whole slew of memoirs. Now what he wanted to do was just stay in one place, build the cabinet he'd been working on for the last three years, and fucking relax.

Having located his gate, he was just about to sit down, when his phone started to warble in his pocket.

He knew before even looking at the caller-ID who it was going to be.

One of the McAllister brothers.

And it was.

Tate.

The oldest.

"Another lead?" he asked, having hit the green button and put the phone to his ear. There was no need for time-wasting pleasantries. He was too fucking tired for them. They were almost as painful as small talk.

"Yeah," Tate said.

"Where?" Barnes ran his hands through his more salt than pepper hair and sat down in his seat with a huff.

"Germany."

Germany.

He'd just been in Scotland.

Why the hell hadn't they called him and told him about the new lead BEFORE he hopped continents?

Fuck.

"Send me the details."

He couldn't say no.

As badly as he wanted to, he couldn't say no.

What they were paying him would set him up for a few years once he found the missing heir or heiress, and introduced them to their family and collected his fee.

As it was, the McAllisters were funding his travel, hotel and meal expenses. And his per diem was very plush.

"Already done," Tate said. "We're really hopeful about this one."

Barnes grunted, put his Bluetooth earbuds into his ears and brought up his email to start reading the details on the latest lead. "We also really wish you'd let us fly you on our private jet. You don't *have* to fly commercial."

"Waste of fuel flying one person around the world. Planet is one fire in case you haven't noticed? Your kids won't have enough fossil fuel left to drive themselves to the grocery store if we keep consuming the way we do." Barnes murmured. "First class commercial is fine." That drew a grin out of him and a chuckle from Tate on the other end.

"Fair enough. But know that if you *do* want to avoid the airports and layovers you just need to say the word. Besides I think by the time my kids are old enough, everything will be electric and self-driving."

Barnes grunted, not in the mood to disagree. "Noted."

Tate let out a heavy sigh. It frustrated him that Barnes wouldn't use their company jet. Well, too bad. The world was going to hell in a flaming hand-basket and a large contributor of that was greenhouse gas emissions and unnecessary consumerism.

People were gluttons nowadays. They took more than they needed. Used more than was necessary. Over bought. Over spent. Over ate.

If he could help contribute to the cause even just a little bit by flying commercial rather than burning a fuck-ton of fuel just for his ass to be flown around the world, then he would.

"We're all heading to Whistler tomorrow for the holiday. It would be really great if you found her and convinced her to come meet us for Christmas. We've got adjoining chalets so tons of room. For our sister, and you of course," Tate said.

Barnes rolled his eyes.

He was avoiding his own family at Christmas, no freaking way was he going to spend the holidays with a loud, crazy family that wasn't even his own.

"I've already had my assistant cancel your flight to Portland and book you another one to Hanover from where you are in Chicago. Leaves in three hours," Tate said. "Hotel is booked. We've procured you a rental car. All the details are in the email."

They always were.

As frustrating as it was turning up empty with each lead he had pursued so far, he had to hand it to Tate and his assistant, they were very thorough and organized.

He started scanning the email.

Name: Dr. Brier Aoife Scofield.

Age: 39

Born: Dublin, Ireland but grew up in Brighton, England

Mother: Ciara Scofield nee O'Leary (deceased)

Father: Unknown (presumed to be Randall McAllister)

Stepfather: Gerald Scofield (deceased)

Occupation: Research biologist for a division of the Cancer Institute of Germany

And that was it.

No address. No phone number.

He shrugged and closed the email. He'd been given less and found his target. This wouldn't take long at all.

"I'll call you when I've made contact," he said to Tate at the same time he spied the bar across the way. The amber bottles called to him like a siren on a pinnacle in the middle of a stormy sea.

He got up and made his way over to the bar and mouthed "whiskey" to the preppy looking guy in suspenders who lifted a brow at him.

"We're counting on you, Barnes," Tate said. "If our dad had another child, not only is that child entitled to her inheritance, but she deserves to know she has family out there. Brothers and a sister. Nieces and nephews. We're creating our own legacy and she deserves to know she is welcome to be part of it."

Tate had said some version of this exact thing on numerous occasions, so Barnes was really only half-listening. He grunted into the phone and thanked the bartender for his drink. Putting the crystal to his lips, he sipped the liquor and held it on his tongue for a moment before letting the rich, caramel notes slide down his throat.

"I'll do my best," he said after swallowing.

"I know you will," Tate replied. "Look forward to hearing from you."

Barnes grunted and the call ended.

He left his earbuds in and brought up a music app on his phone.

In his youth, he liked classic rock and even a bit of punk. In his military days, he got into country music because that was what a lot of his fellow recruits were listening to. Now he preferred the classics. Vivaldi, Mozart, Beethoven, Bach.

After all his time in the trenches, taking out bad guys and protecting the innocent, the only way to drown out the memories, to drown out the sounds of gunfire and screaming that was like Tinnitus in his ears, was to play classical music.

It calmed him.

He soothed him.

It helped him function like a normal human being.

Closing his eyes for a moment, he reached for the lowball glass and brought it to his lips.

The malty, grainy scent wafted up through his nostrils and when it hit that memory node in his brain, he smiled.

The first time he'd ever tried whiskey he'd been fourteen and his dad had taken him out on a three-day hike into the woods. They brought very few rations, slept under the stars and fished for their dinner. They sat around the campfire listening to the embers crackle and his dad told him stories of when he was in the Navy.

It was those stories that prompted Barnes to enlist in the Navy when he was eighteen. He wanted to be just like his dad.

A man who took care of people.

A man who made the world safer.

They'd been sitting around the fire on their first night, the crickets sung and wolves howled far *far* off in the distance, then his dad passed him a worn metal flask.

Barnes knew that flask. He'd seen his dad with it for years.

Faint initials were engraved into the center. But after years of hands holding the flask, the letters were barely visible anymore.

Barnes knew what they were though.

They didn't belong to his father.

His dad's name was Michael Remington Wark and these letters were F.D.W.

His father must have read his mind.

"Foster Dalrymple Wark."

Barnes scrunched up his nose and glanced at his dad.

"That was my *grandfather*. So your *great* grandfather."

Barnes's eyes went wide.

"My father gave me this flask when I turned eighteen and enlisted. Just like his father had given him the flask when *he* turned eighteen and enlisted."

"So if I enlist, I'll get it at eighteen, too?"

His father's smile was small and he didn't look at Barnes, he just stared into the flames. "You'll get it either way. I'm not like them. I'm not going to *force* you to do something. I was told from early on that it was my *duty* to family and country to enlist. But I'm not going to do that to you. There are other ways you can make an impact on the world, son. Other ways you can do good and protect your country. You don't *have* to enlist if you don't want to." He glanced up at Barnes. "And I will not love you any less if you decide not to. Know that, Barnes. Know that if you choose a safer life. A safer career that I will not love you or respect you any less."

Barnes sniffed the inside of the flask. It smelled like cereal. "But what if I want to enlist? What if I want to join the Navy like you?"

His dad shrugged and prodded at the fire with a stick. "Then you enlist. It's your choice." His gray eyes tipped up and he hit Barnes with a look that Barnes felt all the way to his toes. "But always know that it is *your* choice." He jerked his chin at the bottle. "Have you tried whiskey before?"

Barnes shook his head. "Smells like Cheerios."

His dad chuckled. "Made with grain, so I get that. Go slow. Take a small sip and hold it on your tongue, then gently let it slide down your throat. If you drink it too fast it'll burn your throat and your nose and you'll end up coughing."

Barnes nodded, hesitated for a moment then put the open flask to his mouth. The liquid poured across her lips and over his tongue.

It was sharp and had a flavor that he would later learn was called *peaty*. But at fourteen he thought it tasted foul. However, no way in hell was he going to spit it out in front of his dad. He tossed on a manly blank face, let the disgusting liquid sit on his tongue, probably burning a hole through it, then he slowly swallowed it.

As hard as he tried, he coughed and his eyes stung.

He sniffed and shook his head, clearing his throat a few times as he handed the flask back to his dad.

His father was chuckling. "You handled that first sip a lot better than I handled mine. I spat it out, ran to the river and licked rocks until the flavor was out of my mouth."

Barnes's eyes went wide and his bottom lip dropped open.

His dad offered him back the flask, but he shook his head and reached for his canteen full of fresh glacier water. He took a healthy sip.

When he set the canteen back down next to the log he was sitting on, he lifted his head to find his dad watching Barnes through the flames. The gray became silver as the flames danced inside his irises and the look on his face was one Barnes hadn't seen before.

Unease wormed through him.

A small smile tugged at one corner of his dad's mouth. "I'm really proud of the man you're turning into, son. You're going to do a lot of good in the world, no matter what you choose to do."

Barnes blinked at father, the sting behind his eyes was overwhelming, and the cords in his throat felt as tight as a guitar string. He couldn't swallow even if he tried.

With an old-man grunt, his father stood up from his log and patted Barnes on the shoulder. "You'll put out the fire before you go to sleep? Hang up the food so we don't wake up to bears?"

All Barnes could do was nod.

"Good boy. Fish will be up for their breakfast with the birds, so we better be too. Don't stay up too much later."

Barnes fought down the lump in his throat and finally swallowed. He shook his head and croaked out, "I won't."

"That's a good lad." Then his father wandered off into the darkness to go and use the bathroom and retire to bed in his hammock.

One week later, back at home and while out mowing the lawn, his father died of a heart attack. And Barnes was the one that found him.

Back in the present time, Barnes stared at the last sip of whiskey in his glass. It was a peaty and fruity one. His father's favorite kind.

He tipped the glass up to his mouth and drained it, then reached into his duffle bag and pulled out an old, worn flask. The letters F.D.W weren't visible at all anymore. But Barnes's still felt them as he ran the rough pad of his thumb over where they'd once been. Whether it was his mind playing tricks on him and manifesting the feeling of the letters there or not, he didn't know, but he did felt them all the same.

He unscrewed the cap and set it on the bar.

"You can't bring your own alcohol in here, sir," the bartender said, his expression remorseful.

With Vivaldi in his ears, Barnes nodded and tapped the flask. He cleared his throat and bit down hard on the inside of his cheek for a moment to regain his composure before removing one earbud and speaking. "I know. It's empty. Could you fill it up for me, and also pour me another glass?"

The bartender nodded. "That I can do." He unscrewed the whiskey, reached for a small plastic funnel and started pouring into the flask. "This thing seems ancient. I bet there's a story behind it."

Barnes nodded. "There is, but unfortunately, I never got the chance to hear it."

IF YOU'VE ENJOYED THIS BOOK

If you've enjoyed this book, please consider leaving a review. It
really does make a difference.
Thank you again.
Xoxo
Whitley Cox

ACKNOWLEDGMENTS

There are so many people to thank who help along the way. Publishing a book is definitely not a solo mission, that's for sure. First and foremost, my friend and editor Chris Kridler, you are a blessing, a gem and an all-around terrific person. Thank you for your honesty and hard work.

Tara at Fantasia Frog Designs for my Harty Boys covers. You are fantastic, your covers are fantastic and I so appreciate you. Thank you.

Author Kathleen Lawless, for just being you and wonderful and always there for me.

Author Jeanne St. James, my alpha reader and sister from another mister, what would I do without you? Thank you!!

Caroline Scott of World of Books 65 for proofreading. Thank you so much! I truly appreciate your help with this one.

Whitley Cox's Fabulously Filthy Reviewers, you are all awesome and I feel so blessed to have found such wonderful fans.

The ladies and gent of Vancouver Island Romance Authors, your support and insight have been incredibly helpful, and I'm so honored to be a part of a group of such talented writers.

Author Ember Leigh, my newest author bestie, I love our bitch fests—they keep me sane. You helped me SO much with this book, and I am so very grateful for that. Sometimes it just takes talking it through with someone to have the lightbulb come on. Thank you for helping me find the light switch.

My parents, in-laws, brother and sister-in-law, thank you for your unwavering support.

The Small Human and the Tiny Human, you are the beats and beasts of my heart, the reason I breathe and the reason I drink. I love you both to infinity and beyond.

And lastly, of course, the husband. You are my forever, my other half, the one who keeps me grounded and the only person I have honestly never grown sick of even when we did that six-month backpacking trip and spent every single day together. I never tired of you. Never needed a break. You are my person. I love you.

ALSO BY WHITLEY COX

Love, Passion and Power: Part 1

mybook.to/LPPPart1

The Dark and Damaged Hearts Series Book 1

Kendra and Justin

Love, Passion and Power: Part 2

mybook.to/LPPPart2

The Dark and Damaged Hearts Series Book 2

Kendra and Justin

Sex, Heat and Hunger: Part 1

mybook.to/SHHPart1

The Dark and Damaged Hearts Book 3

Emma and James

Sex, Heat and Hunger: Part 2

mybook.to/SHHPart2

The Dark and Damaged Hearts Book 4

Emma and James

Hot and Filthy: The Honeymoon

mybook.to/HotandFilthy

The Dark and Damaged Hearts Book 4.5

Emma and James

True, Deep and Forever: Part 1

mybook.to/TDFPart1

The Dark and Damaged Hearts Book 5

Amy and Garrett

True, Deep and Forever: Part 2

mybook.to/TDFPart2

The Dark and Damaged Hearts Book 6

Amy and Garrett

Hard, Fast and Madly: Part 1

mybook.to/HFMPart1

The Dark and Damaged Hearts Series Book 7

Freya and Jacob

Hard, Fast and Madly: Part 2

mybook.to/HFMPart2

The Dark and Damaged Hearts Series Book 8

Freya and Jacob

Quick & Dirty

mybook.to/quickandirty

Book 1, A Quick Billionaires Novel

Parker and Tate

Quick & Easy

mybook.to/quickeasy

Book 2, A Quick Billionaires Novella

Heather and Gavin

Quick & Reckless

mybook.to/quickandreckless

Book 3, A Quick Billionaires Novel

Silver and Warren

Quick & Dangerous

mybook.to/quickanddangerous

Book 4, A Quick Billionaires Novel

Skyler and Roberto

Hot Dad

mybook.to/hotdad

Harper and Sam

Lust Abroad

mybook.to/lustabroad

Piper and Derrick

Snowed In & Set Up

mybook.to/snowedinandsetup

Amber, Will, Juniper, Hunter, Rowen, Austin

Hired by the Single Dad

mybook.to/hiredbythesingledad

The Single Dads of Seattle, Book 1

Tori and Mark

Dancing with the Single Dad

mybook.to/dancingsingledad

The Single Dads of Seattle, Book 2

Violet and Adam

Saved by the Single Dad

mybook.to/savedsingledad

The Single Dads of Seattle, Book 3

Paige and Mitch

Living with the Single Dad

mybook.to/livingsingledad

The Single Dads of Seattle, Book 4

Isobel and Aaron

Christmas with the Single Dad

mybook.to/christmassingledad

The Single Dads of Seattle, Book 5

Aurora and Zak

New Years with the Single Dad

mybook.to/newyearssingledad

The Single Dads of Seattle, Book 6

Zara and Emmett

Valentine's with the Single Dad

mybook.to/VWTSD

The Single Dads of Seattle, Book 7

Lowenna and Mason

Neighbours with the Single Dad

mybook.to/NWTSD

The Single Dads of Seattle, Book 8

Eva and Scott

Flirting with the Single Dad

mybook.to/Flirtingsingledad

The Single Dads of Seattle, Book 9

Tessa and Atlas

Falling for the Single Dad

mybook.to/fallingsingledad

The Single Dads of Seattle, Book 10

Liam and Richelle

Hot for Teacher

mybook.to/hotforteacher

The Single Moms of Seattle, Book 1

Celeste and Max

Hot for a Cop

mybook.to/hotforacop

The Single Moms of Seattle, Book 2

Lauren and Isaac

Hot for the Handyman

mybook.to/hotforthehandyman

The Single Moms of Seattle, Book 3

Bianca and Jack

Doctor Smug

mybook.to/doctorsmug

Daisy and Riley

Hard Hart

mybook.to/hard_hart

The Harty Boys, Book 1

Krista and Brock

Lost Hart

The Harty Boys, Book 2

mybook.to/lost_hart

Stacey and Chase

Torn Hart

The Harty Boys, Book 3

mybook.to/torn_hart

Lydia and Rex

Dark Hart

The Harty Boys, Book 4

mybook.to/dark_hart

Pasha and Heath

Full Hart

The Harty Boys, Book 5

mybook.to/full_hart

A Harty Boys Family Christmas

October 9, 2021

Upcoming

Quick & Snowy

The Quick Billionaires, Book 5

mybook.to/quick-snowy

Brier and Barnes

November 13, 2021

Rock the Shores

A Cinnamon Bay Romance

Juliet and Evan

May 10, 2022

Raw, Fierce and Awakened: Part 1

The Dark and Damaged Hearts Series, Book 9

Jessica and Lewis

Raw, Fierce and Awakened: Part 2

The Dark and Damaged Hearts Series, Book 10

Jessica and Lewis

ABOUT THE AUTHOR

A Canadian West Coast baby born and raised, Whitley is married to her high school sweetheart, and together they have two beautiful daughters and a fluffy dog. She spends her days making food that gets thrown on the floor, vacuuming Cheerios out from under the couch and making sure that the dog food doesn't end up in the air conditioner. But when nap time comes, and it's not quite wine o'clock, Whitley sits down, avoids the pile of laundry on the couch, and writes.

A lover of all things decadent; wine, cheese, chocolate and spicy erotic romance, Whitley brings the humorous side of sex, the ridiculous side of relationships and the suspense of everyday life into her stories. With single dads, firefighters, Navy SEALs, mommy wars, body issues, threesomes, bondage and role-playing, Whitley's books have all the funny and fabulously filthy words you could hope for.

DON'T FORGET TO SUBSCRIBE TO MY NEWSLETTER

Be the first to hear about pre-orders, new releases, giveaways, 99 cent deals, and freebies!

Click here to Subscribe
http://eepurl.com/ckh5yT

YOU CAN ALSO FIND ME HERE

Website: WhitleyCox.com
Twitter: @WhitleyCoxBooks
Instagram: @CoxWhitley
Facebook Page: https://www.facebook.com/CoxWhitley/
Blog: https://whitleycox.blogspot.ca/
Multi-Author Blog: https://romancewritersbehavingbadly.blogspot.com
Exclusive Facebook Reader Group: https://www.facebook.com/groups/234716323653592/
Booksprout: https://booksprout.co/author/994/whitley-cox
Bookbub: https://www.bookbub.com/authors/whitley-cox

Subscribe to my newsletter here
http://eepurl.com/ckh5yT

JOIN MY STREET TEAM

WHITLEY COX'S CURIOUSLY KINKY REVIEWERS

Hear about giveaways, games, ARC opportunities, new releases, teasers, author news, character and plot development and more!

Facebook Street Team
Join NOW!

Made in the USA
Coppell, TX
23 August 2023

20703780R00194